Impending Love and Capture

by

Laura Freeman

Impending Love Series

This is a work of fiction. Names, characters, places, and incidents are either the product of the author's imagination or are used fictitiously, and any resemblance to actual persons living or dead, business establishments, events, or locales, is entirely coincidental.

Impending Love and Capture

Cover Art by *Debbie Taylor*

The Wild Rose Press, Inc.
PO Box 708
Adams Basin, NY 14410-0708
Visit us at www.thewildrosepress.com

Publishing History
First American Rose Edition, 2017
Print ISBN 978-1-5092-1639-0
Digital ISBN 978-1-5092-1640-6

Impending Love Series
Published in the United States of America

Dedication

To my sons, Pete and Joe.
Live your dreams.

Chapter One

Jessica Beecher fought the growing dread building in her chest as she neared Leesburg, Virginia, where she would gut punch Sergeant Ed Herbruck. Any other woman would have written a letter telling him the news. Although she was fond of him, she couldn't accept his marriage proposal. But Jess was no coward. She would tell him in person.

Ed had been a childhood companion, a dear friend, and her beau since the summer of 1862. She had been sixteen, and he was the first man to kiss her. What had changed in one year?

"You're awfully quiet, Miss Jessica." Sid Wilson slapped the reins on the back of two black draft horses pulling their wagon of supplies. Sid was in his mid-twenties but appeared older with a receding hairline and spectacles. He propped his peg leg against the front wall of the wagon. Sid had joined the Union army in 1861 and fought at Bull Run with the First Ohio Volunteers. Then he reenlisted with the Seventh Ohio until the battle of Antietam when he lost his right foot in the cornfield near Dunker Church. Even after losing his leg, he remained in Washington City, helping with the wounded and gleaning information from soldiers of every rank. Sid gathered facts about the officers, battles, and news of the war. He said he was going to write a book one day.

He had become a family friend, especially to the Beecher sisters. Jess and her five sisters had been born and raised in Darrow Falls, Ohio. Jess and Colleen, or Cole as she was known to family, had traveled to Pierce House on Pennsylvania Avenue last year to help their sister, Jem, who had been expecting a baby. Even after Chauncy Theodora Pierce was born, they had stayed to help with the wounded who flooded the city after every battle. Their father, Dr. Sterling Beecher, had taught them about medicine, but their skills sharpened with each patient.

Cole had married Blake Ellsworth and ran the Mermaid's Mirth hotel on Maryland Avenue near the Long Bridge in Washington City while he fought with the Twenty-ninth Ohio Volunteer Infantry. Ed and others from Ohio were in the regiment. Ed had joined in 1861 and had survived the cold, starvation, and never ending marches up and down the Shenandoah Valley fighting for his life against General Thomas "Stonewall" Jackson's men.

The wagon and team belonged to Blake. Medical supplies and gifts from Ohio were stacked in the back. Jess withdrew several letters from her skirt pocket. She moved the most recent missive with Ed's proposal to the bottom of the stack. "Want to hear a letter from Ed?"

"Don't read the mushy parts," Sid warned.

Jess laughed. Ed was too shy to write anything fanciful. He shared news about the battles and the role the Ohio boys played. Jess unfolded the papers and read.

"Dear Miss Jessica,

President Lincoln fired Ambrose Burnside and

2

replaced him with Joe Hooker as commander of the Army of the Potomac."

Jess turned to Sid. "Why does the president keep replacing his generals?"

"He wants to win," Sid said. "The South may not have as many men as the North, but they have generals who know what it takes for a victory."

Jess turned her attention to the letter.

"That means a battle is brewing. Hooker will want to prove himself. We've asked for furlough, but now there's little chance it will be granted. Two years we've been fighting without a visit home. I sometimes think I'll never see Ohio again."

Jess reread the last lines. Home. Ohio.

"We received new uniforms and added a five-point white star to our kepis to mark us in the Twelfth Corps. I have a new shelter tent half, and Harry is my tent mate. He complains I'm bossy, but I want to keep him alive. Art wrote and said with the metal and leather brace John and your father made him, he can do most chores."

Sid nodded toward the letter. "Harry is Art and Ed's little brother?"

There were four Herbruck brothers. "Yes. Didn't you serve with their brother John?"

"We were at the Battle of Bull Run. He caught a shell casing to the back of his leg. Messy cut."

"He has a bit of a limp, but Art could barely lift his arm with a chunk of bone missing," Jess said. "He was wounded at Cedar Mountain."

"That was a nasty one."

"Do you remember all the battles?"

"I think it's important we don't forget." Sid rubbed

3

his knee, which rested in the wooden hollow of his peg leg.

Jess read the final sentence in the letter.

"Robert E. Lee spent the winter resting at Fredericksburg, and Hooker wants to wake him up.

God bless you and your family,

Ed"

She folded the missive. It was like most of Ed's correspondence, direct and uncomplicated. He was a good man, but marrying the wrong man closed the door to marrying the right man. Ed was not the husband for her.

Jess sorted through the stack of letters for another one to read. "That one was written before Chancellorsville. This one is after."

"Another loss." Sid gripped the reins as a wagon wheel sank into a rut on the dirt road. "The one thing I can say about the boys, they haven't lost hope. Their spirits were high when they marched north."

"How do they do it, Sid?" So many of the Ohio boys had been wounded or killed. Last fall because the Twenty-ninth Ohio Volunteer Infantry had only a couple hundred men and one officer, they didn't fight at Antietam but guarded the railroad bridge instead. The Seventh Ohio had not been so lucky and had nearly been destroyed by the battle. "How can they continue when so many have died?"

"They put one foot in front of the other and march until they're exhausted, and then they march some more." Sid's voice rang with pride. He couldn't fight anymore, but Sid would do what he could until the war was over.

"Are you going to join the Invalid Corps?"

"With my foot gone, I'd be limited to the Second Battalion. I'm not sure if I want to work as a nurse or a guard. Don't know if I could take orders again."

Jess didn't question his excuse. Some soldiers called them cripples and mocked their service. "I appreciate you driving these supplies to the Ohio boys. I'm sure they'll be glad to see them."

"Do you have an ulterior motive, Miss Jessica?" He grinned. "I bet Ed will be happy to see you."

How wrong could Sid be? Jess unfolded the letter written in May.

"Dear Miss Jessica,

A man can only escape death so many times, especially with generals who know nothing about winning a battle."

She glanced at Sid. Some considered questioning generals a crime, but Sid made no comment.

"About a third of the men in the Twenty-ninth Ohio are new, including three troublemakers I won't name. They complain about carrying forty pounds on their backs, but I turn a deaf ear to their childish wails. They don't know what's in store for them even though I've prepared them."

"He's talking about Harry Herbruck, my cousin Ethan Donovan, and their friend Zach Ravenswood."

"Paxton's brother?"

Pax Ravenswood had been in the Seventh Ohio and had played baseball at Mermaid's Mirth during a break in the battles. Death claimed him after the battle of Cedar Mountain. Blake had carried him to his hotel in his wagon along with Art, but the only medicine for a gut shot was opium to ease the pain until he died.

An older brother died, and a younger one took his

place to fight in the war. "They're all nineteen." They probably resented being called boys. She was two years younger and considered herself a full-grown woman. "I can't believe they lied to the recruiter about their ages."

"They didn't lie." Sid pointed at the heel of his single boot. "It's a common trick. A soldier puts the number nineteen in his shoe. When the recruiter asks if he's over nineteen, he says, 'Yes.' "

Jess shook her head. "But why lie? They'll end up being drafted in another year."

"They think the war will be over by then."

"Will it?"

Sid rubbed his knee. "Lee has almost ended it a few times. If we don't start winning some battles, we'll all be singing *Dixie*."

Jess didn't like being on the losing side. She turned her attention to the letter.

"We crossed the Rappahannock River on a pontoon bridge then we crossed the Rapidan River on a foot bridge made from scrap wood. No sense in building anything permanent with Lee's men waiting to burn it. Then we marched along the Orange Turnpike to a brick tavern at the Chancellor's Crossroads near the Plank Road intersection.

"After spending all day digging trenches and building barricades, we waited. I miss your cooking. All we have to eat is salt pork, crackers, and creek water to wash it down. When the enemy didn't show, Hooker ordered us to march out to scout the woods. We found Lee's men and had to double back to the trenches. We've piled rocks in front of us before but never dug holes in the ground to fight from. It's safer than marching through a cornfield."

"I hate cornfields," Sid growled between his teeth.

Sid had survived Antietam, but her cousin, Jake Donovan, had been among the dead lined up in rows in the cornfield, mowed down by the volleys from the enemy's guns. Ethan Donovan, one of the three troublemakers, was Jake's cousin, too. They shared a grandfather, Michael Donovan, who operated a canal boat between Akron and Cleveland, Ohio. He hired his grandchildren to work on the *Irish Rose* during summers. It had bonded them with hard work and idyllic memories but made the loss of Jake a harsh reality.

Antietam had been the worst. Jess and Cole, dressed as men, and Blake at the reins, had joined Clara Barton's wagons to deliver medical supplies and tend the wounded. Soldier after shattered soldier had been transported to the makeshift tables where surgeons sliced and sawed through thousands of bones, tossing the damaged limbs into wheelbarrows until they overflowed. With so many casualties, Antietam earned the moniker, *the bloodiest day of the war*.

Those who survived the battle, begged for water while waiting for an ambulance to take them to a hospital. Jess carried the precious liquid in wooden buckets and offered ladle after ladle to the thirsty men. Their gunpowder-stained faces haunted her. The smell of sweat and blood lingered in her nostrils for days. The memory made her shudder, and she turned her attention to the letter.

"On May 2 we piled our knapsacks and marched out again. The Seventh Ohio joined us, but it was tough fighting in the woods. We couldn't retreat with the Johnny Rebs a breath away, firing at us every time we

stepped out from behind a tree. We fought until our ammunition ran out. Somehow we made it back to the trenches, but we couldn't help our wounded, moaning and crying for water. No one could sleep, and we were ordered on picket duty. We were so close we could hear the enemy talking. Stonewall Jackson had been wounded. Said a prayer. Odd to pray for the other side, but we've gained a respect for the stubborn fools."

"Jackson died May 10," Sid said. "He was a worthy opponent."

His praise for the enemy startled her. "You liked him?"

"The first thing a soldier learns is to respect the enemy. We put the names of the battles we lost on our flag along with any victories. Do you know why?"

Jess shook her head. She didn't brag when she lost a game or contest.

"We fought and stood our ground against the enemy. We didn't run. Some men can't say that." He rubbed his knee. "When Jackson's men saw our colors, they knew the battle was going to be a tough fight. They would have to earn a victory."

She emphasized winning but understood the importance of competing to gain respect. She rarely turned down a challenge.

"May 3 the Rebels attacked after firing their cannon all morning. Our officers ran. Cowards most of them. They left the Ohio boys to hold the line."

Sid stabbed at her letter. "That's courage, girl. Knowing everyone has abandoned you to hold off the enemy alone. We did it at Bull Run when everyone was fleeing. Ohio boys have been at the front, leading the charge, and they've been at the rear, guarding the

8

retreat. And when the order is given, they hold the line."

The words blurred on the letter. Sid's voice rang with pride even though the North had few victories. Whether they won or lost, the soldiers took pride in doing their assigned task. Sometimes that meant guarding a supply train or building barricades, but more often than not, it meant marching into enemy fire.

"The wounded were in the inn when it was shelled, but we couldn't help them. Some escaped before it burned to the ground. After the order to fasten bayonets, we charged several times before retreating to the turnpike and across the Rappahannock. It was hours before the stragglers joined us.

"May 4 we rested and reinforced our trenches. It didn't matter. Rain soon filled them. Crossing the river was difficult, and we had no supplies. Everything had been left behind during the retreat. No coats, knapsacks, blankets, or food. All I had left in my cartridge box was some loose gunpowder. About a third of the Twelfth Corps was wounded, killed, or captured by final count. Hooker won't last long."

Jess turned the paper sideways to read the last part.

"We received new supplies at Aquia Creek landing, and we ate fresh bread with butter. We played baseball, and our spirits soared when we were paid. I had to warn the babies not to waste their money on shoddy Sutler goods.

God bless you and your family,
Ed"

She put away the letters. Jess was weary of war. Too many good men had perished already. Yet the soldiers obeyed their orders and marched into death.

She recalled Lord Tennyson's poem, *Charge of the Light Brigade*. The words repeated over and over in her head.

Theirs not to reason why, theirs but to do and die: Into the Valley of Death rode the six hundred.

When Jess and Sid reached Leesburg, the Ohio boys were gone. While Sid visited with the soldiers to discover the reason, Jess took care of the draft horses. She opened a wooden box on the side of the wagon and removed two feed bags with oats and two metal curry brushes.

After watering and feeding Romulus and Remus, she cleaned their hooves and brushed their black coats. Although her father was a doctor, her family lived on a farm. Taking care of the animals was a priority before any personal needs. The horses munched on grass beneath a shady tree, and Jess ate cucumber slices and carrots while she waited for Sid to return.

His expression was sour. "They're in Maryland heading north for Frederick. Do we follow?"

Jess offered a carrot. "I didn't come this far to turn back."

He sat beside her in the shade of the tree where she had spread a blanket. "Nasty business while they were here."

Jess opened a basket laced with pink dyed bands and offered a sandwich. "What do you mean?"

He hesitated, a scowl marring his sunburned face. "They hanged three deserters."

Jess swallowed a bite. "Why? From the beginning of the war, men have walked away and gone home. Some of them couldn't take the endless marching and fighting. But no one thought worse of them."

"Too many of them didn't return. General Joe Hooker has a new policy. They hang men on leave without permission and order the soldiers to watch. Teach them a lesson." Sid wiped his glasses clean with his kerchief. "I agree with Ed. Hooker isn't general material." He turned to study her. "You want to spend the night here?"

Jess stood and gathered her basket. "The horses are rested, and there's plenty of daylight. Let's advance."

When they reached Frederick, Lincoln had fired Hooker and replaced him with General George Meade. He had his hands full. Lee was marching north on the other side of the Appalachian Mountains west of them. The Union forces had left Frederick and were following Lee in a parallel route on the east side of the mountains. The supply wagons and ambulances were preparing to depart in the morning, and they would have to wait and follow. The army had priority.

Antietam had opened her eyes to the naked horror of war. It no longer was limited to band music and men dressed in bright uniforms, marching along in straight lines. War was torn bodies and men gasping for a final breath. She had hoped to talk to Ed while relaxing in camp. She couldn't deliver bad news before a battle. By the time they arrived, the conflict could be resolved. But if they lost, would Lee head for Washington City and deliver a final blow to any chance of Union victory?

She spent the night in a rented room but had trouble sleeping. No matter how she tried, she couldn't think of words to ease Ed's pain from her rejection. Was she making a mistake? She had no other man in her life. She had fallen out of love with Ed, but was

11

there a chance she would fall in love with him again? Only a face to face meeting would give her the answer.

Chapter Two

Captain Morgan Mackinnon surveyed the battered town of Gettysburg, Pennsylvania. After skirmishes on July 1, Union and Confederate forces were digging in for a decisive confrontation. He removed his slouch hat as he entered Colonel Chauncy LaDonte's tent and saluted.

"Welcome, Captain."

Chauncy's dark hair was streaked with gray, and his beard nestled against his chest. His breathing had a labored quality, like a snore. He'd been shot in the chest, and it had taken nearly a year to recover from the near-fatal wound. The injury was the reason he remained a colonel identified with three stars within a wreath on his collar. But since his return to the field, he had proven himself a capable leader.

"Theo!" Chauncy shouted to a man who stood back from the officers. Theo Jameson moved quickly, eager to please his commanding officer. He was Chauncy's right hand and had stayed with him during his long recuperation. It was rumored Chauncy had taught Theo to read and write during his convalescence. Theo had been promoted to corporal, more for his loyalty than his leadership abilities.

Morgan liked both men. Chauncy had been a riverboat captain on the Mississippi River, and Theo had lived in a small town in the hills of Western

Virginia. They were an unlikely pair who never would have met except for the war. Morgan was a West Point graduate, trained to be an officer with a military career. But three years of fighting were enough. He was anxious for a victory that would end the war. His father had left him the store he owned in Richmond, but he planned to use his training to build bridges and railroads to replace those destroyed by both sides.

Theo rolled out a map of the area on the table. Lee had invaded the North and planned to attack closer to Washington City, but against orders, his men had engaged Union forces at Gettysburg. More men from both sides had arrived through the evening hours. The Confederacy had the town and a line along Seminary Ridge to Warfield Ridge. The Union had the high ground along Cemetery Ridge and Culp's Hill.

Chauncy stroked his droopy mustache and pointed to the map illuminated beneath a lantern attached to the tent supports. "They've positioned their end of the line at Culp's Hill. If we can break through to the Baltimore Pike, we'll flank the entire Union line."

"Do we know who we're against?" Morgan asked.

"Twelfth Corps."

"We've fought them before, Colonel LaDonte," Morgan said. "They won't run."

"Then we won't either." Chauncy looked at the other officers gathered around the map. "I don't have to tell you how important this battle is. General Lee wants to end this war. The battle has to be decisive. We need to break the Union army to force Lincoln to negotiate."

"We'll do it." Lieutenant Otis Baker had been a school teacher before the war. He was quiet and scholarly, the perfect complement to Morgan's fiery personality.

Chauncy shared the orders. Lee's plan for July 2 was to attack each end of the Union's long line. Once Confederate soldiers charged around the flanks, Lee would send the main army to attack the middle. The Union forces would have nowhere to run.

Chauncy asked Morgan to remain behind after the others had left. "What do you think of the plan?"

"It's sound."

"But?"

"The Union soldiers have discovered a new way to fight. Although they didn't win at Chancellorsville, they dug trenches and built barricades. I think they'll do the same on Culp's Hill. I would if I was on the hillside."

"They have to come out of the trenches at some point," Chauncy said. "They did at Chancellorsville, and we beat them."

"But we lost General Jackson."

"Overzealous sentries," Chauncy said. "Yankees wouldn't dare claim to be Stonewall Jackson. They should have known it was the general."

Morgan had added sinew and grit to his tall frame fighting to stay alive during the numerous battles since he joined the Twenty-first Virginia Infantry in the Army of Northern Virginia. He had fought in the Valley Campaign commanded by Jackson. "No one can replace Stonewall," Morgan said. They had followed the man for too long to believe otherwise.

"Lieutenant General Richard Ewell is determined to prove himself," Chauncy said.

Ewell was Jackson's replacement. Morgan preferred experienced leaders. Untried men were unpredictable and dangerous in the middle of a battle. "My men are seasoned. They'll do what's asked of them."

Chauncy signaled to Theo. "Would you like some coffee?"

Theo poured the hot brew into a mug for Chauncy.

Coffee was a rarity among the Southern troops. Morgan nodded and took a cup. Theo wore a handmade coat of dark gray with gold buttons. It was showing wear with a tear along the shoulder that had been badly mended and two poorly sewn on chevrons marking his rank. "Did your mother make that coat for you, Theo?"

"Oh, no, sir." Theo's wide smile revealed a gap where he had lost a couple of molars on one side. Most likely from a brawl he hadn't won. "Miss Jenny made this coat for me."

"Miss Jenny?" He must have searched far and wide to find a woman who would fall in love with his homely mug.

Chauncy leaned back and sipped his coffee. "Miss Jenny. Prettiest woman you ever did see. She had hair close to the shade of yours, Morgan."

A pretty redhead. Morgan ran his fingers through his thick rusty curls. "I like her already."

"She had a voice like an angel," Chauncy added. "Her husband was killed at Manassas."

"In '62?"

"The first battle in '61." His face softened, the lines of war erased by a memory. "Theo had taken her husband's coat when he discovered his body."

"Spoils of war," Theo defended.

"Miss Jenny wasn't a Southern lady?"

"Miss Jenny was from Ohio," Chauncy said.

"Abolitionist country."

Morgan gagged on his coffee. "And you befriended her?"

"Miss Jenny offered to make Theo a new coat if he surrendered her husband's jacket."

Theo stroked the sleeve. "She made this coat, and Mr. Ellsworth delivered it."

"Blake Ellsworth?"

"Yes," Chauncy said. "Do you know him?"

"His father owned a hotel in Richmond close to the store my father ran." They had been best friends. "We attended West Point together. He left his junior year when Loren Ellsworth died. I attended the funeral. I haven't seen him since."

"He never joined?"

"He had to take care of his stepmother and spoiled stepsister. They were determined to bankrupt him of his inheritance."

They finished their coffee, and Morgan headed for his tent. They would have a long day of fighting in a few hours. He walked through the southeastern edge of Gettysburg. Splintered doors and broken glass littered the streets from the first day of fighting. Most of the residents had stayed in cellars but not all. Otis had told him a stray bullet killed a woman baking bread in her kitchen.

Morgan entered the straight wall tent that had been erected a few hours ago on the edge of town. Tootie Mackinnon, dressed in plaid pants and a mustard-colored coat, had arranged the furnishings in his absence. "Hey, Morgan."

"Captain," he reminded his younger half-sister. Tootie had arrived a month ago dressed in men's clothing and a slouch hat covering a bad haircut. She had been exhausted, frightened, and unusually quiet. Tootie said she couldn't return home to Richmond. She couldn't live with her stepfather.

Morgan and Tootie had the same father but different mothers. His parents were dead, and Tootie's mother, Faye, had married Lyle Neely last year while Morgan was away fighting. Morgan owned the store but had told his stepmother the profits would support her and Tootie in his absence. He had never met Lyle, but Tootie had written about financial troubles with the store and Lyle's drinking. Tootie's letters had become anxious about her stepfather and her mother's lack of concern for her husband's shortcomings. Something had driven her to desperation, but he didn't pry. She was eight years his junior, and he had spent most of his time at school or working. They were practically strangers except for the shared parentage of Ian Mackinnon, a towering Scotsman who had arrived in the United States with his ginger-haired wife and three-year-old son. Morgan could speak in the heavy brogue of his father for a laugh or to scare those who thought his temper matched his fiery hair.

Morgan had told his men Tootie was his younger half-brother and too young to enlist. Tootie remained in his tent away from the men. She kept the place neat, his clothes clean, and his meals served on time. But the army was no place for a sixteen-year-old girl. He had written letters to friends asking if she could stay with them, but the civilians in the South were hurting as they gave everything to support the soldiers and couldn't afford to take in another mouth to feed.

He tossed his hat on the table near the opening of

the tent. "You should be asleep."

Tootie placed a blanket on his bed. "They dumped everything in a pile. I couldn't leave it that way."

"It looks nice." He could sleep on the bare ground wrapped in a blanket, but the upgraded living quarters were a required change for his sister. "Ought to be plenty of fighting today. I need you to remain in the tent so you'll be safe. Do you understand?"

She nodded. "What if something happens to you?"

She was frightened. He couldn't blame her. Even seasoned soldiers were nervous before any battle, and this was a big one. He needed a practical answer to Tootie's worries. What if he was killed? "Remember, Colonel LaDonte is our friend. He'll help you."

Chauncy had guessed Tootie was his half-sister. He had mentioned her once in a past conversation, but his commander hadn't betrayed their deception. Chauncy was a widower, and from the way he had talked about Miss Jenny, he had a soft spot for the female gender.

"I know it's been awkward having me around, but I'm grateful you've let me stay."

"I'm your big brother."

Her giggles made her disguise worthless. "You never let me forget it. You boss me around more now than when you visited home during the summer."

"When did I boss you around?"

"Whenever you allowed me to tag along on your adventures with Blake."

"I was trying to save your life. You were the clumsiest child we knew."

Tootie's bottom lip jutted out. "That's not true."

"Don't you remember how Blake and I had to jump in the river to save you from drowning?"

She shook her finger. "You should have taught me how to swim."

"Blake tried. You sank like a rock."

Tootie giggled. She had been a thorn in his side on his excursions with Blake, which is why their father insisted they take her along. He figured Tootie's presence would keep Blake and Morgan out of trouble. He'd been wrong, but Tootie knew how to keep a secret.

She removed her coat. Underneath was a man's clean cotton shirt. She sat on her cot and kicked off a pair of new brogans. She had taken the clothing from the store he owned. He didn't like Lyle controlling the finances that had been allocated for Tootie and her mother. From what Tootie shared, the man wasn't trustworthy.

Tootie relaxed against the canvas bed and arranged her blanket.

Tootie didn't complain, but camp life was hard for grown men let alone a girl. With her face full of freckles and high-pitched giggle, he could never think of her as a young woman no matter what her age. He needed to find her a home with a soft bed and warm meals every day. A place where he didn't have to worry about the enemy shooting her.

"Go to sleep, Tootie." Morgan had rigged a blanket over a rope to serve as a barrier between their cots and offer her some privacy. He sat at his desk and drew a crude map of the battlefield. The Union line looked like a fishhook. Colonel LaDonte's regiment and Morgan's company had attacked the curve near the cemetery today but would try flanking the Union at Culp's Hill tomorrow.

Chapter Three

Jess had the unfortunate position of being at the rear of a long line of wagons which stirred dust from the dry road into the air. She pulled a kerchief, made from an old dress, higher over her nose to block the choking dirt from the supply train. Rumors of a battle seeped back through the teamsters. Lee was in Pennsylvania with Washington City as his target.

General Meade had orders to stop him. No one had to tell him that if he failed, the war would be over, and he would be known as the general who lost to the South.

Jess had taken the reins of the horses to give Sid a much-needed rest. One of the stretchers was placed over the wooden walls of the wagon and he slept, his snores echoing behind her.

A slouch hat protected her fair skin from the sun beating down on the second day of July. Only her eyes showed above the cloth wrapped around her face. Jess wore a lightweight linen jacket over her dress and rested her soft leather boots against the front of the wagon, her shortened skirt the only sign of her femininity.

Clara Barton had broken the gender barrier, and women traveled to battlefields to offer their nursing services or simple humanitarian care. Jess had perfected her medical skills on the countless wounded that streamed into Washington City after every battle. Her bag was smaller than her father's leather case, but it contained an assortment of probes, scalpels, scissors, and saws for most medical needs.

The wagons in front of them pulled to the side of the road, and Jess moved the team to the edge of the Baltimore Pike.

Union soldiers marched toward them, the metal on their bayonets reflecting the evening sun.

Sid woke and swung his good leg over the back of the seat and sat beside her. "What's going on?"

Jess lowered the scarf from her face. "Soldiers are marching this way."

Sid studied the men as they neared. "It's the Twelfth Corps. Look at the star."

A five-point white star was sewn on the front of the kepi hats the men wore. She searched the regiments for familiar faces. The soldiers were ordered to fall out and moved to the side of the road, relaxing in the grass beneath any available shade tree.

Captain Blake Ellsworth of the Twenty-ninth Ohio strode toward them. He'd been promoted from first lieutenant after the Battle of Chancellorsville.

He removed his wide brimmed hat and shook the dust from it. He was handsome with black hair, a close-clipped beard and stormy gray eyes, but she had always regarded Blake as a brother. Would she desire a man as passionately as her sisters reacted to their husbands?

"Sid, Miss Jessica." He examined his team of horses, stroking the white blaze across their foreheads. "Did my wife think Romulus and Remus needed some exercise?"

The words were casually spoken, but his jaw was

tense. He was worried. She needed to explain her presence. "We have supplies," Jess said. "They were piling up at Pierce House."

He cocked an eyebrow. He didn't believe her. "Was it my wife's idea to send them?"

Jess elbowed Sid. "Why don't you ask her?" She gestured to the back of the wagon.

Blake's jaw dropped. He ran to the rear of the wagon and tossed aside a few blankets searching for his pregnant wife. "That isn't funny."

Jess covered her mouth to stifle her laughter. "We searched the wagon three times before leaving to make sure she stayed behind."

He returned, disappointment and relief written on his features. "Tell her I miss her."

Jess withdrew the stack of letters from her skirt pocket and handed him one. "She wrote you."

Blake withdrew a letter from his coat. "Give her this with my love." He tucked his gloves into his belt and ripped open Cole's letter.

Jess had promised Cole to watch Blake's face. She would report on his tender expression as he read her words of love and the moment when he broke into a grin. Blake loved Cole as much as she loved him. Their feelings were evident in the way they looked at each other, the sound of joy when they spoke, and the pain when they were apart. The feelings that had been absent between her and Ed. Jess looked around. "I hope you aren't retreating. We don't have any plans to leave Washington City, especially with Cole in her delicate condition. You better make sure Lee doesn't visit."

He leaned against the wagon. "The battle began yesterday but doesn't look like it'll end soon," Blake said. "We arrived last night and camped on two hills, the Big Round Top and the Little Round Top overlooking a rock formation called the Devil's Den. The Rebs took the town, but we have high ground. It gives us a fine view of the battlefield."

"How important is high ground when you're marching through cornfields?" Jess demanded.

"We learned from Chancellorsville to build entrenchments," Blake said. "We used flat rocks, fence rails, and trees to build breastworks in front of our trenches on Culp's Hill this morning." He pointed behind him. "George Greene's third brigade is tucked in safe and sound, waiting for the Rebs to attack."

"So what are you doing on the road?"

He looked around. "Brigadier General John Geary ordered us to reinforce the center of the line, but someone missed the turn off."

"Why don't you head back the way you came?"

"Not without orders," Blake said. "That means we sit and wait until someone figures out they made a mistake."

Sergeant Ed Herbruck joined them. He saluted Blake and tipped his kepi marked with the Twenty-ninth insignia inside a bugle and the white star beside it. "Miss Jessica." He offered his hand to help her to the ground.

She bumped into him. "Sorry."

Ed blushed. Her heart barely noticed. What had happened to the spark of excitement that had flowed between them? Did he notice its absence?

Blake turned to Sid. "There's a creek ahead if you want to water my horses." Blake tucked Cole's letter away and strode beside the team.

Ed offered his arm, his sergeant stripes sewn onto the dark blue sack coat. His bedroll was attached to his knapsack strapped to his back, and his canteen was strung across his chest. A cartridge box was attached to his black leather belt. He gripped his Enfield rifle in his free hand.

Jess walked with him along the road. The sun was low in the sky, casting its golden rays in long streaks across their path. She prayed she wouldn't say anything to tip her hand and reveal the reason for her visit, especially with every eye upon them. "You look well." Jess meant it. His light brown hair was cut short beneath his cap, his skin was tanned from the outdoors, and his deep set eyes had wrinkles where he had squinted against the sun.

Ed was twenty-two, five years her senior, but they had grown up in the same town, attending the same school and church. She loved him, but as a brother and friend, not as a husband or lover.

Would she be able to say no to his proposal? Would a white lie be kinder than the hurt and disappointment in his face when she told him the truth? She wouldn't think about words now. There would be time after the battle to wound his tender heart.

They walked slowly. Ed was probably tired from marching, but she needed to stretch her legs after sitting all day on the ride to Gettysburg.

"It's grand seeing you," Ed said.

Jess had left her floppy hat on, shielding her face from too much scrutiny. She wasn't good at camouflaging her feelings and feared Ed would guess she didn't share his dreams of a future together. "Sid and I brought supplies."

"Did you receive my last letter?"

The one with his proposal. "Yes. Blake delivered it before he left for Leesburg."

"Nasty business at Leesburg." Ed's voice was harsh.

"Sid told me about the hangings."

"Some men reach a breaking point," Ed said. "No excuse to murder them."

"War is an ugly business." Her voice was bitter.

"I'd like to see some of the officers do what we've done and not want to run away."

She didn't want to stir Ed's anger. Blake and Sid were returning with the team. "Is Blake a good officer?"

Ed nodded. "He kept the boys alive at Chancellorsville." Ed turned toward three young men resting by the side of the road. The eye contact was enough for them to break ranks and gather around Jess.

"That wasn't an invitation," Ed muttered beneath his breath, but Jess wouldn't have to talk about his proposal with the three youths around.

Her cousin Ethan Donovan greeted her by lifting her off her feet and planting a kiss on her lips. His ginger curls escaped his kepi, and his blue eyes sparkled above a wide grin. At one time she could beat him climbing a tree, running a race, or shooting a gun, but Ethan had turned into a man. It was a startling transformation since a year ago, the last time she had seen him.

Harry Herbruck was a smaller version of Ed with sandy hair and deep set eyes. He was the youngest of the four brothers, and their father had been training him to be a veterinarian before he volunteered. He examined the two horses, checking their legs and hooves. "Are these your horses, Captain Ellsworth?"

"Romulus and Remus." Blake patted his team, rubbing each horse behind their ears.

"They're a fine pair." Zach resembled his brother, Pax, with sour apple green eyes, but his hair was blonde instead of light brown. "Eighteen hands high and matched well for pulling a team."

"How do you know about horses, Zach?"

"My grandfather raises horses. He has a dozen brood mares at Ravenswood Farm."

"Probably a bunch of broken down nags," Harry challenged.

"Mostly Morgans with some gait horses from Kentucky," Zach said. "You can visit Ravenswood any time you want, and I'll prove I'm telling the truth."

"Maybe you'll need a veterinarian for all those horses," Harry said.

"I'll ask about a job if you want it."

"Zach, why aren't you in the Seventh?" Sid asked. "Pax served with me."

He nodded toward Ethan and Harry. "It was two against one. I didn't want to fight alone."

Jess put her hands on her hips. "Sid told me how you put the number nineteen in your shoes so you could lie to enlist."

"It worked," Ethan said. "We're fighting men."

"You should have seen us at Chancellorsville," Zach said. "I bet I shot a hundred Rebs."

"That's nothing to brag about," Blake reminded them.

Zach bowed his head. "Yes, sir."

"Sounds like you have your hands full keeping

27

them alive," Sid said.

"Ed helps."

Ed shook his head. "When they listen."

They gathered around the wagon, searching its contents. "Anything good to eat in here?"

Jess retrieved the basket. It belonged to their mother, but Jem had carried it east when she traveled to find her first husband, who had fought at Bull Run. Jem claimed it had special powers to never be empty, and the battered hamper accompanied them on all their journeys. "There's a berry pie you can share." She cut the pie with the knife she stored in a leather sheath tucked in her boot and served the slices.

She found a loaf of bread and brick of cheese. "I should have served this before dessert." She made sandwiches and offered lukewarm tea.

Jess could stay all day with the Twenty-ninth Ohio, but Sid reminded her they had supplies to deliver. "Do you know where the Twelfth Corps field hospital is located?"

"We passed two on the Baltimore Pike. The nearest is ahead about a mile after you pass a sawmill near a loop in Rock Creek," Blake said. "The next one is in a barn on the Spangler farm near our position. Shouldn't be many wounded. We've been digging and marching instead of fighting."

"Captain!" a rider called. Blake excused himself to talk to the messenger.

Ed slapped his kepi on his head. "Want to bet we have orders to turn around?"

Sid pointed. "If you keep marching on this road, you'll end up in Maryland."

Blake returned to the wagon. "We'll escort you to

the farm. We've been ordered back to Culp's Hill."

Sid waited until the soldiers formed their ranks and marched in the direction they had come. Blake had been wrong about the wounded. Men from the Twelfth Corps were being delivered to the field hospitals in ambulances as soon as they could be gathered from the battleground.

"What happened?" Blake demanded from the first man he met.

"The Rebs in General Ewell's Second Corps attacked Culp's Hill," he said.

"Ewell attacked!" Blake's jaw tensed. "Geary never should have led us on this fool's errand. Now we have to find our way back in the dark."

"We have lanterns in the wagon," Jess said.

"You may mean well, Jessica, but I do not wish to make my lovely wife a widow by carrying a bright light and giving the enemy an easy target." Blake looked at his men. "We'll sneak back to our trenches and pray we don't stumble into any Johnny Rebs."

Jess hugged Blake before he could protest. "Take care of yourself. I don't want to have to face Cole if anything happens to you."

He grabbed her chin and kissed her on each cheek. "You keep your head down, too. And run if there's fire."

He was thinking of the wounded in the inn at Chancellorsville. "I'll be careful."

Ed hesitated to leave her. "I wish we had time to talk."

"After the battle." She gave him a quick kiss on the cheek. Ethan, Harry, and Zach whistled from the ranks.

"They shouldn't let children fight in wars," Ed said

loudly as he joined the men.

Jess waved before boarding the wagon. She turned to Sid. "Who's Geary?"

"The Twelfth Corps is commanded by General Henry Slocum with Brigadier General John Geary in charge of the Second Division and Colonel Charles Candy in charge of the First Brigade. The Twenty-ninth Ohio regiment is in Candy's brigade along with the Fifth, Seventh and Sixty-sixth Ohio, and two Pennsylvania regiments."

"He said Greene's brigade was left behind at Culp's Hill."

"Brigadier General George Greene is in charge of the Third Brigade. New Yorkers."

"Are they the wounded the ambulances are bringing in?"

"Most likely."

Chapter Four

The large barn near the Baltimore Pike on the Spangler farm served as the surgery area for the Twelfth Corps. Canvas wall tents were filled with cots for the wounded. Others with minor wounds were sprawled on blankets in the grass.

The surgeon general had implemented a standard procedure to divide the wounded into three groups. Those who needed surgery, usually amputation; those who had belly or severe head wounds and would die; and those with minor wounds who could wait. She carried cards and wrote a soldier's name, hometown, regiment, division, and corps to pin to his shirt in case he didn't survive.

Jess removed her slouch hat and coat. She put on a long apron and wrapped her hair in a scarf to keep it clean. She placed the haversack filled with medical supplies and bandages over her shoulder and grabbed a bucket and ladle. After filling the bucket from the water barrel on the side of the wagon, she was ready to go to work. She looked at Sid. "Do you think you can find someone to unload the supplies?"

"I already have a few volunteers," he said. "I'll put the horses with the others." He pointed to a line where several horses were tethered, their shapes illuminated by the moon.

She offered the men water but wasn't allowed to

serve food until after a doctor assessed their injuries. Most soldiers didn't have time to eat during a battle and marching rations barely staved off starvation. They complained about hunger but accepted the water instead. Their canteens had run dry in the heat of July.

From conversations with the men, she pieced together what had happened at Culp's Hill. The Confederates had attacked soon after the First Brigade with the Twenty-ninth Ohio had left and continued their onslaught until they occupied the lower trenches. Blake and the boys could be walking into enemy lines.

"You're needed in the barn." Sid took her water bucket and ladle.

Jess could kill a chicken, skin a rabbit, and field dress a deer so the sight of flesh and blood was nothing new. Mangled limbs needed amputation. Wounds needed cleansed and sewn. She entered the barn. Lanterns hung from the cross beams supporting the structure. It took time to adjust to the bright light. Jess joined a doctor at his operating table. His tools were laid out on a smaller table. The saws and knives were covered in blood. He wiped his soiled saw on his blood-stained apron.

A soldier carried a bucket of water to rinse off the portable surgery table. "Could you fetch a bucket of water to wash the medical instruments?" Jess asked.

He stared without answering. Didn't he understand her simple request? "They're covered in blood and need to be cleaned."

"Yes, miss." He nodded, hurried away, and returned with two buckets.

Jess poured water into a long flat pan and rinsed the tools between operations. She dried the handles so the doctor's hand wouldn't slip.

A patient was carried in. The young soldier stared at the surgeon and panicked. "Don't cut off my leg. Please don't cut it off."

Even with the ambulances recovering the wounded and bringing them to the hospital within hours, it was often too late to save a limb. The lead balls did too much damage to the bone. The splintered ends would never mend.

Sometimes a doctor didn't amputate in the field, but the saved limb ultimately was removed in Washington City hospitals after infection and gangrene gave the surgeon no choice.

The orderlies held the man down as a male nurse lifted a green glass bottle from a crate by the head of the table. The doctor placed a small device in the man's nose and added a drop of chloroform to cotton on the wider oval end. The man convulsed, shaking as he inhaled the chloroform. The second drop sent him into a deep sleep.

Jess cut away the soldier's pant leg, exposing the damaged limb. The lower leg bones were shattered, the splintered ends sticking through the shredded skin. Someone had tied a tourniquet below his knee to stop the bleeding. The leg couldn't be saved. She removed his shoe and sock and tossed them into a barrel. Other soldiers would claim the footwear later.

The surgeon cut through the flesh and peeled it back, saving a length to cover the bones after amputation. Blood splattered her apron as Jess struggled to tie off the severed arteries. The doctor sawed back and forth, metal scraping against bone until the two bones in the shin were severed. Jess placed the useless limb on a pile of twisted body parts in a nearby wheelbarrow. She threaded her bent needles and stitched the flap of skin covering the remaining bone. She loosely wrapped the stump with a clean bandage, and soldiers carried the man to one of the tents. Then the process began again with a new patient.

****

Sid tapped her on the shoulder. She had closed her eyes for a brief moment. "There's food for the medical staff. Most of the wounded are taken care of."

"I'm too tired to eat." She rinsed her hands in a fresh bucket of water and wiped them on one of the remaining clean towels. Jess didn't know what time it was or how long she had stood in the blood-soaked mud below the surgery table. The muscles in her back throbbed, her arms ached, and her eyelids drooped. But when she stepped out into the star-filled sky, the cold night air revived her. "I am hungry." She looked around. "Where is the mess tent?"

"I'll fetch the food to the wagon," Sid said.

"Thank you." The words were a whisper. She was too exhausted to speak louder. Jess stumbled to the wagon and removed her soiled apron and headscarf. Sid had removed all the supplies and piled straw in the wagon with several blankets to form a bed. She sat on the end of the wagon floor and kicked off her soiled boots. The straw pile beckoned to her exhausted body.

"Don't fall asleep, yet." Sid handed her a tin plate with a thick slice of smoked pork next to a generous portion of beans. A wedge of cornbread was on the edge. "I don't think these men know how hard you work."

She gripped the fork, but her fingers were numb

from thrusting needles through thick flesh. She tore the meat apart and ate it with her fingers between bites of cornbread. She used a spoon to shovel the beans into her mouth. It wasn't ladylike, but Sid wasn't offended.

She gulped water from her canteen.

Sid took the empty plate and spoon. "Sleep. I made my bed under the wagon. No one will bother you."

Jess wore no crinoline, and her corset wasn't as stiff as those worn with formal gowns. She had slept in her clothes before and knew how to dress for comfort. The bed of straw was as comfortable as most beds, and she drifted off to sleep.

****

Wounded arrived at daybreak. Jess washed the sleep from her eyes. She brushed and braided her hair, arranged it in a chignon at the base of her neck, and covered it with a scarf. She donned a clean apron and gathered her belongings.

Wounded surrounded the barn as if none had been tended during the night. "Where did they all come from?" she asked Sid. "Isn't it too early for casualties?"

"Fighting began a couple of hours ago and hasn't slowed." Sid looked worried. "The Ohio boys have been fighting all morning to retake the lower trenches they lost to the Rebs yesterday."

Gunfire echoed from the higher ground north of them. "Where are the Ohio boys positioned?"

"From what I can determine from the wounded, they're on a high spot behind Greene's New Yorkers. If the Rebs break through the lines, they could reach the Baltimore Pike and flank the entire Union army. Do you want me to hitch the horses to the wagon in case we need to flee?"

"They won't let them break through." Most of the time battles were fought on worthless pieces of ground, forsaken after the fighting ceased, but this was different. The Union had established its line between Lee's army and Washington City. The outcome of the war was at stake.

Sid wrinkled his brow. "No shame in a woman being afraid."

"I know when to pull the tent stakes and retreat, Sid. And remember, I'm a fast runner."

He chuckled. "You better marry a military man, Miss Jessica. No civilian would understand what you're saying."

****

Jess took a break from surgery at noon and served water to the men resting in the shade. She turned at the sound of her name. It was Harry. He took a long draw from the ladle. His uniform was dirty and smelled of sulfur. Blood was smeared on his sleeve. "Are you hurt?"

Harry wiped his eyes, smearing black powder from the battle with his tears. "It's Ed." His voice trembled, and his body shook.

Jess grabbed his arm. "Is he dead?"

Harry choked back tears. "Not yet."

"Where is he?"

He pointed toward the large medical tents.

"Tell me what happened." Jess dashed across the yard.

"The Twenty-ninth Ohio was in a ravine along Rock Creek," Harry said. "It was a good position until we had to replace the Irishmen in the One-hundred-thirty-seventh New York regiment. We fired volleys to give them cover so they could retreat, then we yelled and ran up a swell to replace them in the lower trenches. The Rebs opened fire on us when we were in the open. Lost most of our men during the transfer."

"Is that when Ed was shot?"

"No. Two hours later the Twenty-eighth Pennsylvania regiment relieved us. We had to rip our shirts for rags to clean our guns 'cause we'd fired them so much. We were down to a few canteens of water. Not more than two hours later, we prepared to relieve the New York boys again. That's when we were hit hard. Ed rose up to lead the charge and took a volley of shots." Harry wiped the sweat from his brow, leaving a clean streak on his forehead. "He collapsed. Blake ordered me to accompany him when the ambulances were loaded."

They passed the large walled tents where cots were filled with wounded. "Ed sent me to find you. He said it was important he spoke to you."

Jess paused at the opening of the last tent.

"Over here." Harry pointed to men laid out on blankets or stretchers outside the tent. The group with mortal wounds. Harry knelt by Ed's body and clasped his hands in prayer.

Jess examined Ed as if he were a patient. His skin was grayish in color. A sign of impending death. The sergeant stripes on his upper sleeve were intact but below the elbow his arm was shattered by a lead ball. He would lose his hand and wrist. Another blood stain darkened his jacket. She unbuttoned the single row of military buttons and folded back the dark blue wool fabric. The dull white and blue linen shirt was stained a dark crimson with a yellow stain higher, blending the two colors like a late night sunset. A gut shot. He wouldn't survive.

Harry paused in his prayers, his face streaked with rivers of tears. "He's going to be all right, isn't he, Miss Jessica?"

She couldn't lie to him so she didn't answer. Ed's breathing was shallow and labored. She reached across his torn body and took his good hand in hers. "It's Jessica. Can you hear me, Ed?"

His eyes flickered, vacant at first, but then recognition registered. He smiled and blood dribbled between his blackened lips. "Miss Jessica." He raised his injured arm and groaned. "Pocket."

Jess ignored social rules and put her hand into his trouser pocket. She retrieved a small leather coin purse. "Is this what you want?"

"Open it."

Among the coins was a gold band.

"Do you see the ring?"

Jess removed it and waved it across his line of vision. "Is this a wedding band, Ed?"

"I didn't get a chance to ask you in person."

She had planned to turn down his proposal with a compliment, a few tears, and a firm refusal. But the reason no longer mattered. The truth wasn't necessary. "Ask me now, Ed."

The gray pallor faded for a moment under his blush. "Miss Jessica." He labored to catch his breath. "Will you marry me?"

He didn't have the strength to declare his love. His proposal had been simple and straightforward. Characteristics they shared. "Here's my answer." Jess slipped the ring on her finger and kissed him on the lips.

"I'm the luckiest man alive." Ed's chest heaved with a shudder and a gush of air escaped his lungs. His final breath.

Ed Herbruck was dead. They had been friends and more. He was the first man to ignite the euphoric wonder of being in love. She cherished his kindness, strength, and patience as they stumbled through their awkward courtship and would miss him. The loss of her best friend hit her like a cannonball, and she bent forward, clutching herself as her body convulsed. Grief welled in her heart, and she poured out her emotions, sobbing. She didn't want Ed to be dead. He should have gone home, bought the farm he always talked about, and married a woman who would have loved him for the rest of his days.

Harry sobbed. "What am I going to tell Ma?"

John and Art had returned home, wounded but alive. How did anyone soften the news that a strong, brave son had been killed? "Tell her he died a hero."

Jess caressed Ed's cheek. His face was strong with a wide generous mouth and a high ridge nose bordered by deep set eyes that stared without seeing. She closed his eyelids.

"How can Ed be dead?" Harry's grief had turned to anger. "He was the biggest and strongest of us!"

Jess remained curled in a ball. All the strength in her limbs had left her. She was like a rag doll and didn't trust her legs to hold her if she stood. She was weary of war. She'd seen death and destruction at Cedar Mountain, Antietam, and now, Gettysburg. She'd cared for the sick and wounded in Washington City with her sisters. But she also had played baseball, ate dinner, and written long letters to the soldiers from Ohio. Too many deaths had been loved ones. She wanted the killing to end.

Harry rose and balled his fists. "I'm going to kill all those dirty Rebs!"

Jess rose to her feet and grabbed his arm to steady them both. He didn't need to add more misery to his family. "There's a time to kill and a time to show mercy, Harry."

"But what about avenging Ed's death?"

"We have to make sure Ed is taken care of first," she reminded him. By the time Harry returned to the lines, the fighting would be over, and he would be safe, at least for a little while.

"Do you think we can send him home?" Harry asked. "I'm sure the men will donate. They admired Ed."

They had sent Jake home, but it would cost more than a hundred dollars for the coffin, embalming, and shipping to Darrow Falls. Jess withdrew her purse from her skirt pocket. She gave Harry all the money she had brought, nearly ten dollars, and added it to the money in Ed's purse.

"You'll need money for your trip to Washington City," Harry reminded her, handing her a few dollars.

She dropped the coins into her purse and shoved it into her skirt pocket. She had made the trip to break Ed's heart, but her heart was the one broken.

An orderly approached. "Is this one dead?"

"Could you carry him to the embalming tent?" Jess asked.

"I'll help." Harry took the end near Ed's head.

"We can't send Ed home in a dirty uniform," Jess

said. "Why don't you remove it, and I'll clean it and make repairs."

Jess stood a respectable distance outside the embalming tent. Harry handed her the clothing and Ed's haversack. "The doctor says he won't start until I give him fifty dollars."

"I'll find Sid. He'll collect enough." She laid her hand on Harry's arm. "You stay with Ed."

Jess found Sid at the rear of the wagon bawling. "Cinder in my eye," he excused.

"Flush it with some water. I need you to collect money for Ed's embalming. Harry is waiting at the tent for the money. The doctor won't start without it."

"Vultures," Sid said. "I'll get it if I have to turn the fellows upside down and shake it out of them." He headed toward the medical tent.

Jess sat on the end of the wagon and examined Ed's uniform. She had half a yard of dark blue fabric for jacket repairs and a good length of light blue cloth to patch the holes in his knees for the trousers. The embalming doctor would sew up any holes in Ed's body, and he would be dressed in his uniform when he arrived at Darrow Falls. She washed the uniform and strung some rope on the side of the wagon to dry the clothing before mending it.

She had finished the repairs to Ed's uniform when Harry and Sid returned. The money was paid. Harry had written a letter to his parents while waiting and showed it to Jess. It was filled with the love a brother has for his older sibling. A few tears smeared the ink. His parents would understand.

Jess penned a letter to her sisters to explain why she was in Gettysburg and about Ed's death. She told them she didn't know when she'd return from the battlefield but not to worry. She was among friends. They gave the letter to the mail carrier who was riding to the nearest train depot in Union possession. Jess included the letter to Cole from Blake.

Chapter Five

Jess shared some food from her basket with Harry as they sorted through Ed's personal belongings. They agreed to place Ed's Bible and a few items in the casket that would transport him home. Harry handed her the photograph taken at Matthew Brady's Shop on Pennsylvania Avenue last summer. She had given it to Ed, and he had carried it in his jacket pocket. The edges of the mounting cardboard were worn, and blood stained one corner.

Jess stared at the woman in the photograph. She didn't recognize herself. She had arrived in Washington City anticipating a glorious adventure. Men in uniform, parading down the streets in step to lively band music, were replaced by the endless flow of wounded arriving by train or boat and delivered to the hospitals in and around the capital.

Antietam had aged her as she waded through blood in the surgery barn. The desperate cries of wounded men trapped helpless and wounded in the cornfields haunted her dreams. The death of her dear cousin Jake had taken joy from her heart. Jake had taught her how to tie ropes to secure the lines for the *Irish Rose* and how to play the fiddle. Dear Ed had taught her to hunt and set snares. The woman in this image was younger, not by a mere year, but by the miles traveled between battles.

Jess was putting away the lunch basket when cannon fire erupted. Not one or two, but hundreds of shots in a boom louder than she had ever heard. Harry pulled her outside and shoved her under the wagon, where he joined her. The ground shook from the impact, and the noise was deafening from the continuous blasts that followed the initial round.

A young soldier stood in the open, looking around, unsure what to do.

Jess had seen too many bodies mangled and broken by the balls packed in a canister. The metal casing was ripped apart, and shards tore flesh and organs. She bolted toward the confused man and grabbed his arm. Harry pushed them beneath the wagon.

"What's happening? It's my first battle," the soldier said.

"Artillery," Harry shouted above the deafening noise. "Must be more than a hundred guns firing."

Jess flinched at the screaming noise of the missiles launched across the battlefield. The resulting burst when the shells hit a target made her close her eyes and cover her ears. Although most of the shells landed farther away along Cemetery Ridge, a stray canister hit nearby, killing two horses tethered to a line. Another horse was wounded, one leg blown off and another shattered. It writhed on the ground, screaming in pain.

"That's too close for comfort." The soldier they had pulled under the wagon sprinted across the field.

Jess removed the gun from the holster hidden beneath her skirt. It was the gun Ed had given her when she had gone to Antietam.

Harry put his hand over hers. "I know how to put a horse down."

She might not be able to do it in one shot. She nodded and handed him the weapon.

Harry approached the frightened animal and killed it. He returned and handed her the gun. "Pa always said it was a sin to allow an animal to suffer."

Jess studied the weapon. "This was Ed's gun. You should keep it."

"He gave it to you," Harry said. "Besides, you're a better shot than I'll ever be."

She returned the revolver to her holster. Jess retrieved a blanket and spread it on the pile of straw Sid had used for his bed under the wagon. They made themselves comfortable and waited. Both sides continued their battle of big guns for an hour and then the federal guns fell silent. It was nearly three o'clock when the constant firing of Rebel cannon ceased.

Jess looked to Harry for an explanation. "Now what?"

"Usually infantry fights after a display of artillery power. I wonder if we're preparing to attack."

They crept out from under the wagon and looked around. Others remained under cover, waiting for what would happen next.

"Maybe we should see what's going on." Harry searched through Ed's haversack. "The war could be over."

"That's unlikely."

He grabbed Ed's field glasses. "You can stay here if you're afraid."

Afraid? Jess had never shirked from danger. According to her sisters, she treaded too close for their comfort. Protective Sid was nowhere in sight. She had never seen a battle, only its aftermath. "Let's take a look." She kept pace with Harry's brisk walk.

They arrived at a path. Harry grinned. "Hey, race ya!"

It was as if they were back in Darrow Falls when Jess could outrun most of the boys. She had always left Harry eating her dust. She sprinted down the narrow lane.

She halted as the path emptied onto Taneytown Road. Harry passed her but stopped. He whistled as he surveyed the sight. The Union line was spread along Cemetery Ridge, which had been hit hard by the Confederate artillery. The shells had created so many holes, it looked like a farmer was preparing the ground for planting. Yet the men on the lines had survived without too many casualties. They had remained on their bellies, protected behind piles of rocks and wood.

"Looks like the Johnny Rebs fired high." Harry found a spot with some trees for protection that gave them a clear view of the open field stretching from the Union lines, across Emmitsburg Road to Seminary Ridge in the distance. He stared through the field glasses. "I think I see movement in the trees."

Jess stared across the wide expanse between the lines. "That's a stretch of ground to cross."

"Got to be a mile at least," Harry said. "Looks like the Johnny Rebs are coming out of the woods."

Jess squinted beneath her wide-brim felt hat as heat radiated in waves from the sun's bright sunshine, the temperatures peaking in mid-afternoon. Men emerged from the shadows and silently formed straight lines. "What's happening?"

"They're preparing to fight." He handed her the field glasses.

Men in gray, brown, and faded blue lined up by companies, regiments, and brigades in front of the woods. Soldiers stood shoulder to shoulder, their bayonets and metal trimmings on their guns reflecting the bright sunlight. "Look at all of them," Jess said. "How many do you think there are?"

Harry did a quick calculation. "At least ten thousand."

"I've never seen a battle," Jess said. "What happens?"

"They'll march across the field, and the Union soldiers will march to meet them. Then they'll shoot at each other. And men will be dead when it's all over." He reddened. "Sorry. The winning side takes prisoners and claims the ground."

"I don't understand the prize," Jess said. "No one wants to own Gettysburg. No one is going to claim this land once the fighting is over."

"But one side will claim victory when the smoke clears, and the dead and wounded are counted," Harry said. "Prepare yourself for the slaughter."

"I've seen the wounded and dying," Jess said. "I want to understand why men will line up and march into death. Lord Tennyson makes it sound so pretty and yet so final. You'd think after the first battle, men would run as far away as possible."

"One word keeps us here," Harry said. "Courage. None of my older brothers were cowards. I'm not going to be the first."

The Union lines remained in their protective shelters. "I don't see our soldiers forming lines."

"If Meade is smart, he won't order the men to meet the Johnny Rebs on the field," Harry said. "The men will stay behind the breastworks like we did at Culp's Hill."

"Is Meade smart?"

Harry shook his head. "We'll find out."

"How can you have a battle if one side doesn't fight?" she asked.

"They'll shoot from where they are," Harry explained. "We shot for two hours before being relieved. Johnny Rebs died in piles at Culp's Hill."

"Won't they stop marching when they see the Union isn't budging?"

"Like the six hundred Tennyson wrote about, the Johnny Rebs will march into the depths of hell."

"You like Tennyson?"

"We had to memorize that poem in school, Miss Jessica. Don't you remember me reciting it?"

"Who would have thought we would be living it?" The lines of soldiers stepped forward. "They're moving."

The men in gray marched across the green expanse in the hot sun. They maintained straight lines, their guns at their shoulders. No one played the drums or fife. No one shrieked the Rebel yell. "Why are they so quiet?" Jess whispered.

"They're waiting to get closer," Harry said. "See how their lines are converging. They're going to focus their attack on our middle."

A cannon fired from the Union lines and plowed a furrow across the ground in front of the advancing army. Jess grabbed Harry's arm and turned to the high ground on their left.

"Those cannons are on Little Round Top." Harry pointed to the smaller of two hills. "I thought they were out of canisters when they quit firing the cannons earlier. I think they were bluffing Old Bobby Lee."

The big guns were positioned on the high peak and aimed downfield instead of at the woods. As the soldiers marched, a hollow cannonball exploded or a canister released its deadly cargo along the length of the lines. Groups of four and five soldiers were caught in the blasts and thrown into the air, their bodies torn in a puzzle of arms and legs.

Harry shouted and waved his kepi as a cannon blast took out a group of Confederates. "That's for my brother!"

The cannon fire was replaced by gunfire. Union soldiers shot in ordered precision. A cloud of smoke filled the air and afterward, Confederates littered the ground. The Southern lines continued to converge, filling in the gaps of wounded and dead. The Rebels reached the fence near Emmitsburg Road, and Union gunfire targeted those climbing over it.

A flagbearer dropped his colors, but another man picked up the flag, raising it into the air to show where the middle of the line was located, a gathering point as soldiers marched forward to their destination.

The Union lines fired back, picking off men. Harry cheered as several Rebels fell. Harry wanted revenge for Ed's death, but Jess could only think of the mother somewhere in the South who would never see her son again. Was her sympathy misplaced? She had cared for Confederate wounded, but that was after a battle, after surrender. This was the contest, and she wanted to win. The North needed a victory.

Hundreds of Confederates had fallen and yet they continued on. Smoke from the guns made it more difficult to see the soldiers. Jess silently waited for movement to emerge from the black cloud. An officer with his hat on his sword burst out of the confusion and waved his men forward. Those in the lead broke through the Union line. Guns were useless in the close quarters, and the men fought hand to hand, screaming in pain as they struggled for ownership of a small section of land near a cluster of trees.

Outnumbered and exhausted, the Confederate soldiers who had made it across the field surrendered. Those able to escape, headed back across the field, gathering the wounded who hobbled or were carried to Seminary Ridge. In between, the dead lay scattered like crumpled leaves blown by the wind on a field of green.

A strange silence fell upon the air. The battle was over. A loud cheer roared along the Union lines and was repeated in a wave of euphoric cries.

"What are they doing?" Jess asked.

"Celebrating." Harry grabbed Jess and swung her around. "We won, Jessie girl. We won!"

Jess threw her hat into the air and echoed the jubilant cries of victory.

Harry collapsed to the ground, and Jess sat beside him. "This one was for Ed and Jake and Paxton." Harry bent forward, his kepi gripped in his fists, and wept.

Hot tears blinded Jess as she leaned against Harry's shoulder. Through misty eyes, the field was strewn with the wounded and dead of the enemy. The Union, which hadn't won a major victory since the war began, was celebrating. Lee wouldn't march on Washington City. The Army of Northern Virginia would have to return to the South. She touched the ring Ed had given her. The North had won, but it had come at a staggering price.

Jess stood and offered Harry her kerchief. "We better return to the hospital." Even victors had wounded or dead. Once a truce was called, the orderlies would gather the bodies.

Chapter Six

Morgan urged his men to relinquish their positions as he gave the order to retreat from Culp's Hill. Victory had seemed within their grasp after the first day. On the second day of fighting, Morgan and his men had taken the lower trenches on Culp's Hill when two brigades from the Twelfth Corps marched away.

But they had returned during the night, and it had been a bloody battle back and forth to claim the slope the morning of July 3. The Union soldiers were dug deep in the trenches except when they relieved the men in the front barricades. He was watching through his field glasses to give the order to shoot when the men raised up to exchange positions and were sitting ducks. He focused on a captain urging the men forward and recognized Blake Ellsworth on the open rise above the ditches.

"Don't shoot," he ordered.

"Looks like an officer," a sergeant argued.

"He's my best friend," Morgan said.

"He's the enemy."

Morgan stared at the sergeant. Who had decided his best friend had become his enemy, and he had a right to kill him? What moral principle supported war?

Blake had dropped safely into the trenches along with his men. He had spared Blake's life. His conscience was guilty free.

Morgan ordered his men to the rear while a group of Jackson's boys in the Fourth Virginia occupied the trenches. Everyone called them Jackson's boys even though Stonewall had been dead for months. Old Jack had declared that *war was the sum of all evils,* but he was a military genius, and Lee missed his advice at Gettysburg. Now that Jackson was dead, something had gone out of the fight the general had inspired.

Ewell, who had lost a leg the year before, led the Second Army Corps in Jackson's absence. He had positioned the Corps on the northern end of the line of Culp's Hill and west of Cemetery Hill. The Confederates had attempted to flank the end of the line, but the Union soldiers were dug in deep and not willing to yield. Officers continued to order men to attack up a slope and into a narrow rocky opening where the bodies of dead and wounded Confederate soldiers littered the ground.

Without rhyme or reason, hundreds of Jackson's boys surrendered to the Seventh Ohio. Maybe they were tired of fighting or maybe they didn't want to fight without Stonewall leading them. Others followed their example. A squad of Confederates surrendered to the Twenty-ninth Ohio. Capture was better than being killed.

Ewell ordered retreat. The general had sworn he would take Culp's Hill, but he had failed to break through the Union defenses.

Morgan asked his squad leaders to report who had survived, who had died, surrendered, or been wounded. Some squad leaders never reported. The entire group was gone. He wrote their names, hometown, and fate in a bound book he carried. Later, he would write letters to the families.

They had failed in their mission to flank the Union forces but didn't have time to dwell upon it. Cannon fire boomed farther south. The work at Culp's Hill was taking second place to the attack on the center of the Union defenses. Morgan studied his map. Lieutenant General A. P. Hill, who had served under Jackson, was newly appointed to the Third Army Corps positioned in the middle of the Confederate line. All they could do was wait for news that Hill broke the middle. Then they would gather the fleeing Union soldiers.

The men cleaned their guns, chewed tobacco, or slept during the artillery fire. Morgan checked the watch his father had given him when he left for West Point.

When the cannon fire ceased, Morgan removed the cotton he had stuffed in his ears. The silence was unnerving. What was happening? He left Lieutenant Otis Baker in charge while he reported to Colonel LaDonte.

"Should we prepare to attack, sir?"

Chauncy was reading a report. He shook his head. "George Pickett's division and ten of A. P. Hill's brigades marched across the field to Cemetery Ridge." Chauncy choked back tears. "The Federals remained in their trenches and waited to slaughter our men. The loss was enormous."

They had lost. It seemed impossible. "What should we do, sir?"

"The men are to withdraw to new positions closer to town and Seminary Ridge. They are to build breastworks and prepare for an attack by the Union army tomorrow on the Fourth."

"We lost a large number of men, sir."

"Do you have a report of your company?"

Morgan gave him the numbers his squad leaders had reported. He gave him a written report of the battle he had prepared while in the trenches.

Lee had planned to destroy the Union army and capture Washington City. Now, they were fighting to stay alive. "Colonel, if Meade attacks, and our defenses hold, we might strike a hard enough blow to turn this defeat into a victory."

"His inexperience could work to our benefit," Chauncy agreed. "Let's hope he comes out into the open. He'll find out what it's like for the opponent to remain entrenched."

Morgan's men had picket duty. They dug in for the night. A few men fired shots at the Union lines, and the boys in blue returned fire, but no skirmishes broke out. His men were too hungry and too tired. The wounded cried out for water, but no one dared to go forward. A few crawled to the picket line, and Morgan shared his canteen until the container ran empty.

Another company relieved the men of picket duty near dawn. Morgan helped carry the wounded to the medical tent. He grabbed some hard crackers and filled his canteen from a rain barrel before returning to his tent. After undressing in the dark so he wouldn't wake Tootie, he collapsed on his cot and fell asleep.

****

Morgan woke with a start. The sun was shining. How long had he been asleep? He turned to Tootie's cot, but it was empty and neatly made. Why hadn't Tootie awakened him? She normally cleaned his clothes, but they remained in a pile where he had removed them.

He splashed water on his face to wash the remaining sleep from his eyes and dressed. Morgan brushed the dust and gunpowder from his double-breasted gray frock coat and checked his watch. Where was his sister?

He walked to the mess tent and grabbed a plate of fried potatoes and ham chunks. After gobbling the food, he strolled through the neat rows of canvas shelters toward the medical tent. Was she helping with the wounded?

A young physician's assistant was examining a patient. Tootie had befriended Romeo Greystone who had been drafted to fill the diminishing ranks. He was nineteen and had been attending college to become a doctor. He was learning the trade the hard way. His apron was soaked with blood. His eyes were dark from lack of sleep. He wobbled as he bent over another patient, unwrapping the bloody bandage placed on the mangled leg of a soldier wounded in the field.

"You need to lie down," Morgan warned.

"They keep coming," Roe answered.

"I'm Tootie's brother. Have you seen him? He was wearing a yellow coat and plaid pants."

"I saw Tootie late last night, or was it early this morning?" Roe rubbed his eyes. "I can't remember."

"What was he doing?"

"He visited last night to see if you were among the wounded."

Where was Tootie? Theo entered the tent and strode across the space between them. "Have you seen Tootie?"

"Last night he asked about you," Theo said. "He

was scared you might be dead. I told him you were on picket duty near the cemetery."

That should have reassured Tootie. She wouldn't be foolish enough to go anywhere near the battle lines. He missed what Theo had said and asked him to repeat it.

"Colonel LaDonte requests your presence in his tent."

"I need you to find Tootie," Morgan said. "I haven't seen him all morning, and it's not like him to leave the tent for so long."

"I'll find him." Theo saluted and left on his mission.

Morgan stopped at his tent. Tootie hadn't returned. He didn't like being afraid. Especially over a wayward girl who should have known better than to wander off during a battle. "She's fine," he repeated as he headed for the colonel's tent.

Colonel LaDonte had called a meeting with his officers who were gathered around a map. Morgan was taller than most men and could see over the shoulder of the man in front of him.

"Early this morning Lee ordered Brigadier General John Imboden and his cavalry to escort the wagon trains of wounded out of Cashtown to Greenwood and then south to Williamsport." He traced the westward and then southern route on his map. "They are assembling the wagons now and loading the wounded." Chauncy looked at Morgan. "Major Mackinnon will accompany them."

Major? He'd been promoted. He hadn't done anything warranting the higher rank. Most likely a superior officer had died on the battlefield, and he was being promoted to fill the gap.

"Lee anticipates an attack today, but if Meade hesitates, we will slip away during the night. The army will take a southern route to Hagerstown and keep them occupied enough to allow the wounded to travel unmolested. We'll meet at Williamsport and help the wounded cross at Falling Waters." Chauncy pointed at the South Mountains. "It's a more difficult pass than the one the wounded will use, but we have J.E.B. Stuart's cavalry to scout for any Union forces."

"Where was he two days ago when we needed him?" Otis Baker demanded.

"Stuart made an error, but he wasn't the only one to cost the Confederacy a victory. This wasn't our turn, men. We'll retreat and gather our forces to fight another day."

"Should we pack up?"

"No. We don't want the Union to know we're leaving. It would be a slaughter if they attacked us in the open unprepared. Keep your men in the barricades until they're given the order to retreat. Keep them quiet. We'll be most vulnerable on the road. We want as much of a head start as possible."

"We could surprise them with an attack of our own," Otis remarked.

"We tried for three days. Lee doesn't want to lose any more men."

"Do we know the casualties?" Morgan asked.

"Estimates are twenty thousand killed, wounded, or captured," Chauncy said. "The wagons are carrying about eight-thousand wounded men, but more than six-thousand are too severely injured to transport. They'll remain in Gettysburg and rely on the care of the residents or mercy of the Union army."

"Some of our men surrendered at Culp's Hill," Morgan said. "They thought this would be their final battle."

"So did Lee," Chauncy said.

Morgan turned to leave, but Chauncy called his name. He handed him two gold stars, one for each side of his collar. "You'll need these, Major."

"My men don't care what rank I am. *They fear mah Scotsman's fury.*"

"Your men won't be traveling with you and the wounded. There isn't room."

"I don't understand. Why am I abandoning my men?"

"Imboden is inexperienced," Chauncy said. "Frankly, we don't know how he'd react in a crisis. I recommended to Ewell, who proposed it to Lee, that you accompany the wagon train to advise if necessary."

"Is that the reason for the promotion?"

"You've earned it, but make sure those stars are sewn on before you report to Imboden. If your towering size and Scottish temper don't intimidate him, the stars will." He handed him a folded paper. "These are your orders. Be diplomatic but help Imboden avoid any costly mistakes."

"Can I take Tootie with me?"

"Yes, but you'll have to ride with the teamsters. We lost too many horses today to spare any."

"Who will be in charge of my men?"

"I already promoted Otis Baker to captain. I bet he has his bars sewn on his collar before you replace yours with those stars."

"Otis is efficient." Morgan needed time to search

for Tootie. "When do the wounded leave?"

"Hopefully, the first ambulances have already departed. You can't miss the wagon train. I hear it's longer than ten miles and growing."

"How is the Union army going to miss a target that big?"

"We're going to distract them," Chauncy said. "That's why the army is taking the southern route. Lee wants it to appear we may attack Washington City after all."

"Are we?"

"The men are willing even after being beat, but Lee wants to return to Virginia and regroup. He wasn't expecting this awful carnage. I've never seen the old man shaken this much."

"The Union lost plenty of men, too."

"Their resources are deeper than ours. We can't afford to lose so many. It causes discord among the generals. Pickett blames Lee for the decimation of his division, and I heard Longstreet advised against the attack. Old Pete has grown weary of war like most of us. I had hoped this would be the final chapter."

"We will recover," Morgan said. "We can't allow the Federal generals to build on this single victory."

"Let's hope Meade is like all the generals before him and hesitates to pursue us."

Morgan folded his orders and placed them in his inside pocket along with the stars for his uniform. He saluted the colonel and headed for his tent to gather his belongings and Tootie. She was still missing. He threw his belongings into a wooden travel chest. His tent would be packed with the others and transported with the army. He checked his revolver. It was loaded and primed. Two more cylinders were in his ammunition pouch on his belt. He strung his haversack over his shoulder and searched the surrounding area and then expanded his search.

No sign of Tootie, but he recognized Theo talking to a group of men and approached. "Do you have any news on Tootie?"

Theo pointed to one of the men. "He was seen heading toward the cemetery."

"When was this?"

"After midnight."

Morgan turned on the private. "Why didn't you stop him?"

"He said he had to find his brother. Is that you?"

Morgan walked away without answering. Why couldn't his sister obey orders? He should have checked her cot before he fell asleep. He should have lit a lantern to make sure she was in the tent. He should have sent a messenger to inform her he was alive and on picket duty. If anything happened to her, it was his fault. He checked his watch. He'd catch up to Imboden and the wagon train. He had to find Tootie.

Evergreen Cemetery was between the town and Cemetery Hill with Culp's Hill to the east. The large stone gatehouse had escaped serious damage, but the ornate headstones had been toppled by Union forces, and artillery had destroyed most of the remaining headstones, leaving fragments scattered on the ground.

This was a high point overlooking the battlefield but neither side occupied it now. He searched among the standing headstones and tall grass. He stumbled across a body. It was a Union soldier. If he wasn't careful, he would stumble upon Union forces. He withdrew his field glasses from his haversack and scanned the area.

On Culp's Hill, Union soldiers had left the security of their breastworks and were burying their dead, gathering guns, and hunting for souvenirs among the Confederate bodies. Was Tootie among them? He searched through the glasses for a body in Tootie's clothing but no plaid pants and yellow coat were among the fallen. If they took Tootie prisoner, what would happen to her? She couldn't keep her gender a secret for long. "Tootie, if I find you alive and well, I'm going to…"

He stopped his rant when he heard a groan. He swirled around, expecting an attack. A soft whisper of his name greeted him. A hand moved above the grass growing around a broken tombstone. He knelt by the marker. Tootie was hidden behind it. Blood covered her hip and leg.

"I'm sorry, Morgan. I'm so sorry."

All harsh reprimands fled his lips. She was hurt and apologizing. "I should have sent word."

"I had a vision," she said. "You know how superstitious the Scottish can be. I was sure something dreadful had happened to you."

"I'm unharmed," he said.

"I searched for your line, but it was too dark. Then I heard a voice and a shot." She touched her hip.

She was pale and beads of sweat covered her face. He touched her forehead. He couldn't tell if she was warm from the heat of the sun or had a fever. He needed to take her to a doctor. "I'll get you out of here." He put his arms under her, but when he lifted her, she screamed. He lowered her and looked around. Had the

Union soldiers heard her cries? He stroked her short hair from her face. "You'll need a stretcher."

"Don't leave me." Tears flowed freely, and her body shook. "I'm afraid. I don't want to die alone."

Morgan took her hand. He'd fetch Theo and a stretcher, and they would carry her to safety. But first he had to reassure her she would be safe. He could hide her. He looked for some brush to cover her and saw a wagon approach from the south on the Baltimore Pike. It turned off on a narrow lane that led to Spangler's Spring. Confederate forces had temporarily taken it along with the lower breastworks on Culp's Hill on the second day of fighting. He lifted his field glasses and watched.

Chapter Seven

Harry had told Jess the men of the Twenty-ninth Ohio hadn't eaten since the fighting began and were still in the breastworks on July 4.

She convinced him she should take supplies and care for any wounded. Harry wanted to return to the regiment and didn't argue. Besides, Independence Day had been unusually quiet. The Union officers congratulated the men for defeating the enemy. Broken guns, empty canteens, and the remnants of the battle were scattered on the field. Soldiers and civilians searched for souvenirs along the edges of the battlefield.

Sid had met a few wounded friends from the Seventh Ohio and was celebrating the victory with them. Harry had helped Jess pack food and medical supplies in her wagon and hitched the team. They traveled along Baltimore Pike and turned off on a dirt road leading to Spangler's Spring. When Harry halted the team behind the lines of the Twenty-ninth Ohio, they did not receive the welcome they had anticipated.

"What are you doing here?" Blake helped her down from the seat. "The battle isn't over."

She ignored his angry retort. "If you don't want something to eat, I can take it back to the hospital."

"Food!" someone shouted behind him.

"Unpack everything, and don't stop to examine it,"

64

Blake ordered the men who had gathered around the wagon. He pulled Jess toward a trench and lowered her into its depths. "As soon as they're done, Harry can take you back."

"He can stay here," Jess said from the hole. "Ed has been taken care of, and Harry needs to be with his friends."

"Where's Sid?"

"He's celebrating the victory," Jess said. "I hadn't heard anything about the Ohio boys. I was worried."

"We've been twiddling our thumbs since yesterday. We only ventured out of the trenches this morning after the Rebs had withdrawn."

Jess raised her arms. "Then I should be safe out of this hole. It smells like an outhouse."

Blake pulled her to higher ground and examined the ring on her hand. "What is this?"

"Ed gave it to me before he died." She wasn't ready to offer a full explanation.

"I'm sorry. He was a good man."

"I know." Jess brushed away a stray tear and turned from Blake. She surveyed the gradual slope in front of the breastworks. Bark had been stripped from the larger trees while smaller ones were stumps, broken by the lead balls from the muskets. Debris of shoes, blankets, knapsacks, ramrods, caps, and paper littered the ground.

Flies buzzed over the black and bloated bodies. Jess covered her nose and mouth with her scarf to quell the suffocating odor of death lingering in the hot humid air. "Aren't you going to bury the Confederates?"

"After our own boys are laid to rest," Blake said.

Harry had joined Ethan and Zach on burial duty.

They had replaced their Enfield rifles with shovels as they dug the holes for fallen comrades. Each grave was a stark reminder of the cost of war. "There's so many of them."

"More than a thousand in this area alone," Blake said. "I don't want to add you to the number."

"There was no sign of Rebels on the road," Jess said. "The ambulances have been transporting wounded all morning."

He raised his hands in surrender and sighed. "I wish you and my wife knew when to be afraid."

"Fear won't lengthen our lives. Does anyone need medical care?" She patted her haversack. "I have bandages."

"I'll check." Blake signaled for Ethan to join her.

Her cousin was sunburned, dirty, and smelled of gunpowder. He grabbed the canteen on her shoulder and took a long swallow. "Harry told us Ed died."

"Sid gathered enough money to send him home to Darrow Falls."

"Will they bury him in the same cemetery as Jake?"

Jess nodded.

"He was a hero, Jessie," Ethan said. "Ed promised we would survive this war, and he took that shot for us."

Jess hugged Ethan. "Don't make him a liar, cousin. Stay alive."

Ethan nodded. "Harry said you witnessed the battle. I wish I'd seen our victory."

Jess fought back tears. "Oh, Ethan. I celebrated all those men being killed, and now I'm ashamed. I've never seen a battle. Only the aftermath. It was worse than I imagined. They kept coming even when those next to them were blown apart. I wanted to scream at them to turn around and run away, but they kept marching until they fell. The field was littered with bodies. I don't know how they'll bury them all."

A soldier was lowered into the long trench Ethan had helped dig. "One body at a time." Ethan put his arm around her shoulders. When had he grown so tall? They had spent long summers working on Grandpa Donovan's canal boat, laughing and enjoying carefree summers. Now life was filled with chaos and death.

"When are you heading back to Washington City?"

"I'll stay to take care of the wounded. Sid will probably want to transport those we know to the Mermaid's Mirth." Jess surveyed the battle-torn countryside. "How long will you remain here?"

"Until we're given orders to march," Ethan said. "In the meantime, we'll bury the dead and gather the weapons." Thousands of guns were piled in numerous stacks already.

Blake returned with a few wounded men. She cut off their dirty bandages, cleaned the wounds with water from her canteen, and wrapped them with clean strips of cloth. A few needed stitches, but she was done quicker than she had expected.

Ethan took her canteen. "Let me fill this for you."

She packed her supplies, replaced her apron with her worn but comfortable coat, and covered her loosely-braided hair with her hat. The men thanked her for the food and shared some with the Confederate prisoners, the same men who had been the enemy yesterday. She was familiar with contests. Most losers congratulated the winner, but war wasn't a friendly game. The stakes were life and death. How could the men ignore the blood on their uniforms as they ate and laughed? How could they forget the past three days? A young soldier in faded gray burst into tears. Harry put his arm around him. "I lost my brother, too."

Her chest heaved with the pain she knew both men felt. Hot tears coursed down her cheeks. She rubbed her scarf across her face. Ethan startled her when he returned with her canteen. She gulped a drink. "This is cold."

Ethan pointed to a low spot below them. "Spangler's Spring is nearby. Blake watered the team."

Blake led his horses toward her. She dampened her scarf and cleaned her face.

"Say your goodbyes." Blake hitched the team to the wagon. "The sooner I return you to the camp hospital, the better I'll feel."

Was he planning to escort her? "You need to stay here," Jess said. "You're their captain. Harry and I didn't see any Rebels along the Baltimore Pike. Everyone says they've retreated to lick their wounds."

Ethan hugged and kissed his cousin. He signaled Harry and Zach to join them.

Jess hugged Harry. "We both loved Ed, and we'll cherish his memory. Write me when you can. I'd like to hear from you."

Zach grinned at her, his sour apple green eyes begging for a hug. She opened her arms and embraced him. "Take care of your friends."

"Can I write, too?"

"I'd be upset if you didn't."

Blake kissed her. "Give my love to Colleen." He lifted her into the seat of the wagon and handed her the reins. "Take care of my horses."

Horses? "You're not concerned about me?"

"Aren't you the Beecher sister who won a five-dollar gold piece in a shooting contest? Do you have your gun?"

She patted the side of her skirt. Beneath its folds was her gun secured in a holster strapped around her waist.

"Knife?"

She pointed. "In my boot."

"Do you know how to return to camp?"

She could have reminded him they were the ones lost a couple of days ago. "Take the path to Baltimore Pike and turn north."

"North? That'll take you into town. The Rebs hold it."

She laughed at his unease and tugged her hat down to shade her eyes. Blake was easy to bait. "I go south, Captain." She saluted, but her gaze lingered on clouds gathering in the sky. "I better hurry. It looks like rain is coming."

"That's good," Blake said. "We can't fight when the powder is wet."

****

Jess passed a few curious Union soldiers but most were busy eating, sleeping, or burying the dead. She tucked a stray blonde curl beneath her slouch hat. Her coat was warm as the sun peaked, but it protected her dress from the dust the horses stirred on the path.

She was within a wagon length from the Baltimore Pike when a lump trembled on the side of the road and groaned. The blue wool coat exposed through the tall grass belonged to a Union soldier. Had the ambulances missed a man? Jess didn't see a rifle near the body and pulled back on the reins with her gloved hands. "Are you hurt?"

The man groaned and rocked in pain. "Help."

Jess left her gloves on the bench seat and gathered her bag and canteen before jumping to the ground. The weight of the revolver hung on her hip beneath her skirt. She had access through a slit in her skirt pocket if she needed to defend herself. She glanced around and knelt by the injured soldier. He was on his side with his back turned toward her. Blood stained his blue coat. His trousers were gray. Gray?

The soldier rolled to face her. A large hand clamped over her mouth, and a thick arm pinned her to the ground.

She kicked and twisted to escape. Before she could scream, he shoved a sweaty rag into her mouth. She gagged and reached to remove the cloth. He grabbed her wrist and wrapped a rough, scratchy rope around her flesh. He tied the other one so she could barely wiggle her hands. She couldn't reach her gun or knife.

The big brute yanked her off the ground and threw her in the back of the wagon. Jess landed on the straw piled on the wooden floor and scrambled to a sitting position. She glared at her attacker.

He was a huge man who filled the opening at the back of the wagon. His hair was long, the tight reddish-brown curls framed his fierce countenance and a short ginger beard outlined his square jaw.

She tried spitting out the gag but only made the filthy rag wet as her spit mingled with a manly scent. Her knife was in her boot. If she could raise it out of the sheath, she could rub the ropes against the blade.

He returned with her sack. He had removed the bandages and medical bag. "Are you a nurse?"

Jess nodded, hoping her medical training would save her.

He tossed her bag inside but kept the canteen. She turned to see him climb onto the driver's bench. The wagon jerked forward, and she fell on her side. Instead of turning south, her captor had turned north toward town and the Confederate camp. He was taking her into enemy territory.

Jess rolled to the side of the wagon and sat, bracing her back against the wall. She bent her knees to her chest and raised her hem. If she could reach her boot, she could cut the ropes with her knife. She had raised the blade about an inch from the sheath when the wagon stopped. She lowered her skirt and covered her knife before her captor saw what she was doing. He grabbed a stretcher tied to the side wall and pulled it free. "I'm going to need your help."

He didn't wait for her response but grabbed the front of her coat and yanked her to the edge of the wagon and dropped her to the ground. She stumbled but didn't fall. They were in the cemetery. Broken stones littered the ground. He pushed her forward to a lump beneath an officer's gray frock coat. It was absent of any braiding, but she'd cared for too many Confederate wounded not to recognize the double row of buttons and three bars on the collar that signified a captain. Light blue trim identified infantry. He placed the stretcher beside the body and offered water to the wounded man. Boy. A freckled face with short brown hair didn't belong to a man or officer. Who was he? He moved the boy to the canvas carrier. "Take that end."

She showed him her hands and shook her head, trying to spit out the rag in her mouth. He loosened one wrist and tied the rope to the stretcher pole. They loaded the boy into the wagon on top of the straw. He freed her hand but bound it with the other before lifting her in the wagon. He was taking her prisoner. He returned with the canteen and an officer's wide-brimmed hat, which he tossed into the corner of the wagon. He discarded the Union jacket on the ground and slapped the dust from a worn felt hat.

"I'll take the gag out once we're clear of enemy lines." Without his military coat and wearing the floppy hat, he could pass for a civilian. He climbed into the driver's seat and urged the team forward. Jess rolled with the motion then braced herself against the wagon wall. She glanced at her captor's back. He was hunched over, pretending to be small and insignificant. Would the Union soldiers be too busy to stop a lone driver on the road? She moved her skirt aside and rubbed the ropes against the edge of her raised knife.

She nearly cut her wrist when the wagon hit a rut, and she fell to the side. The boy cried out, and the man turned around. Jess pulled her skirt over her blade. "You all right, Tootie?"

"Let me die, Morgan."

"That's not going to happen, Tootie."

Knowing their names didn't lessen the danger. Morgan was a brute. He had taken her captive. What were his plans? She shuddered as she recalled how his big hands had caught her and made her a prisoner. What else could his callous paws do to her? Jess waited until the team jerked the wagon forward. She returned to cutting the rope. Finally the fibers unraveled under the sharp edge, and her hands were free. She yanked the filthy rag out of her mouth and gasped for clean air. She considered her options.

She could jump and run, but Blake's team would fall into the hands of a ruthless enemy. And she didn't like to lose any contest, especially to a ruffian, who would be caught off guard by a mere girl. She pulled her knife out of the sheath and inched closer behind Morgan, keeping low in the wagon bed.

She took a deep breath and sprang to her feet, placing the blade against Morgan's neck. "Stop the wagon!"

He pulled on the reins. They were in the town of Gettysburg, but the streets were deserted. The citizens had remained in cellars or hidden in inside rooms, expecting another day of fighting. Not many of the homes had escaped damage. Broken windows, dislodged shutters, and debris littered the streets. "It looks like I'm not the first civilian to suffer at your hands."

"Maybe you missed the three days of battle."

"Your fighting days are over if you don't jump off."

He didn't budge. "Don't nurses save lives? Why are you intent upon taking mine?"

"You attacked me," Jess reminded him. "This is my wagon and my team of horses, and no one is going to take them from me."

"Tootie will die without medical care."

"We have good doctors at the Union hospital."

"She isn't a soldier."

"She?" Jess turned to examine Tootie. The smooth skin, the slight build. She had mistaken feminine attributes for a youth. It had been nearly a year when she and Cole had dressed as men to travel to Antietam. She should have seen immediately through the disguise.

The distraction was enough for Morgan to grab her hand and prevent the blade from slicing his throat. He tried wrestling the knife from her grasp, but she wouldn't let go. He'd have to break her hand to loosen her grip.

But in the end all her struggling was useless against his superior strength. She had lost the element of surprise, and by distracting her with Tootie's gender, he had gained the upper hand. She managed to cut his shirt, which elicited a cry of outrage and renewed his determination to subdue her.

Morgan pulled her across his rock hard thighs. He bent her arm back and wrestled the knife from her numb fingers. She needed to escape, but he held her firm against his legs. He wrapped a kerchief around her wrists.

"Let me go you stinkin' polecat!"

His deep rumbling laughter mocked her feeble attempt to escape. "You have more fight than a dozen soldiers." He leaned forward, trapping her with his body. "What do you have hidden beneath your skirt?"

A draft of air cooled her body as Morgan tossed her skirt and petticoat upward, nearly covering her head. Was he going to rape her on the seat of the wagon? His hand moved upward along her linen bloomers.

"Get off me, you oaf!" She kicked, but he crushed her with his greater weight. None of her weapons, none of her skills at besting boys would help her. He was too strong, too intent upon harming her. Jess fought a sob in her throat, steeling herself for the assault.

"You have the most interesting toys."

"You touch me, and it'll be the last thing you do." Jess arched her back and threw back her head to butt him, but her jerk met empty air, and her hat fell to the ground.

"You are intent upon ending my life, of which I am fond." His fingertips caressed the curve of her hip before moving to her waist. He reached beneath her belly and fumbled at the buckle of her holster. *He wanted her gun.* The leather slid against her bloomers. "I only wish to disarm you." He checked the cylinder. "This gun is loaded. You could have killed someone."

"I would have shot you if you didn't sneak up on me like a snake."

His weight was gone from pinning her, but her skirt and petticoat were still tossed over her head. She rocked on his thighs and pushed against the floor board, but the action propelled her forward into empty air. Her hands were pinned behind her, and she landed with a thump on the hard ground, the wind knocked from her body.

Morgan jumped to the ground and grabbed the back of her coat. He yanked her to her feet. "You fool. Were you trying to kill yourself?"

Jess gasped for breath, each intake a painful struggle. Morgan brushed off the front of her coat, pausing when his hand encountered the curve of her breast. He stared at her as if seeing her for the first time. "Who are you?"

Chapter Eight

Morgan had seen a formless coat, stained skirt, and low-fitting slouch hat on the driver. He had expected a tobacco-spitting crone at the reins, not the fair-haired beauty with a murderous expression. He had discovered the gun strapped to her thigh during their wrestling match for the knife and had to disarm her. She'd put up a fight, and the fall had knocked the wind out of her, but she had yet to shed a tear.

Her chest moved up and down, her breathing labored, but she found her voice. "Jessica Beecher. My father is Doctor Sterling Beecher, and if you think you can kidnap me, you'll find you've met your match. I have important friends."

Her father was a doctor. "So you know medicine."

"He taught me enough to help the wounded."

He looked at the wagon. "This isn't marked as an ambulance."

"This is my personal wagon." She struggled against the bindings on her hands. "It doesn't belong to the army, and it doesn't belong to you."

"I can't carry Tootie without her screaming in pain. I need your wagon to reach camp."

She paused her struggles. "The Confederate camp?"

"That's where I'm heading."

She nodded south to the Baltimore Pike. "We're

not traveling in the same direction."

"Then I guess you're going along for the ride."

"It's against the law to kidnap someone," Jess said. "They'll hang you."

"It's perfectly legal to capture someone during war," he countered. "I have no intention of ransoming you."

She planted her boot-encased feet on the ground. "I told you my name was Beecher."

The implication finally registered. "That's an abolitionist name. I don't have to ask what side you're on in this war." He frowned. "You're not related to Harriet Beecher Stowe, the woman who started this war with her distorted fairytale?"

"She's a distant cousin, and she didn't start the war. Slavery did."

He leaned down, his face inches from hers. "My family never owned slaves."

She didn't cower under his stare. "Then why are you fighting for the South?"

He raised his voice. "Because Virginia is my home."

She looked around, a look of confusion on her face. "Are you lost? This is Pennsylvania."

She had him there. They were invading the North to put an end to the war. Only a newly promoted Meade had bested a seasoned Lee. He sighed. The tactics he used to intimidate his men weren't working on this slip of a girl. Woman. Maybe. She had the innocent face of a child but the curves of a seductress. A raised eyebrow terrified Tootie so why wasn't Jessica Beecher trembling and crying for her mother?

"If you help Tootie, I'll let you go." It was a lie.

With the Southern army withdrawing from Gettysburg, he couldn't let her leave until hours after the last soldier marched away. Besides, he needed her wagon to transport Tootie to the wagon train carrying the wounded.

She looked at her gun and holster in his hand. "What about my gun and knife?"

He waved toward the wagon. "I'll return them when you've helped Tootie."

Jess frowned. "Is she your wife?"

"My half-sister."

"What sort of brother are you to make her live among soldiers and worse, put her in danger?"

How could a woman with a face like an angel attack his honor with such a viperous tongue? His answer was laden with sarcasm. "Yeah, I was having so much fun being shot at I wanted to put my baby sister in the line of fire. What sort of man do you take me for?"

"The sort who kidnaps defenseless women."

"Defenseless?" He tossed the gun and holster onto the seat next to her knife. "You have more weapons hidden on your person than a mercenary."

She stared him down, her full lips pursed. Jessica Beecher was a rare beauty up close. Blonde curls escaped a thick single braid and framed a delicate pointed chin and big green eyes that flashed when she was angry, like now. "You're going to be popular at camp."

Her face reddened. "I'm not a camp follower." She blew a stray lock of hair from her face. "If I help Tootie, you have to promise no harm will come to me, including any molesting."

"Do you promise to behave?"

A sly smile formed on her plush lips. What was the imp thinking?

"You don't know what you're asking."

For an instant Morgan forgot he was in the middle of a war-torn town. Her husky voice and softened features reminded him he was a man who had entered the war soon after graduating from West Point. His experience with women was limited but had been pleasurable from what he recalled. His search of her body had determined she had long legs, firm and well-shaped hips, and breasts that could satisfy his appetite. Then there was her face. How many men pictured her lovely features in their dreams?

She turned her back toward him. "Are you going to untie my hands?"

He grabbed her wrist and pulled on the kerchief to free her. He retrieved her hat and crammed it over her head. "Even covered up, that face is going to be a problem."

Her hands brushed her cheeks. "What's wrong with my face?"

Nothing. A gold band decorated her left hand. She didn't look old enough to be courted. "Are you married?"

She looked confused by his question. "No."

He pointed to the wedding ring. "Why are you wearing that?"

Jess hid her hand with the other. "It was a gift from a dying friend."

Gift? The band on her finger gave him an idea. One she would balk at. "My job will be easier if you wear it."

Her eyes slanted in an exotic tilt. "What job?"

He chuckled at her suspicious tone. With her not being gullible nor fearful, he'd have to convince her of his plan. "To keep you safe and unmolested."

She smoothed her skirt into place. "I was most concerned about you."

He'd been raised to be a gentleman, but his reaction to the defiant wagon owner was rooted in his Scottish ancestors. His father had bragged about his heritage. Highlanders were bold raiders who defied authority. They struck fear in the hearts of their enemies and made women faint in their arms. He wouldn't allow a delicate flower to challenge his superiority. He would conquer her. She would surrender her sweet lips for him to claim.

"Did you hear me?" Jess snapped her fingers in front of his face. "If you give me back my gun and knife, I can take care of myself."

Her petal-shaped lips were likely coated with poison. He put the gun and knife in his haversack. "Even fully armed, you're no match against the entire Confederate army, Mrs. Mackinnon."

Jess looked around at the deserted town of Gettysburg. "Who's Mackinnon?"

He pointed to his chest. "I'm Major Morgan Mackinnon. Your husband."

She put her hands on her hips. "I'm not marrying you."

"It's in name only." He didn't want to calm her fears too much. "Would you prefer I tell everyone you're a Beecher abolitionist? All the men in camp lost brothers and friends the past three days. They don't need much of an excuse to take it out on someone. I'd hate for them to use your hide to vent their anger."

A gasp escaped her trembling lips. His words had frightened her. "I'll borrow it."

Morgan swung her onto the wagon seat and joined her. He moved his haversack as far from her reach as possible.

She sat with her back straight, her hands in her lap. "Is Mackinnon Irish?"

Morgan slapped the reins on the back of the black draft horses and imitated his father's Scottish brogue. "*Dorn't insult me, lass. Mah faither was a fierce highlander.*"

She tilted her head with a teasing smile on her face. "Hah, if you're a Scotsman, where's your kilt?"

"*It's nae th' kilt that's important.*" He clucked at the horses and winked in her direction. "*It's what's underneath.*"

She slid to the far edge of the bench seat. "You said this marriage was in name only. No kilt lifting."

Morgan laughed. A dainty lass would have fainted at his remark. She might enjoy a few wifely duties. He had never seduced a woman into sharing his bed, but it couldn't be difficult. Men bragged about it all the time.

****

Jess turned to look at Tootie. Even with the bed of straw, the girl grimaced with every jolt and bump. "Maybe I should look at her now."

"We're almost at my tent. It'll give her some privacy. No one knows she's a girl."

"How long has she been in camp?"

"About a month."

"Why?"

His square jaw clenched and his dark brown brows

knit in a frown. "That's none of your business."

Morgan's tenderness only extended to his sister. He'd show her no mercy. He had one foot on his haversack. He wasn't taking any chances of her recovering her arsenal. But he'd have to lower his guard at some point, and when he did, she'd snatch her weapons and take her wagon to freedom.

They passed the breastworks of the Confederate camp. They were preparing for another fight. Rocks and brush were piled high in front of trenches. The men stared in her direction. If they wondered why a woman was in the camp, they didn't ask. Was it common for Morgan to be seen with a strange woman? She pulled her hat lower to hide her face. What was worst, being a prisoner or being considered an officer's play thing?

He stopped in front of a walled tent. He jumped and pulled her down from the bench seat. "You can help carry Tootie inside."

She glanced around for an escape route.

He must have read her mind. "Remember you're surrounded by Confederate troops. You won't get far no matter how fast you run."

Morgan's hand encircled her wrist, and he dragged her to the back of the wagon. He lowered the back and pulled the stretcher part way. Tootie groaned. "Can you manage this end?"

She should have refused, but Tootie was in pain. She also was a woman. Life was difficult enough for the female gender in a world dominated by men. She wouldn't make it harder. She grabbed the ends of the stretcher and pulled.

Morgan grabbed the opposite ends, and they carried her into his tent. He directed her to place the stretcher on the nearest cot.

She turned toward the opening. "I'm going to need my bag."

He followed her and tossed her into the wagon. She fell forward from the force. "I'm not a bag of flour."

He jumped onto the bed. For a big man, he was light on his feet.

While he searched, she gathered her haversack and canteen.

He retrieved his haversack and grabbed Jem's basket. "What's in here?"

"My supper." Jess didn't wait for his help and jumped from the wagon to the ground. He followed, his hand on her waist to guide her inside.

When she opened her haversack, Morgan snatched it and dumped the contents on a small table. He sorted through her belongings.

Morgan examined the photograph Ed had carried in his pocket. He compared the picture with the real woman. "Is this you?"

She wasn't the same inside but had her outward appearance changed so much he couldn't match her to the girl who had arrived in Washington City a year ago? She shrugged. "That girl doesn't exist anymore."

"Too bad. She was pretty."

Her pride wouldn't allow the slander. "Plenty of men think I'm pretty."

"Pretty is for a girl." Morgan studied her. "You have the beauty of a woman who knows what she wants and how to obtain it."

How wrong could a man be? A chapter of her life was closed with Ed gone. What words would the ink form on a clean page?

Morgan stared at her belongings. "What do you need?"

"I need you to stay out of my way." The sooner she completed her task, the sooner she could return to Union lines. She removed her coat and placed it around a wooden folding chair near the table.

Her work dress was plain with wide straps that crossed in front and tucked into a belt. The sleeves were narrow and she pushed them to her elbows. She examined the two aprons she had washed after helping the wounded and put on the one with fewer stains. She wrapped a scarf around her hair and arranged her medical supplies on a clean cloth as Jem had taught her.

Unlike surgeons, midwives emphasized cleanliness. Her instruments were mismatched, gathered a few at a time, but she took time to wash and dry them after tending the injuries of the soldiers.

Although she had participated in countless surgeries, if she made a mistake, nicked an artery or vital organ, she would be helpless to correct her error. "You should fetch a doctor."

"They're busy chopping off arms and legs." Morgan stared at her with strange golden eyes. He looked like a hawk, his focus on her while chewing on a sandwich he had stolen from her basket.

"That's my supper."

He offered her what remained.

She ignored his generosity. "I've lost my appetite."

"Suit yourself. I eat when the opportunity allows. I barely filled my belly after the battle." He finished off the sandwich and searched the basket for more.

Jess removed the gray officer's coat covering Tootie and handed it to Morgan. He had removed the

84

felt hat he had worn during the ride and placed it on the table next to his gray military hat. His rusty hair was tightly curled while Tootie's darker locks were straight. She leaned close to Tootie's ear. "I'm going to have to remove your clothes."

"No." She pointed at Morgan. "Wait outside."

Jess straightened. "She wants you to leave."

Morgan leaned toward his sister, his voice tender. "Why, Tootie?"

"Leave me some dignity, Morgan."

"Dignity?"

"I was shot in the butt."

Jess snickered. She liked Tootie. Morgan, not so much. She expected Morgan to agree to his sister's request, but he remained nearby. "I won't look at your wound, but I'm not leaving."

"I'll cover you with something." Jess retrieved a blanket from the other cot. She eased her out of the yellow coat, which was stained with blood on one side. She examined the torn trousers. "I'm going to need my knife." She offered her hand to Morgan, palm upward.

Morgan grabbed his haversack and retrieved her knife. He patted the holster on his hip with his other hand. "I have a gun if you slip."

Jess took the knife. "I don't hurt women. The world has plenty of men to do that."

"Women can cause pain, too."

"They don't start wars and blow each other to pieces. Why do men enjoy violence?" She stabbed the knife in his direction. "Why do they find pleasure in punching a hole in a man and watching him writhe in pain? I would like to know the answer. Ninety percent of men are wonderful creatures. It's the remaining ten percent that terrify me."

He stared. "No woman scares me."

Jess waved the knife in the air. "The boys are smarter back home. They're terrified of me."

Her words startled him. "Why?"

Jess grinned and hummed a tune as she cut away the bloody cloth. She paused. It was the Scottish Air, *Comin' Thro' the Rye*. Why had that tune invaded her thoughts?

Jess had cut along the seam from the cuff to mid-thigh, but the plaid wool cloth stuck to the dried blood. She cut around it, discarding the extra material on the ground. She moved the blanket to cover bare skin. The remaining patch of fabric needed to be eased off her hip. "I'll need my canteen."

Morgan took a swig and offered her a drink. She dampened the cloth, but when she tugged to remove it, Tootie cried in protest.

Morgan stepped forward. "Do you have something for the pain?"

"I have ether, but I'll need help administering it." She removed a tin container holding the ether from her medical bag. Tootie was on her side, her face toward her. "Don't be afraid," Jess reassured her. She handed Morgan a copper funnel with a stem to hold over Tootie's nose and mouth. Jess placed a few drops on a wad of cotton in the narrow opening. "Breathe deeply."

"She's asleep," Morgan said.

"Add a drop if she stirs." Jess added water to what was left of Tootie's trousers and used a smooth stone scraper to loosen the cloth. The wound's blood was mixed with yellow pus, and the surrounding area was red and swollen. There was no exit wound. She would have to find the lead ball. Jess selected a probe. The long metal pick had a porcelain ball on the end to separate torn tissue and search for the misshapen lead. Tootie twitched. "More ether," she reminded Morgan.

She enlarged the hole with a scalpel and pressed folded bandages into the wound to absorb the blood so she could see. She probed deeper for the lead ball. The porcelain tip hit something solid. The bullet was nearly flattened against the hip bone. She switched to tweezers to remove the distorted lead and pieces of Tootie's clothing that had been driven into the wound. She removed a chip of bone and tossed it in a small bowl. The bleeding was slow. No squirts or heavy gushers. None of the major arteries or veins had been severed. She washed the wound with the spring water.

Jess turned to Morgan. "In my medical bag is a flask. Hand it to me."

Morgan reached toward the bag and retrieved the flask. "Medicinal purposes?"

"Make sure she's asleep," Jess warned. "This will sting."

She washed the wound with the alcohol. Most doctors believed it was a waste to clean a wound. Pus was needed for proper healing. But Jem, as a midwife, emphasized keeping everything as clean as possible to prevent the fevers that often took a mother's life. When they couldn't boil the medical instruments, they used alcohol on the wounds.

Jess soaked the needle and thread in the alcohol and stitched the wound closed except for a small opening for drainage. She examined Tootie for any other injuries and found a cut on the back of her leg. The jagged edges needed trimmed and sewn. She tied off the knots and wrapped a bandage around her leg.

She instructed Morgan to remove the cone from Tootie's face. "We can't put those dirty clothes back on. Does she have a nightgown?"

Morgan's retrieved a clean shirt from a wooden chest at the foot of the cot. "It's my nightshirt. Will it do?"

It was large and loose, the perfect gown for Tootie. After slipping it over her head and tugging it down over her hips, she placed clean socks from her bag on Tootie's feet and covered her with the blanket. She stirred slightly but remained asleep.

Morgan, who had avoided viewing his sister during her undress, turned to study her sleeping form. He brushed Tootie's short hair away from her face. "How long have you been an army nurse?"

Jess cleaned her tools and packed them in her bag. "I don't work for the army. I'm a volunteer."

Morgan studied her. "That explains it."

She pulled the end of the silk thread through a notch on the top of the wooden spool to secure it and thrust the needles through a scrap of fabric before storing them. "Explains what?"

"I was told Union army nurses were ugly."

She understood his backhanded compliment but wasn't going to reward him. "I was told Southern officers were gentlemen. I guess we were both wrong."

"Before you put away your needles and thread, I have a favor to ask."

The man was insufferable. "What now?"

"I need stars sewn onto my coat." He handed her his military jacket.

The three bars were the rank of a captain in the

Southern army. "You were promoted?"

"It was nothing I did." His words were bitter. "A major died. I'm filling the ranks."

"Union soldiers pay for laundry or repairs to their uniforms."

Morgan handed her a Confederate dollar bill.

"I'm not going to the outhouse."

He snorted to cut off a laugh. "This paper money is good in Virginia."

"We're not in Virginia."

He flipped her a coin. It was Confederate but silver. She retrieved her scissors and clipped the threads holding the bars on the collar. It took her a few minutes to attach the stars.

Chapter Nine

A soldier stood in the tent's opening. "Major Mackinnon, sir."

"Come in, Corporal," he ordered.

He saluted. "The colonel thought you'd left by now. He sent me to pack your tent and belongings."

Morgan stepped between the corporal and Jess. "I was delayed."

"The colonel said if you were still here, he wanted to see you. It's about the retreat."

Morgan turned. Jess lowered her gaze but not before he briefly locked on hers. She dried her medical tools, avoiding his scrutiny. The Confederate army was moving out. She needed to return to Union lines and warn them of Lee's plans. If Meade attacked now, victory would be complete. The war would be over.

Morgan examined his coat before slipping it on. "Corporal, I need you to remain here and guard my wife."

Had Morgan guessed her plans? How? Could the man read her mind?

"She's not to leave the tent. That's an order."

"Yes, sir."

Morgan turned to Jess, a smile playing on his lips. "I won't be long." He jerked her close and patted her behind. "Be a good girl or the corporal will have to shoot you."

She stiffened at his familiar touch. He rested his hand on her waist, keeping her close. She recognized the familiar scent of his skin from the gag he had shoved in her mouth. It should have been repugnant, but the manly odor was more subtle, almost earthy. It stirred a womanly reaction she failed to repress. He rubbed his other hand across his beard. It was short, more closely resembling stubble than the long flowing beards most officers sported. Ed had always been clean shaven. She'd never kissed a bearded man. She shook her head. She wasn't going to allow Morgan Mackinnon anywhere near her lips.

"Don't keep the colonel waiting, darling."

He grabbed his hat and haversack, met her gaze with a warning look, and departed.

Her hands trembled as she packed her haversack. She'd celebrate the torn and bloody body of Major Morgan Mackinnon on the next battlefield of the war. She lifted the well-worn picnic basket. It was light. Morgan's greedy appetite had left her little to eat.

The corporal stared at the basket and then at her with a strange look that was unnerving. He had a bowl-shaped haircut and scraggly brown growth of hair on his chin. How was she going to get away from him?

"Miss Jenny?" All the Beecher sisters bore a strong resemblance that bound them as sisters. Even people who knew them in Darrow Falls often confused them. Did he know Jem?

Jess grabbed the tattered sleeve of his coat. The cuffs and detail stitching were familiar. "Where did you get this?"

"Miss Jenny made it for me." He squinted. "You look like her."

Could it be? "Theo Jameson?"

He removed his kepi and fumbled with it. "You know me, ma'am?"

"I sewed the buttons on this coat. I'm Miss Jessica."

His eyes widened. "You're Miss Jenny's sister." Theo smiled, revealing a few gaps. "Only your hair is like wheat and hers is like fire."

The jacket was two years old. Most soldiers replaced their coats after six months, sooner if in a battle. "It looks like your coat could use some mending."

He removed it so fast Jess couldn't stop him. "Would you mind fixing a few tears? I don't have a coat to replace it."

She needed to escape before Morgan returned. But if she mended Theo's coat, he might help her leave. Her needle was still threaded from sewing Morgan's stars. She used the light blue cloth to repair a large hole on Theo's sleeve, but every time she fixed one hole, she found another.

Theo told her about meeting Jennifer and Logan Pierce at Manassas where he had claimed Ben's coat from his dead body. Jem had promised to make Theo a coat in exchange for Ben's velvet-trimmed jacket. Ben had saved and stored letters from Jem in an inside pocket of his coat, and she had read them to her Confederate captors. In them, Jem had written about her sisters and life in Ohio. "Did you win a five-dollar gold piece in a shooting contest?"

Had Jem written about that? And how did he remember? She nodded. If only she had her gun now, but Morgan had taken it with him. She finished the repairs and returned Theo's coat. She tossed her remaining belongings into her bag and moved to the opening in the tent. The wagon and team were outside, and there was no sign of Morgan. She needed to gain Theo's trust so she could sneak away. Dark clouds threatened to storm. "It looks like rain. I should take the team to a shelter."

"I can do that, Miss Jessie."

Miss Jessie? She'd won his friendship. "I wouldn't want to take you away from your duties." Jess put on her coat and hat. She grabbed her bag and basket. "Please stay with Tootie. I won't be long."

"Major Mackinnon said I should guard you."

"He didn't mean guard." She smiled and touched the sleeve of his repaired coat. "Why would you have to guard me? I'm your friend."

He squared his shoulders. "That's right. You fixed my coat. That makes you my friend."

Jess nodded as she stepped through the opening of the tent. "I'll be back in the time it takes to whistle *Dixie*." She threw her belongings on the floor in front of the driver's bench seat and climbed aboard. As she reached for the reins, two hands yanked on her coat. She reached for a secure hold and snatched the basket. It tumbled to the ground, spilling the remaining items.

"Where do you think you're going?"

It was Morgan. He had a firm grip on the back of her coat, straining the buttons in front.

She pointed to the sky. "It looks like rain. I was going to put the team in a barn."

He spun her around and pulled her close, his face inches from hers. "Liar."

She looked to Theo who had come outside.

"I told you to guard her," Morgan barked.

Theo backed away, tripping over the basket. He snatched it and ran away.

Jess struggled out of his grasp. "Don't shout."

"I'm not yelling."

She put her hands on her hips. "That booming noise isn't you?"

Morgan looked around. "Where's Theo?"

He was gone and so was her basket. "You scared him."

"I don't see you running."

"I recognize hot air when it blows in my face."

A crack of thunder echoed their argument. Heavy droplets pelted them. Morgan pushed her inside the tent. The storm had arrived.

They turned and stared out the flap. Rain gushed in sheets. The dry ground bounced in dusty splatters with each heavy drop. He pointed at Jess. "Don't move." He opened his travel chest and removed an oil cloth blanket. "Put this over Tootie."

He placed an oil cloth poncho over his head and loaded his travel chest into the wagon. When he returned, the poncho was dripping. Morgan bent over his sister and listened to a raspy exhale. "Is Tootie going to be all right?"

"The wound is deep but will heal with time. But her breathing is labored. How long was she on the field after being hit?"

"She was in the cemetery all night. I was on picket duty and didn't realize she had left the tent until morning." He paused. "Picket duty is where…"

"I know what picket duty is. You need to keep her warm and dry." She glanced outside. "Are you sure you want to transport her in this downpour?"

"The colonel was not happy I was still in camp," Morgan growled. "I have orders to depart immediately, and I'm not leaving Tootie here with the dying."

Confederates sorted their wounded the same as the Union. They were evacuating the casualties who would survive. Those left behind would be cared for by civilians until they died. "You could leave Tootie with me. I'll take care of her."

"I'm not leaving my sister behind."

If she helped Morgan transport Tootie to the wounded being evacuated, she could take her wagon and return to Union lines. Jess draped the oil cloth blanket over Tootie, shielding her face. "You may borrow my wagon until we reach your ambulances. After we transfer her, we'll part ways."

Morgan grunted as he made another trip to the wagon with a few more belongings. When he returned, Theo was with him. He was empty handed.

"Where's my basket?"

He smiled. "I put it in the wagon."

"Help me load Tootie." Morgan signaled Theo to lift the other end of the stretcher.

Jess grabbed the remaining blanket from the cot. "Where's your rain coat, Theo?"

"I don't have one, Miss Jessie."

Morgan looked at her with a peculiar expression. "Miss Jessie?"

Jess shrugged. "He knows my sister."

Theo gripped the handles of the stretcher. "Miss Jenny made my coat."

Morgan looked from Theo to Jess. "Who are you?"

"Apparently, I'm your wife."

95

Morgan lifted his end of the stretcher, and Theo followed. "Come along, Mrs. Mackinnon."

Jess dashed for the wagon. They had Tootie loaded. Morgan tossed her in the back. He turned to Theo. "Tell the colonel I'm on the road."

The clouds had turned the afternoon sunshine into a murky darkness. The rain pounded on the canvas of the wagon, but the material was strong and held against the wet onslaught. Morgan slapped the reins on the backs of the team, and they plodded forward. Tootie groaned with the movement. Jess removed the heavy oil cloth blanket and replaced it with a wool cover. She tucked the straw around her body to add cushion against the hard floorboards. Jess retrieved a small bottle of laudanum from her medical bag and gave Tootie a spoonful followed by a sip from her canteen. "That should help with the pain."

"Thank you. I hope I can repay you some day."

Once Tootie fell asleep, she gathered the oil cloth blanket around her shoulders and secured her wide-brimmed hat with a scarf. She needed to know how to return to the Union lines. She climbed over the front of the wagon and joined Morgan on the bench seat.

"You're going to get soaked."

She retrieved her leather gloves for the side box on the seat and gripped the waterproof blanket. "I can take it if the horses can."

"They're beautiful animals. Did you steal them?"

The man was insufferable. "You're the thief."

"I didn't steal you. I took you prisoner."

"I was talking about my gun."

"What's a little girl like you doing with a big revolver?"

She needed to divert his attention from her weapon. "The horses belong to my brother-in-law."

"You said you weren't married."

"I'm not. Blake Ellsworth is married to my sister Colleen."

"Did you say Blake Ellsworth?"

"Do you know him?"

"Must not be the same man. The Blake I knew would never marry." His tone was disbelief. "He had a parasitic stepmother and stepsister. He swore he'd never take on a shackle for any woman."

"Cole is not a shackle."

"Cole?"

"Colleen. Miss Colleen to you."

"What do they call you?"

"Miss Jessica."

"You're a Jess."

"Only my sisters call me Jess."

"So what made Blake marry your sister? Is she expecting a baby?"

"Yes, but they're in love."

"Love." He spat the word. "I'll wager she trapped him into marriage. How early will the babe be born?"

"Their baby is due next month, eleven months *after* the wedding."

"I don't believe it," Morgan scoffed. "All Blake talked about was being a soldier when he was at West Point."

"My sister didn't marry him to stop him from joining the army. It was important for him to fight. He's a captain in the Twelfth Corps."

"He was standing on Culp's Hill." He turned when she gasped. "My sharpshooter wanted to kill him, but I ordered him to stand down."

The brute had a conscience? "Why?"

"He was my best friend."

Blake had talked about his best friend from West Point. "You're Mac?"

He shook his head. "So he spoke of me."

"He made you sound like a nice man." She stared at the rain pelting the horses. "He won't like Romulus and Remus being in this downpour."

"Blake loved the classics. I'm sure my best friend won't mind if I borrow them."

Jess made note of the route. "You promised to let me go when we reached the ambulances."

"And have you tell the Union generals about Lee's plans to sneak out tonight?"

"What makes you think I'd do that?"

"You should never play poker, Mrs. Mackinnon. You blush when you're plotting a coup."

"I promise I won't say a word about your departure."

"Liar."

She needed to return to camp before Sid noticed she hadn't returned from Culp's Hill. She didn't want anyone to risk their lives in an attempt to rescue her. "What are you going to do with me?"

His golden eyes studied her. "I wish I knew."

She would bide her time for now. Somehow she'd get away and warn the Union.

****

The rain continued its torrential downpour all the way to Cashtown. Jess looked around. "Where are the ambulances?"

A young private braved the downpour and left a

building that had served as a hospital. "The last of the wagons left two hours ago," he said. "Brigadier General Imboden said he was ordered to travel the forty miles to Williamsport non-stop, but you might be able to catch up to them. They're heading toward Greenwood and then south to Waynesboro."

"I know the route, Private. You said two hours ago?"

"Before the rain started. I hope it lets up before the rest of the army heads out. Monterey Pass is going to be tough riding in this weather."

Jess had studied the map of the area when guiding Sid to Gettysburg. Monterey Pass was south of Cashtown. The Confederate army would retreat in a different direction from the wounded. Now she had to escape with her urgent news.

"Looks like we're going for a ride, Mrs. Mackinnon." Morgan slapped the reins on the horses. "I hope it doesn't ruin your plans to warn the Union about the news the private so graciously shared."

Was her expression so transparent? She resorted to sarcasm. "I've already penned a note and attached it to the carrier pigeon I keep in the back of the wagon, Major."

"Morgan," he corrected. "A wife doesn't address her husband by his military rank."

"I've never been married to a soldier before."

"I've never been married to a woman so intent on seeing me dead."

"It should keep you on your toes, *darlin'*."

Morgan laughed. "*Ah hae' a feelin' it will, mah bonnie lass.*"

Jess gripped the side of the wagon. His rumbling

deep voice had sparked a spontaneous flame that was burning hot in response. But he was the enemy and a formidable foe. The man had bested her at every turn. She didn't like losing. Eventually her luck had to turn for the better. Then she'd show Morgan what it was like to be at the mercy of Jess Beecher.

Chapter Ten

Morgan followed the muddy trail west out of Cashtown. Searching for Tootie had caused him to miss the wagon train. Colonel LaDonte had chastised him for putting personal matters before duty and threatened to demote him to captain. But after hearing about Tootie's injuries, Chauncy suggested it would reduce Brigadier General Imboden's suspicions about his superiors' lack of trust if Morgan joined the wagons because of Tootie's wounds.

The teamsters were driving teams of mules or horses through the rain-drenched roads. Blake's pair of draft horses were strong, but the thick mud, churned by hundreds of wounded-filled wagons, slowed their progress.

Jess had given in to exhaustion and had joined Tootie in the back of the wagon. She was curled next to his sister to keep her warm against the damp night air. Both were asleep. Morgan urged the team forward, a flash of lightning illuminating the narrow road.

Blake wouldn't approve of pushing his team through the storm. He certainly wouldn't approve of kidnapping his sister-in-law. Jess was under the impression once they reached the wagon train, Tootie would be transferred, and she would be given the reins to the team. That wasn't going to happen. He couldn't let her return to the Union forces until Lee's army was safely in Virginia. If his comrades had left during the night, they would reach Williamsport a day or two later than the wounded. He'd have to hold her at Williamsport until the army crossed the Potomac River.

The wind whipped the rain in his face, stinging his skin like tiny needle pricks, and his beard was soaked. Even with his oil cloth poncho and thick leather gloves, the harsh elements should have chilled him to the bone. But the curvaceous image of Jess Beecher behind him on a bed of straw warmed his body with a growing heat. "Don't go soft on the treacherous wench," he warned himself. He laughed at his choice of words. Soft was not his problem.

****

The rain had slowed to an annoying drizzle by morning, but the damage was done. The downpour had filled small creeks and tributaries that flowed into larger streams. Water flowed in the ditches along the roads leaving thick rivers of mud that sucked the wooden wheels into its depths. There was no sign of the wagon train and no way of knowing how far ahead it was located.

Jess poked her head through the canvas opening. Her blonde curls were in disarray, and she rubbed the sleep from her eyes. She'd been asleep a few feet from him wrapped in a warm blanket while he had been wet, cold, and tired. He'd been tempted to join her. She would have put up a fight, but he could tame the wildcat. He chuckled.

"You're in a good mood this morning." Her sweet voice reminded him she was under his care even as a prisoner, and he banished any lascivious thoughts for the moment. "Where are we?"

Her breath was a warm breeze against his cold face. "Near Greencastle," he said. "About half way."

She raised her hand to her forehead and peered through the rising mist. "Where are the other wagons?"

"Ahead somewhere."

"You didn't catch up to them?"

Her accusation reminded him why he disliked the company of women. They could point out the obvious and destroy any shred of confidence. His mood turned foul. "Look at the blasted road."

"Romulus and Remus must be exhausted."

"Thank you for your concern," Morgan said. "I'm tired, too."

"Do you want me to drive?"

Was she serious? His shoulders ached from fighting the reins to keep the horses trudging through the muck. He glanced over his shoulder. "How's Tootie?"

"She's sleeping. I gave her some laudanum for the pain after I checked the wound. She has a slight fever but no signs of infection." She looked at the sky. "We need to get her out of this dampness."

"Thank you for taking care of her." He sneezed.

Her warm hand was on his forehead. She brushed back his soggy curls. "You need to rest."

"I'll be fine." His stomach growled. "Anything left in your basket?"

"I think you ate everything." She disappeared into the back. A scream carried forward. "I can't believe it!"

He turned his head. "What's wrong?"

She showed him the basket. "Someone filled it with food. It must have been Theo when he disappeared with it."

Morgan removed his glove with his teeth and reached for a chunk of cornbread. It was dry and hard but took away his gnawing hunger.

"I didn't believe her, but my sister was right. This is a magical basket."

Did she say magical? "I know little girls enjoy fairytales, but you don't seriously believe in magic?"

"Jem took it with her when she searched for Ben after Bull Run, and everywhere she traveled, someone filled it with food."

"Who's Jem?"

"My sister, Miss Jenny. My eldest sister Cory gave us nicknames when we were small: Jem, Cole, Jess, Cass, and Jules."

Had he counted correctly? "Six sisters?"

Jess took a bite of a fruit tart and nodded. Some filling dripped on the edge of her mouth. He nabbed it with his finger and sucked on the sweet taste.

"Where did Theo get these pastries?"

"When we took the town, we confiscated food from the pantries."

Jess choked on the bite in her mouth. "You stole it?"

"Stole?" Morgan shook his head in denial. "The residents of Gettysburg generously donated their surplus. How else was Theo going to fill your magical basket?"

"You're making fun of me."

Morgan grabbed several chunks of cheese and popped one into his mouth. "If I eat all the food in the basket, fairies won't fill it?"

Jess made a face. She didn't appreciate his humor. She took a cornbread loaf and bit into it. Her mouth moved in a subtle chewing rhythm that was mesmerizing. What was it about a woman's lips that tempted a man to taste them? He'd always considered canoodling a waste of time. His lovemaking had been efficient, fulfilling his needs for the moment. He preferred seasoned women who didn't expect love sonnets or return visits. Was she too young to be practical about a short-term tryst? "How old are you?"

"Seventeen, but I'm not too old to believe in magic or the luck of the Irish."

She was a child. Except his hands had discovered womanly curves beneath her skirt. Jess didn't act like an ingénue. Where Tootie was shy and frightened, especially of men, Jess had challenged him at every turn. She was fearless. She had attempted to escape more than once, and she knew too much for him to allow her to succeed. He reviewed her comment. "You're Irish?"

"On my mother's side. Her surname was Donovan."

"You don't look Irish."

"I resemble my German grandmother."

Germans conquered by Vikings. A delicate beauty forged in fire. He needed to douse his lustful thoughts. "Looks like the rain has stopped." Morgan removed his other glove and hat. He struggled to remove the rain poncho.

"All you have to do is ask."

Had she read his mind? The horses did need a rest, and they could find a dry spot beneath a tree. He'd enjoy a frolic of pleasure before completing his assignment.

She disappeared inside the wagon and returned

with a towel. She was a practical girl. She dried off the seat and climbed over it and raised her hands. "Hand me the reins."

Reins? "Why?"

"So you can remove your poncho."

Her jacket was unbuttoned, and her movements hinted at feminine secrets he longed to discover. A poncho wasn't the only thing he wanted to remove. A few rays of morning sunshine broke through the clouds and illuminated her pale locks like a halo, framing her angelic face. Temptation and trial. The carnal invitation died on his lips. He hated rejection and doubted Jess would exchange a few dollars to lift her skirt willingly. "Put on my gloves."

She pulled on the oversized gloves and took the reins.

"Promise not to bolt in the other direction."

"The poor darlings have been pulling all night. We should let them rest."

"No one rests until we reach Williamsport." Morgan struggled out of the wet poncho. He slapped it on the side of the seat to rid it of droplets and hung it on a hook on the outside of the wagon.

He put on his hat and took back his gloves and the reins. "Look out for any cavalry."

"Wouldn't we see the wagons first?"

"I was talking about Union cavalry."

Jess turned to look past the opening in the back of the wagon canvas. "They wouldn't attack wounded men."

"I almost wish they were following us," Morgan said. "By now Lee has left Gettysburg and is heading toward Washington City."

"He's attacking the capital?" She was hysterical.

He maintained his ruse. "We can't win the war sitting on the front porch sipping mint juleps."

She frowned. "Your army was meeting the wagon train in Williamsport."

She had overheard the plan. Morgan didn't want to frighten her, but misinformation would make her less of a threat if she escaped. Colonel LaDonte had said Lee would travel south to make it appear they would attack the capital and ensure Meade followed. "When I was called away by the colonel, he informed me that Lee was going forward with his original plan to attack Washington City."

"My sisters are in Washington City."

"We don't kill women."

"No, you kidnap them and hold them against their wills."

Morgan countered her passionate outburst with a calm retort. "I have the impression you don't enjoy my company, Mrs. Mackinnon."

"You represent the war, and I hate it. I've had my fill of butchered men and boys too young to rest in a grave. I want the war to end."

He'd seen good men die in the past three years. "This battle was supposed to end the war." He studied her. "Why are you here?"

"You stole my wagon..."

"No, why are you in the middle of a vicious battle instead of sitting in a parlor surrounded by young gentlemen reciting poetry and comparing your beauty to angelic creatures?"

His question had startled her. "When I was sitting in the parlor, I was the chaperone." Her smile disappeared and a shadow crossed her delicate features. "Besides, all the good men are away at war. Or dead from it."

He nodded toward her hand. "What about the man who put that ring on your finger? Who is he?"

"Edward Herbruck. He was a sergeant in the Twenty-ninth Ohio Volunteer Infantry."

Was? "You said you weren't married. Engaged?"

"Not exactly."

How could a woman take a simple question and make it complex? "How can you not *exactly* be engaged?"

"He proposed, and I put the ring on my finger."

"I believe that makes it official. Congratulations."

"I didn't intend to say yes." Jess swiped at a stray tear. "He was dying, and I wanted to ease his last moments."

"When did he die?"

"The morning of July 3. His brother Harry carried him in from the battlefield."

"At Culp's Hill?"

Her voice broke. "Yes."

The fighting had been fierce for possession of a few holes in the ground. "Were you in love with him?"

"I was at one time. Back in Darrow Falls, Ohio, he taught me how to set a snare and dress a deer."

"Did he think you were a boy?"

"I had no brothers and enjoyed the outdoors." A soft smile charmed him. "He was the first man to kiss me."

A stab of jealousy hardened his words. "Must have been some kiss for him to want to marry you."

"A bit ordinary." Jess shrugged. "I guess that's

why I didn't want to marry him."

"So why are you wearing his ring?"

"Because he was my friend. He was dying, and when he asked me to put it on, I couldn't refuse."

Her gentle actions were a contrast to her combative behavior toward him. "And I thought you were a tough, cold-hearted Yankee. You couldn't hurt him."

"If he had lived, I was going to tell him the truth."

She twisted the dead man's ring. Did she love him? He must have loved her. "Why didn't you write him a letter like every other woman?"

"It would have been cruel." Her lip trembled. "Did you ever receive a letter from a woman telling you she no longer was in love with you?"

"Me? Never. But I've seen plenty of men bawling like babies after some woman writes to say she can't wait any longer or she's found someone else. A canister ball to the gut would have been kinder."

"That's why I traveled all the way from Washington City. I had to tell him face to face." She swiped at a tear. "I'm glad I didn't have to hurt Ed."

"Maybe it was better he died."

"No, it's not!" Jess shook with anger. "Ed had dreams of a farm, and he deserved a wife and children. He should have grown old and bounced grandchildren on his knees." Jess searched for a kerchief in her skirt pocket. "I don't understand how life can be so unfair. He was a good man. He deserved to live."

"We lost good men, too."

"Then why are you fighting this war?" Jess wiped her cheeks clean of all tears. "Will the slaves be free when it's over or will their owners shackle them in some other way? Will the states unite into one union or will they continue to strive against each other? A war doesn't change anything. It only delays the decisions that should have been made before the war started."

"A decision requires a majority to agree on a subject," Morgan said. "That's what makes our government so complicated. The more diverse its people, the more difficult for a consensus. We should have made George Washington a king or maintained him as a general. When Lee gives an order, we follow it."

"But his last order nearly destroyed your army."

"We're not beat, yet."

Jess stood and pointed in the distance. "I see a wagon!"

Morgan halted the team when they were abreast of the wreckage abandoned by the side of the road. The wooden spokes in the wheels had been broken apart. The canvas had been torn away and the wagon stripped of its accessories.

"What happened?"

Morgan jumped to the ground and examined the splintered spokes. "Looks like someone took an axe to the wheels." He looked inside. The floorboards were stained, and a wadded rag had been left behind.

"The Union cavalry would have taken the wagon." Morgan joined Jess and looked around. "Must have been angry civilians."

Jess scanned an open field. "Do you think they'll attack us?"

"Without a guard we don't look like a military wagon, but we better keep moving."

"But Romulus and Remus need a rest."

"Do you want someone attacking you with an axe?

110

We can't stop in enemy territory."

"I'm not the enemy."

Morgan smacked the reins against the horses' backs. "I don't think they'll take the time to ask for proof of your allegiance."

"If you're expecting trouble, you should give me Ed's gun."

"Ed's gun? Did he give you that with the ring?"

"He gave me the gun before Antietam."

The bloodiest day of the war. "You were at Antietam?"

"With Clara Barton."

The Angel of the Battlefield. Clara Barton helped wounded on both sides of the conflict. Is that why Jess had agreed to help Tootie? Gettysburg wasn't her first battlefield. She had traveled to Culp's Hill before a truce had been called to visit the boys in the Twenty-ninth Ohio. Was it courage or stupidity? He studied her cat-like green eyes for an answer. How many men had fallen in love with the wild cat, her hair an unruly mass of blonde curls surrounding an angelic face marred by the pain and horror of war?

Morgan Mackinnon was determined not to be one of them.

Chapter Eleven

They had nearly reached Hagerstown on a route parallel to the railroad when more signs of hardship appeared. A Confederate was lying on the side of the road. Morgan halted the team and jumped from the seat. After examining the man, he shook his head. "He's dead." Another casualty was nearby.

Morgan returned to the wagon with a somber expression. "We can't do anything for them."

"Why would your soldiers leave the dead on the road?"

"No time to bury them," Morgan said. "Hopefully, civilians will lay them to rest."

"Even though they're the enemy?"

He slapped the reins on the horses' rumps. "They're no threat now."

When they approached another bundle of gray fabric, the body moved. Jess grabbed Morgan's arm. "He's alive."

He grabbed a stretcher from the back of the wagon. "I'm going to need your help."

Jess knelt beside the shivering man. His clothes were torn and wet. "Let me die," he begged.

"You can die in Virginia." Morgan rolled him onto the stretcher, and they carried him to the wagon.

Morgan lifted her into the wagon and resumed his place as driver.

Jess grabbed a blanket and covered the wounded man. "Why did they leave you by the road?"

"I couldn't take the jostling." He pointed to his leg where the shin was bent in a bow instead of straight. The pant leg had been torn away, but the bones had not broken through the skin.

"No one set it?"

"No time."

Jess searched her medical bag and gave him some laudanum for the pain.

They added two more wounded abandoned on the road. They were a miserable lot. The men shivered from lying on cold, damp ground. She took a blanket from Tootie, who had awakened. "What's going on?"

"We're entertaining some guests," Jess said.

Morgan chuckled. "How are you feeling, Tootie?"

"Better than yesterday. It was yesterday?"

"This is July 5. We'll be in Virginia soon."

"Don't you mean West Virginia?" Jess asked.

"There is no such state."

Most of the soldiers' injuries were broken bones that had not required amputation but jarred with every bounce and jolt of the wagon. Jess fashioned a sling for one man and pushed straw beneath another man's leg to cushion it. Jess examined the remaining laudanum powder. It wasn't enough for all of them unless she diluted it. She took her canteen and mixed the powder with a measured amount of water and made Tootie and each man drink an equal portion. "That should help a bit with the pain."

"Are you a nurse, miss?"

"That's my wife, Mrs. Mackinnon," Morgan announced from the front.

Jess met his gaze. She hadn't agreed to pose as his wife, but the ruse was practical. He was an officer, and they would respect her because of his rank.

"Who's in the stretcher?"

"That's Tootie," Jess said. How much should she reveal? "Has a doctor seen to your wounds?"

"No time except for a quick look and a bandage to stop the bleeding."

"I couldn't take the crowded wagon with all the jarring and thumping," one man said. "Not even a bit of straw to cushion the ride. It was torture."

"This isn't much better," Jess warned.

"Your medicine has eased the worst of the pain," he said. "Maybe I won't choose to die today."

It was late afternoon when they reached Hagerstown and heard gunfire. "Take the reins." Morgan handed the leather straps to Jess, who had joined him to make more room for the wounded.

Imboden's cavalry were fighting off the Union cavalry. Morgan fired a few shots from his revolver, but the Union riders were departing. A lieutenant in the Confederate cavalry joined them. "Major, what are you doing here?"

"I have orders." He gave the paper to the lieutenant. "I picked up a few of the wounded left on the road."

He rode to the back and looked inside. "It's been a nightmare journey. We're resting at Williamsport, and then we'll cross the river at Falling Waters."

Morgan turned to Jess. "We can transfer the wounded into other wagons at Williamsport."

"And I can reclaim my wagon." She looked at Morgan's haversack beneath the seat. "And my other belongings."

****

When they reached Williamsport, the wounded were being unloaded and camps erected.

Jess looked around. The arrangements appeared permanent. "How long are you resting?"

Morgan left her with the wagon but returned shortly. "The Union troops destroyed our pontoon boat bridge," he said. "And the river is too swollen from the rain to rebuild it. We're staying here."

"You and Tootie," she corrected. "You promised I could leave."

"It won't take long to rebuild the bridge, and Blake's horses need a rest."

He was right about the horses. It would be a long trip to Washington City. "A few days rest would do them good but only a few." By now the Union army would have figured out Lee's forces had retreated. Her chance to end the war had passed.

Morgan helped her down and called to a couple of able-bodied soldiers. They loaded the injured men onto stretchers and carried them inside the church, which had been converted to a makeshift hospital.

The women of the town helped with the wounded, offering food to the soldiers. It didn't matter what side the men had fought on, they were wounded and needed care. Jess grabbed her haversack. Tootie was still in the back of the wagon. "Do you think one of the women will take Tootie in?"

"I'll find out." Morgan was gone before she could remind him to ask about a barn for the horses. The man wasn't much of a conversationalist. He was all action. She offered Tootie some food while she waited.

115

A hand reached in and snatched an apple. Jess slapped at it before she realized it was Morgan. "A widow named Donna Shultz said we could use a cabin nearby."

"We?"

"You're my wife, remember?"

She looked around at all the men in uniform. "Does anyone know you're not married?"

"I'm infantry, and these men are cavalry," he said. "We don't socialize unless necessary. They think we're stupid for walking instead of riding a horse."

"And what is your opinion of the cavalry?"

"They make a mighty fine target astride a horse."

Jess hid a smile by turning toward the church. "What about the wounded? Any of them know?"

"Enlisted men don't question officers, especially about their personal lives. Everyone thinks Tootie is my little brother. They'll accept you as my wife."

"Why?"

His gaze raked her from head to foot. "Because you're the type of woman they would expect me to marry."

What did that mean? "You don't even know me."

"Good, we won't get bored with each other."

The man was insufferable. His rank had gone to his head.

He led the team to Donna's home. It was made of hewn logs and had a stone fireplace. A lean-to beside a chicken coop served as a barn and offered protection for the pair of draft horses. She helped carry Tootie inside.

The single-room cabin had basic furnishings, a table and chairs in front of the fireplace, a double bed in the far corner with a single bed in the opposite corner. A folding screen separated the double bed from the rest of the room. A dry sink and shelves with dry goods completed the furnishings.

"Nobody lives here?"

"Mrs. Shultz is staying with her daughter and newborn grandson. Her son-in-law is fighting for the Union."

"And she let you live in her home?"

"She's a romantic," Morgan said. "I told her we haven't seen each other since marrying six months ago."

"You can spend your honeymoon with Romulus and Remus."

"Why don't you share a bed with Tootie, and I'll take the smaller bed in the corner."

The sleeping arrangements weren't perfect, but he could hardly molest her in the same bed as his sister. They helped Tootie roll from the stretcher to the feather-filled mattress.

Jess propped Tootie's leg with a pillow so she could rest on her side. "How do you feel?"

"A lot better now that I'm in a real bed."

"Do you want anything more to eat?"

"Not now." Tootie yawned. Jess checked the bandage and wounds. No infection and the stitches had held during the journey. She covered her when the door opened. It was Morgan, who had retrieved their belongings.

She sorted through her haversack and removed her medical supplies. "Tootie is going to sleep. I'd like to help with the wounded."

"Aren't they the enemy?"

"Women don't look at the color of the uniform when someone is hurting. But our compassion makes us vulnerable." She tied on her apron, covered her hair with a scarf, and gathered her supplies. "We make stupid decisions."

"Or else you wouldn't have stopped when you saw me lying on the side of the road."

"I thought my knife and gun would protect me, but no woman is safe when caught by surprise. You overpowered me before I could react. But I don't like living in fear even if my compassion puts me in jeopardy."

"I needed your help." Morgan tucked a strand of hair into her scarf. "I wish I could let you go, but for now I offer my protection."

"That's another falsity. Women think they're safe if they have a father or husband to protect them, but you can't be at my side every minute of the day, and I won't be shut behind the walls of a fortress no matter how prettily it's decorated. Until men respect women and realize they can't attack them or claim them, women will be vulnerable to violence."

Morgan removed her knife and sheath from his bag and returned them. "I'll take care of Romulus and Remus."

Jess placed the sheath and blade in her boot and followed Morgan outside. "Blake would appreciate it."

"I'm not doing it for Blake." His face reddened as if his words had conveyed more. "They performed a herculean task pulling us through that mud."

She opened a bin on the side of the wagon. "I have oats and some old apples for them." She removed a pair of curry brushes. "Do you know how to groom a horse?"

"I'll make them look so pretty, Blake won't recognize them."

"Romulus likes being brushed first. He's impatient."

Morgan raised an eyebrow. "Which one is Romulus?"

"The larger one."

Morgan unhitched the team from the wagon but paused to study her. "Go help the wounded." He pointed toward the church. "Git."

"Try to treat the horses better than you treat your wife."

The church was crowded with wounded, women, and medical staff. To a stranger, chaos reigned, but Jess recognized the system the Union hospitals utilized. The most urgent cases were prioritized for surgery. She headed for an operating table where a young man was examining a soldier's broken arm.

"It's not going to do any good to straighten the bones without a splint to hold them," a senior doctor barked as he paused behind the young man.

"Where am I going to find any splints?"

Jess answered, "A picket fence is out front."

The older doctor stared at her. "What good is that?"

"You can use the slats for splints."

"They'll need to be cut to size and wrapped in cloth," the older doctor said. "Roe, take care of the broken bones. I have surgeries to focus on."

He pointed at Jess. "You can help wrap splints. I don't need a woman getting under foot while I'm saving lives."

The older doctor moved to an operating table near the pulpit. He wiped a saw on his apron and began to cut into a patient. Jess extended her hand to the young man. "I'm Jessica Bee...Mackinnon." She had almost forgotten her role. "I'm married to Major Morgan Mackinnon."

"Lieutenant Romeo Greystone."

"Romeo?"

"My parents like Shakespeare. I go by Roe."

"My sister Juliet gets teased about her name."

"Juliet is more common than Romeo." Roe had long, dark brown hair tied at the nape of his neck to keep it out of his hazel eyes.

"You don't seem old enough to be a lieutenant."

"I was made a lieutenant because I planned to be a doctor. My father was a professor, and I graduated preparatory school when I was sixteen. I was nearly done with college and was hoping to attend medical school, but my skills were required in the service of my country."

He was the same age as Ethan, Harry, and Zach with a boyish exuberance the war had yet to destroy. She looked around. "You're doing the duties of a doctor."

"I do what is needed. Are you a nurse?"

"Not an official nurse, but my father is a doctor and trained me to care for the sick."

"Is he serving in the army?"

"No. With so many other doctors serving the military, he was needed at home to care for civilians."

"Where is home?"

"Ohio."

He was startled by her answer. "You're

sympathetic to the Union?"

"Yes, but don't hold that against me. I've discovered blood is red no matter what uniform the soldier is wearing."

"Why did you marry the major?"

How did she explain their ruse? She shrugged. "I fell in love."

"He's a lucky man." Roe blushed at his declaration. "I shouldn't have spoken so boldly."

"Your compliment is from the heart," Jess said. "And since we are in the same profession, I would like to be friends."

"Thank you." Roe selected a saw from the surgical instruments he had laid out on a table. "I better cut those boards."

Jess placed her hand on his arm. "Better use an axe. You don't want to dull the blade on the saw."

His face paled, and he dropped the saw. "Is there a tool shed nearby?"

"Try in the back."

The man with the broken arm groaned. "Where's the doctor?"

"He'll return shortly." Jess covered him with a blanket and cut away the fabric of his sleeve so the arm was fully exposed. The arm was limp, curved in the middle between the elbow and wrist. The ulna and radius were broken and the ends jammed together.

Roe returned with an armful of fence boards. She grabbed several before they fell to the floor. She chose two and measured them against the man's arm. "These should do." She removed a roll of bandages and began wrapping the boards.

"How did you break your arm?"

The soldier on the table was breathing shallow. "A cannonball exploded near me. I flew into the air and landed on my arm." Beads of sweat mixed with the gunpowder remaining on his skin. "No one had time to set the bones before leaving. I thought I was going to die in that wagon."

"We picked up a few men who couldn't endure the jarring any longer."

"If they're not set, infection will set in, and the surgeon will have to amputate." Roe glanced toward the older doctor sawing off limbs.

"Let's save him some work." Jess pointed to the curve in his arm. "His radius and ulna are jammed."

"You know your bones."

"I broke a boy's arm once."

"Remind me to stay on your good side."

"They'll have to be separated."

Roe examined the man's arm. He cried out. "If he thinks that's painful wait until I tug them apart to set them." He retrieved a bottle of chloroform and a nose inhaler to administer the liquid. The first drop often caused convulsions, but the second drop put a grown man out instantly.

"Where do you obtain chloroform?"

"Humanitarian aid from the North," Roe said.

People could be kind and show mercy, even during a war. "What do you want me to do?"

"You can place the splints." He looked around. "I'm going to need someone strong to hold him in place while I tug."

"I'll fetch my husband." She passed two soldiers breaking apart the picket fence and gathering the pieces. Morgan was walking toward her. A few ladies, gathered at the community well in front of the church, stared at the big Scotsman. His size commanded attention, but he had removed his hat in deference to the ladies, and the sunlight highlighted the red in his darker curls. He was a handsome devil, and one woman sighed when he smiled. Jess frowned until she realized the smile was directed at her.

He bowed slightly. "Did you miss me, Mrs. Mackinnon?"

"The doctor needs your brute strength." She grabbed his hand and led him inside.

He stopped after entering. "Whew. What's that smell?"

She was used to the urine and vomit mixed with blood and pus. Chamber pots and buckets were already full, waiting to be emptied.

"I need you to empty all the containers."

He waved his arms. "Didn't you notice the star on my collar? That's work for a private or orderly."

She laughed and tugged on his hand. "I was joking."

"That wasn't funny."

"Most people say I have a clever sense of humor."

"I didn't marry you for your personality."

He'd insulted her, or had he? She stopped at the table where Roe was wrapping more splints. "Here's our anchor."

Roe stared at Morgan. "You might want to remove your coat, Major Mackinnon. Sometimes men throw up."

Jess offered her hand. "I'll hold your coat, *darlin'*."

Morgan removed his belt with his revolver and ammunition pouch. He handed Jess his coat and put the belt back on.

"I don't think you'll need your weapon," Roe said.

"I wouldn't want it to fall into the wrong hands."

Jess met his gaze. She tossed his coat over one of the chairs.

"What do you want me to do?" Morgan asked.

"I need you to stand behind the man and wrap your arms beneath his armpits and hold his shoulders firm."

Jess placed the wrapped splints on each side of the arm with a bandage running beneath in three places. She looked at the doctor when she was ready.

"Hold tight!" Roe gripped the man's wrist and braced his hips against the table as he pulled as hard as he could. Even under the influence of the chloroform, the man cried out in pain. Morgan, to his credit, didn't let go. Roe turned the arm to align the broken bones. "Wrap it!"

Jess placed the splints, securing them in place while Roe held the arm to prevent any movement. She tied the last knot and moved back.

Roe examined the remaining contents in the bottle of chloroform. "I won't be able to use this on all the men. Better do the worse breaks first and let the rest scream."

Jess folded a cloth to make a sling. She cradled the arm in the material and tied the ends around his neck.

Morgan and Jess worked as a team with Roe setting broken bones or amputating the limb if gangrene has set in. Jess threaded her needles and began the task of tying off bleeders and stitching the flap of skin over the shortened leg or arm.

"You're good with a needle," Roe said. "Could you help me with the cuts and gashes?"

Jess threaded the curved needle she used for stitches and laid her scissors, scalpel, and a shaving razor on a cloth with a pan of hot water nearby. "Hot water?" Roe asked.

"As hot as you can stand," Jess said.

The men lined up, and one sat by Roe while the next sat on the chair by Jess. "Why do I get a woman?"

"Lucky," Morgan said.

Her patient had a bloody rag wrapped beneath his jaw and knotted on the top of his head. He couldn't remove the knot and pulled the cloth off. He'd been shot in the face. His long, dirty beard was matted with blood. She chose the razor.

"What are ya goin' do with dat?" he mumbled.

"I have to shave the hair around the wound. It'll grow back."

He stood. "No."

"Sit," Morgan ordered. "It's only a shave."

The razor cleaned the area around the wound. The lead ball must have gone through another soldier before hitting this man or the damage would have been worse. The ball had pierced his cheek and broken several teeth.

"Did you spit the ball out?"

"Alon' wid mah teeth." The words were mumbled through swollen lips.

She added laudanum to the wound to numb the area. He jerked with the first stitch. "Are you a drinking man?"

He nodded.

Jess signaled for a woman to approach. "Do you have any liquor?"

"Communion wine."

"I need something stronger."

125

"I know where the pastor keeps his home brewed corn liquor."

"That'll work."

She removed the cork from a jug the woman gave her and filled a cup halfway. "Drink it down and grip the chair."

"You want us to hold him?" the next man in line asked.

She nodded. Two men grabbed his shoulders, but the pain killer was working. He barely flinched when she stuck the bent needle through his face, hooked the opposite jagged side, and pulled the needle out to bind the two edges together. She tied each strand with a French knot.

"Mighty pretty needlework," one of the soldiers remarked.

"I'll embroider your initials if you like." She looked inside his mouth at the jagged remains along his gum line. "You're going to need those teeth pulled when you find someone strong enough to yank them out."

She placed a clean bandage over her work and secured it with a long strip of cloth tied on top of his head. He mumbled a thank you.

The next man took a seat, and she cleaned her needles and soaked her thread before making the repairs from bayonets, bullets, and shards of canisters.

Chapter Twelve

Morgan was helping a man into bed when Roe pointed toward Jess. She was teetering, her hand supporting her against the end of a pew. She had worked without interruption except for a quick meal of stew and bread. She was ready to collapse.

He put his arm around her waist. How could such a slight woman be so strong? She looked up at him, her eyes fluttering with exhaustion.

"Time for bed, Mrs. Mackinnon." He lifted her in his arms.

"No!" She fought against his chest.

"She'd work until she dropped," Morgan explained to the others.

"I'm not too tired to walk," Jess said.

He lowered her. She gathered her belongings, and Morgan put on his coat.

Roe held out his hand to Morgan. "Thank you for all your help. Your wife did you proud, sir."

"Thank you, Lieutenant."

Jess stared at him through narrowed eyes. "I do all this work, and you receive the credit?"

"That's how marriage works." He took her bag and bowed, signaling her to go through the door first. It was night, and the cool air revived them.

Jess inhaled and stretched, rolling her slender shoulders. "You act as if all my accomplishments are for your benefit."

"I take credit for all your abilities." Morgan admired the way her back curved to her waist and the crinoline-free skirt flowed over her hips. "After all, a wife cannot do anything without her husband's permission."

Jess had a queer smile on her face. "Including my misdeeds."

He offered his arm as they walked. She grabbed on when she nearly tripped. "What do you mean, misdeeds? You can't include criminal actions. A husband can't be blamed for a wife who breaks the law."

"My brother-in-law, Tyler Montgomery, would disagree." She had a deceitfully sweet smile and lips he wanted to pluck with his own. "He's a lawyer and argued a case where the man was responsible for his wife's crimes. She couldn't do anything without his authority, so he must have given her permission to break the law."

He had to concentrate on her words instead of the way her mouth puckered as she spoke. "What crime did she commit?"

"She murdered him."

"What?" Morgan stopped in the road. Had he heard correctly? "She killed her husband and blamed him for the murder?"

"That's how the law works according to Tyler." Jess studied Morgan with a playful glint in her eye. "Men claim they own their wives. If they own them, they control them, and they're responsible for their actions. He made a logical conclusion for his case."

Was she telling the truth? "I don't like your

brother-in-law."

"He's a Virginian like you, or he was." Jess paused. "I believe the town he's from is in West Virginia now."

"We don't recognize West Virginia separate from the Commonwealth of Virginia," Morgan said. "Did Tyler Montgomery have a part in splitting the state?"

She didn't answer. "Did he?"

She dismissed his question with a wave of her hand. "He wrote a few letters."

"I'm sure that made Miss Jenny proud."

She laughed. "No, Tyler is married to my sister Courtney. Logan Pierce is married to Jennifer."

"And Blake married…"

"Colleen."

"Cory, Jem, and Cole. It's your turn to find a husband, but you said you weren't going to marry Ed."

"I have a few good years left to snare a man."

"Did your sisters marry well?"

"A lawyer, a politician's secretary, and a hotel owner. I never thought about besting them. I want to marry for love like they did."

He examined her hand with the wedding band. "Ed loved you."

"It wasn't enough."

"Why not?"

"I didn't imagine my future the same as his." Tears welled in her eyes. "I thought he would have a future. I thought Jake would have a future."

"Who's Jake?"

"My cousin Jake Donovan. He was killed at Antietam."

"That was a bloody mess."

"You were there?"

"Marched from Harper's Ferry." Morgan paused. "We didn't march. We ran straight into the jaws of hell."

"We weren't allowed to go into the cornfield to retrieve the wounded because there wasn't a truce. All night I heard the men crying out for water."

"Why were you there?"

"Clara Barton inspired us. Only she wasn't taking female nurses, so we disguised ourselves as men." Jess tugged on a shorter strand of hair. "We wanted to help the Ohio boys, but the Twenty-ninth Ohio didn't fight. That's why Ed gave me his gun. The Seventh Ohio fought near Dunker church. Jake died in the cornfield near it."

"I'm sorry."

"Sorry? You and Blake attended West Point. You live for war."

"We never wanted to fight each other."

"But you wanted to fight. Fame and glory. That's what a soldier lives for. And the blood pools around your feet and rises until you choke on it."

He pulled her close even though she fought against him. "Hush."

The tears flowed. "I hate this war."

Morgan opened the door to the cabin. "So do I."

"I don't believe you."

"I attended West Point for an education. I wanted to build bridges, but instead I've blown them up or burned them to the ground. There's no fame or glory in killing another man. I'm fighting now to survive and to end this war."

"Then surrender."

"We've been asking the North to do that for the past two years."

Jess left her belongings on the table and checked on Tootie who was asleep. "No fever. When will you be crossing the river?"

"There's a problem," Morgan said. "The engineers can't build the pontoon boat bridge until the water is lower. With all the rain, it's a raging torrent."

"But I want to return to Gettysburg. Blake and the others must be frantic with worry."

Morgan removed his coat and sat on a chair to remove his boots. "I'd like to believe you wouldn't say anything, but if the Union finds out we're stranded with the river behind us, they could attack."

"They wouldn't attack wounded men."

"The cavalry attacked at Hagerstown," he reminded her. "Besides, Lee isn't heading for Washington City like I told you. He's coming here. We're retreating to Virginia."

"Why did you lie to me?"

"In case you escaped." He stood and pulled off his suspenders. He tugged his shirt out of his trousers and pulled it over his head. "If you told Meade we were attacking the capital, he'd be on the defensive instead of chasing us down."

"Does Lee know the river is impassable?"

"No," Morgan said. "It's easy to jump into a dangerous situation. It takes a plan to escape unscathed. We're going to have to take a defensive stand in case Meade attacks."

"Another battle?"

She was frightened or angry or a little of both. "You said Blake would be worried. Who are the others?"

Jess dumped the contents of her haversack on the table and grabbed her nightgown. "My cousin Ethan, Ed's brother, Harry, and Zach Ravenswood. His brother Paxton died from injuries at Cedar Mountain last year. We fed them, washed their clothes, and played baseball at the Mermaid's Mirth."

Her voice cracked with pain. Morgan wanted to take her into his arms and offer comfort, but she wouldn't accept it. She was angry.

"Children are carrying on the fight that men started. They were my playmates growing up. We attended school together and enjoyed hot summer days climbing trees, exploring the woods, or riding on my grandpa's canal boat, the *Irish Rose*. We didn't have a care in the world. Now this." He handed her his kerchief. "How can you kill someone and go back to the life you knew?"

"You can't," Morgan said. "Your life is never the same."

"So many men are dead. So many maimed." Jess gasped. "I forgot about Sid. He's going to be furious."

"Who's Sid?"

"Sid Wilson. He was in the Seventh Ohio. He lost his foot at Antietam. He drove the wagon when we need supplies for the Mermaid's Mirth. He drove me to Gettysburg. He's responsible for me."

She was near hysterics. He laid his hand on her shoulder. "He sounds important."

"He helped Ed's brother John when he was wounded, and he waited for Logan and Jem to return from Richmond. He's a dear friend, and I've caused him so much grief."

"I wish I could help."

"I could write a letter."

"And tell them where we are and what we're facing? No letter writing." He stabbed his finger in her face. "I'm putting a guard on the post office. No mail goes in or out until we leave."

"That's the meanest thing you've done. My sisters will be worried sick about me."

"They're in Washington City, aren't they?"

Jess nodded.

"You can write them," Morgan said. "But I read the letter first."

She looked surprised by his offer. "Thank you, Morgan."

Her words were simple, but the look of gratitude nearly buckled him. "Thank you for keeping Tootie alive."

"Roe is going to visit tomorrow and make sure I didn't miss anything." Jess hesitated. "Do you mind waiting outside while I use the chamber pot?"

Morgan yanked off his socks. "I'll go find a bush."

When he returned, Jess was in bed with Tootie. He headed to his bed in the corner. "You don't mind sleeping with my sister?"

"I've slept with a redhead since I was two but…"

Morgan stopped midstride. "What?"

"Until Blake married her. My sister Cole is a redhead."

"If you're partial to redheads, I won't complain if you want to share my bed." His bold invitation was met by silence. "I was only joking about…"

"That bed is barely big enough for you let alone two people. You should be worried I might slit your

133

throat while you're sleeping."

"And I bet you'd use that fancy defense your brother-in-law made up to say I forced you to slit my throat." Especially since he had returned her sharp blade. "You wouldn't consider surrendering your knife until morning?"

The ropes beneath the mattress creaked as Jess settled in the bed. "Tyler is a brilliant lawyer."

Morgan arranged the screen, his head above it as he stared at the shadow of the bloodthirsty woman. Would she cut his throat? "That defense won't work in the Confederate army."

"Don't worry, Morgan. I'm too tired to kill you tonight."

Morgan plopped onto the bed. He placed his gun nearby. In case she was lying.

The room was dark but light filtered through the windows from camp fires outside. The cavalry was keeping watch. A scouting party would search the area in the morning. No news had reached them about Lee's progress. Without the army, they were vulnerable to attack.

****

Jess groaned as she stretched. Every muscle protested any movement. She rolled to the other side. The bed was empty. Where was Tootie? She was standing at the end of the bed, holding onto the bed post as she squatted. A stream hit the chamber pot. "How are you feeling?"

Tootie looked in her direction. "Better, but I have to nearly stand to piss."

"I was worried you might not be able to walk."

"I don't think you call this walking. I step and

drag." She leaned against the bed and let out a sigh. "I don't remember if we were formally introduced. I'm Tootie Mackinnon."

"I'm Jessica Beecher."

"Beecher?" Her eyes widened. "Not the Connecticut Beechers?"

"Distant relatives." Jess stood, smoothing her nightgown. "Your brother didn't think my name would be popular so he told everyone I was his wife."

"Wife?" Tootie stared. "How is he going to explain that?"

"How does he explain you?"

"I'm his baby brother." She examined the oversized nightshirt. "Does anyone else know I'm a woman?"

"No. I took care of you. What are you doing in the Confederate army?"

All the color left Tootie's face. "What did Morgan say?"

"That you were his half-sister and not much more."

She relaxed. "Perhaps when I know you better, I'll share the details."

"You're both Mackinnons. So you have the same father?"

"Yes," Tootie said. "Ian Mackinnon was a big handsome man like Morgan. My mother was in love with him, but Ian didn't return her passion. He was mourning his wife."

"How did she die?"

"She was murdered. I don't know many of the details. No one would talk about it, even Morgan, and he was there when it happened."

"What?"

"Brianna was tending the mercantile they owned. Ian was at the train depot." Tootie took a deep breath. "Two men entered the store and demanded money. They shot Brianna. I think Morgan was hiding, but like I said, nobody talked about it. He had a stutter for years. His friend Blake helped him overcome it."

"Blake Ellsworth?"

"You know him?"

"Blake married my sister, Colleen. She's expecting a baby."

"Married? Blake said he would never marry. He had a horrible stepsister."

"Valerie."

"You know her?"

"We met. She's in Europe trying to nab a rich lord."

"Valerie wanted to marry Blake after he inherited his father's hotels. Does he still have them?"

"He has three, but Colleen is running them."

"Why? What happened to Blake?"

"Blake joined the army. He's a captain in the Twelfth Corps."

"In the Union? He spent so much time in Richmond."

"His main home was in New York, but he wanted to be part of Ohio's regiments. He promised our friends he'd watch out for their younger brothers. Ethan, Harry, and Zach are a handful. I was leaving them at Culp's Hill when I was confronted by your brother."

"Morgan can be very persuasive."

"He better worry about Blake finding out his team of horses has been traveling with the Rebel army."

"Blake and Morgan were inseparable. I was eight

years younger than Morgan and worshipped him. An early baby is what my mother said, but I can count the months between the wedding and my birth. She offered comfort to Ian, and I was the result. He was a decent man and gave me his name. Too bad I look like my mother. Plain. I had no trouble disguising myself as a boy." She tugged on her short brown hair. "Morgan doesn't have one freckle and here I am with a face full."

"They're lovely."

"I wish I looked like you."

"Me? I was the forgotten sister. Stuck anonymously in the middle."

"How many sisters do you have?"

"Five, and they're all prettier than me."

"I don't believe that."

"Mama always warned that the exterior could attract the wrong type of man who wouldn't appreciate the beauty within." Jess shook her head. "With six daughters, she had her hands full keeping the wrong men away."

"Sometimes that's impossible," Tootie said. "That's why I don't want to look pretty."

Jess looked around and lowered her voice. "Do you mean the Confederate soldiers?"

"No. Morgan's last visit home was for our father's funeral. My mother didn't like the responsibility of running a store and married Lyle Neely." Tootie trembled. "Lyle is a smooth-talking con man who took over the store and our lives."

"Is he the reason you left home?"

She nodded, tears brimming her eyes. "Too much attention. My own mother wouldn't believe me. She took his side."

"I'm sorry." Jess put her arms around her. "Not all men are like that."

"I know. Morgan didn't ask any questions. He took me in even though I'm nothing but trouble. He told me to stay in the tent, but did I listen? No. I was worried something had happened when he didn't come home at nightfall. I should have been more patient like he is. I deserved to be shot. He should have left me in the cemetery to die. But he searched for me and found me. He didn't yell or remind me how foolish I was. I don't deserve such a wonderful brother."

Wonderful? Patient? Doesn't yell? "I must have missed that side of him."

Tootie defended him. "His men love him. He takes care of them and tries to keep them alive. It must have been difficult for him to leave them to take care of me. I hope he doesn't hate me."

"I'm sure he doesn't." He had a new target to direct his anger toward. Jess changed Tootie's bandage and put her to bed.

"It was nice of you to loan your wagon to Morgan and help us."

Tootie was ignorant of the details resulting in her kidnapping. She would never think ill of her brother. "I couldn't leave you in the cemetery. You weren't dead."

Chapter Thirteen

Jess prepared a spot in front of the fire for her bath. The days of traveling and working with patients had left a nasty mixture of sweat and dirt on her skin. She would have preferred a long soak in a tub, but a sponge bath was the next best thing. She stood in the tin washtub after arranging her sponge, brush, buckets of warm water and towels within arms' reach. She had a bar of lavender soap and scrubbed every inch of her body to rid it of the grime. She used a ladle to spoon warm water from a bucket over her shoulders to rinse the soap off.

She was enjoying the steamy luxury, letting the hot droplets cascade down her body and pool around her aching feet when the door opened, and Morgan barged in. She dropped the ladle and snatched a towel to cover her torso. "Don't you knock?"

Morgan was in full uniform. His frock coat was wide in the shoulders and stopped mid-thigh on his long legs. His boots reached mid-calf and had a shine to them. When did he have the time to polish them? He strode to a storage chest near his bed and opened the lid. "A scouting party reported Buford's men heading this way."

"The Union cavalry?" General John Buford had fought the first day of Gettysburg. Sid had told her Buford was credited with keeping the Confederate forces contained until reinforcements arrived.

Morgan retrieved his sword and Ed's pistol.

"Has my gun been in that chest the whole time?"

A thick dark brow rose above one gleaming eye. "You didn't think to search?"

No, she hadn't. She could use a gun now. He stood barely five feet away and the only thing between them was a wet towel. "What are you going to do?"

"Imboden has twenty-three cannons. He'll place them on high ground. We don't have time for the men to dig trenches, so we'll place the wagons in a semicircle to create a barricade for the men to fight behind." Morgan checked the cylinder in Ed's gun. "Any wounded man able to tug a trigger will be armed."

She was worried about being molested, and he was telling her the battle plans. Was the man immune to any feminine temptation? "Why are you telling me this?"

"There's going to be more wounded." His gaze caressed her. Her body betrayed her and reacted to his lustful grin. How could she be attracted to an enemy officer? Her captor? Her heartbeat accelerated behind her flimsy cloth.

He stepped toward her. Should she scream? Would it wake Tootie? And what would Tootie do? She could barely move.

Morgan paused a few feet away, one side of his generous mouth rose slightly and his golden gaze appraised her. "With company on the way, you might want to put on some clothes." He turned, opened the door, and left.

Jess shivered. Stark naked, and he had barely noticed. What was wrong with the man? What was wrong with her? Did she expect Morgan to treat her with anything but polite disdain? They barely knew each other. So what if he was the most handsome man she had ever seen? He was arrogant, loud, and worst of all, had no interest in her. She sighed and stepped out of the tub.

The door opened, and she gave a short shriek. It was Morgan, again. "Forget something?"

He strode toward her. Jess held the towel with trembling fingers in front of her body. "I don't like the look in your eyes."

"If I survive the battle you can punish me, but I'm facing death, and I don't want any regrets."

His arms surrounded her, pulling her against his chest. Jess attempted to maintain the towel between them and a fraction of her dignity as his hands touched bare flesh. He didn't bother to remove his hat. His wide grin bared his teeth. He looked hungry. His mouth claimed hers in fierce possession.

His mustache tickled, but before she could be repulsed, his mouth urged her to respond. This was a primal attack, the mating of survival that near death nurtured in desperate times.

His hands cupped the curve of her hips, pressing her against him in a rhythm she had never experienced except through bedroom walls. Her sisters and their husbands had coupled in breathless cries during the night, sparking her imagination and desire to experience the same.

She hugged his neck, urging him to continue when he broke to take a breath. Their gazes locked, neither one admitting victory nor defeat. Her mouth sought his, drawing him to her, refusing to lose the battle he had begun.

He released her, and she acknowledged disappointment as he strode to the door. He grabbed his rain poncho on the hook by the door. "I knew I'd forgotten something. Looks like another thunderstorm is blowing in. I'd prefer that to Buford." He turned and saluted her before opening the door and leaving her wondering what had happened.

Her towel was gone. But on the table was Ed's gun.

****

When Tootie woke, Jess told her about the attack. Buford's not her brother's assault on her senses. They waited nearly an hour before the silence drove Jess to go to the hospital to discover any news. They were picking threads from fabric to create lint and charpies to staunch wounds. Others were rolling strips of cloth for bandages. Donna Shultz was one of the volunteers. They talked as they worked and took turns checking on Tootie. Near noon, women arrived with food. They fed the volunteers and the men too injured to join the fight who rested in pews or blankets spread on the floor.

Jess was helping wash dishes when the first cannon fired. She dropped a tin platter, and it rattled like an echo to the gun. After all the cannon from July 3 at Gettysburg, she should have been used to the booms, but it was a signal more men would die. She prayed a big Scotsman wouldn't be one of them. For Tootie's sake, she added after her "amen."

A few wounded were carried to the hospital on stretchers. The wagons remained along the battle line to protect the men against the assault. By nightfall news filtered back through the wounded arriving at the church that more Confederate cavalry had arrived and drove Buford's men away. Some of the wounded were returned to the hospital, excited they had played a role in the victory. Others remained with the wagons in case Buford returned.

When she arrived at the cabin, Tootie was resting in a wicker rocking chair, a thick pad beneath her hip. She was wearing a nightgown and summer robe. Donna stirred the coals beneath a large pot resting on a metal rack in the fireplace.

Tootie licked her spoon. "This is delicious, Mrs. Shultz."

"I made plenty for you, girls."

Girls? Did Tootie reveal her gender without consulting her brother? Tootie was as headstrong as Morgan.

"Tootie said you didn't have anything to wear but the clothes on your back, and my daughter can't wear these anymore." Donna opened the lid to a large trunk. "You two looked to be the right size."

Clothes. Jess had packed two dresses and both were worn out from work. The shoulder seam was torn on the one she wore. She knelt in front of the trunk and searched through the garments. She lifted a lace trimmed camisole. Clean underclothes. "Are you sure your daughter won't want these?"

"She nearly doubled her size when expecting the baby. These clothes only remind her of what she used to look like."

"She could lose the weight."

"Perhaps in time. But for now, you should enjoy them."

Among the work dresses and undergarments was a

red silk dress. "What's this?"

"That was her last party gown," Donna said. "She wore it when her husband left for war."

"Do you know what happened to him?"

"He was at Gettysburg. We haven't heard if he survived it." Donna gathered her belongings. "There's chicken and biscuits warming over the coals of the fire. Any time you need me to sit with Tootie, it would be my pleasure."

Jess waited for Donna to leave and turned to Tootie. "You told her you were a girl?"

Tootie shrugged. "She knew without asking. When I told her I had nothing else to wear, she brought the trunk. Now I can leave the cabin."

"I didn't think you could walk."

"Soon. For now, I can rock." She moved the rocker forward and back before groaning in pain.

"Let's take it slowly." Jess fixed a plate. "Do you want more?"

"I'm full."

Jess sat at the table and ate. "This is delicious."

"I should have helped you."

"We had plenty of volunteers. You need your rest."

"Not that," Tootie whispered. "I saw Morgan kiss you."

"Your brother has no sense of propriety. He stole my towel."

"It looked like you were kissing him back." Tootie struggled to stand. Jess hurried to her aid. "Or did he force his affections upon you?"

"No." Jess put her arm around Tootie's waist and helped her to the bed. "I've been kissed before."

"Does that mean a man has bedded you?"

Her sisters had shared their marital experiences so Jess was far from ignorant of lovemaking between a husband and wife. Other women weren't as knowledgeable. She arranged the covers around Tootie. "No. A kiss is as far as it's gone." Ed had never seen her naked or roamed her bare body with his hands. His kisses had never burned with the intense fire that Morgan's touch had ignited.

"Then you're not soiled."

It wasn't the words. It was the tremble in Tootie's voice that alarmed her. "What happened, Tootie?"

She clutched the covers. "Promise not to tell Morgan."

Jess crossed her heart.

"I ran away from home because of my stepfather."

"Lyle Neely?"

Tootie nodded. "I told you he married my mother."

She had described unwanted attention. Jess sat on the bed and waited for Tootie to talk. "Morgan wasn't around. He was too busy with the war, but he wrote. He said if I ever needed anything, he would help. But I don't think he meant for me to join him."

"He loves you," Jess said. Tootie was Morgan's soft spot. Was that a pang of jealousy she felt?

"I had no choice." She sobbed.

Jess fetched a handkerchief. "Do you want to talk about Lyle now?"

She nodded and gathered her composure. "At first he was charming. He began managing the store, which is one of the reasons my mother married him. I helped stock the shelves and clean up. He paid me half of what my father paid me, and I worked twice as hard."

She balled her fists in the covers. "When Lyle

waited on certain ladies, he placed his hand on their arms or on their waists. It was scandalous, but Mother dismissed it as a way to encourage sales. I ignored his behavior until I caught him with a woman in the dressing room. He was seated in a chair, and she was bouncing on him. When I told my mother, she said I was mistaken and should forget it."

Tootie blew her nose. "About two months ago, he started touching me. Innocent gestures like wiping a smudge off my cheek or placing his hands on my waist to help me off a ladder. I ignored him, but I should have done something. Or said something. I think he was testing my reaction. One night he asked me to work late after the store was closed to restock the merchandise."

She reached for Jess and took her hand. Her fingers were cold and trembled. Jess squeezed. "Something was wrong. I should have listened to my instincts, but a girl is taught to submit to her parents and to men. When he told me to go in the back room and fetch the box of threads, I did as I was told."

She sobbed. Jess put her arm around her. "Hush. You don't have to tell me any more."

Something in her eyes stated otherwise. She needed to unburden herself and rushed on in a trembling voice. "He was suddenly there in front of me. He pushed me down on the floor and was on top. I struggled, but he was so heavy. I was crushed beneath the weight. I screamed, but he covered my mouth with his." She cringed, and Jess pulled her tightly into her arms. "He pushed into me hard and fast. I thought I was going to die. When he rose, he cleaned himself with my petticoat. He said he'd married both of us, my mother and me. He'd teach me to be a good wife."

Jess gently rested her forehead against Tootie's. "I'm so sorry."

"The next day while he was gone I worked up the courage to tell my mother. She didn't believe me. I showed her my bloody clothes, and she called me a whore for stealing her husband."

"What?" Had she heard correctly? "How could she take his side after you showed her the evidence?"

Tootie gulped a ragged breath. Her body shook with a tremor. "That's what hurt the most. She loved him more than she loved me." Tootie wiped her tears with the sleeve of her nightgown. "I took clothes from the store and cut my hair. Then I packed a bag and took what money I could find. Morgan's camp wasn't far from Richmond. I told him I couldn't go back. He never asked why. He took me in. He looked for me when I was missing. He's a good man."

Jess would make up her own mind about Morgan Mackinnon, but he had accepted Tootie's arrival without any questions. Maybe he wasn't as awful as she thought.

Tootie grabbed her arm. "But sometimes men can't control themselves. When Morgan kissed you, did he hurt you?"

She helped Tootie settle in the bed. There was a fine line between a man's amorous attentions and unwanted touching. "Men choose not to control themselves. Sometimes they use liquor as an excuse, but most of the time they take a woman because they think they can get away with it. No one will stop them."

"I didn't stop Lyle."

"It wasn't your fault, Tootie. He overpowered you. When a man decides to attack a woman, he catches her unguarded so he has the advantage. Even with a gun, a woman isn't safe if he prevents her from using it. Until the law protects all women from men like Lyle Neely, we're all vulnerable. And even then, we have to depend upon the protection of good men."

"Then Morgan didn't hurt you?"

"No. I didn't give him permission to kiss me, but he was going off to fight and became bold."

"Did you like it when Morgan kissed you?"

"Tootie Mackinnon." She was going to reprimand her for asking a personal question, but she had shared her trauma freely. "My sister said you can't tell if there's any attraction between you and a man until he does kiss you, but I will have to make it clear your brother must ask my permission before he kisses me a second time."

Tootie giggled. "Then you did like it."

"A man has to respect you, or he won't marry you."

Tootie sobered. "Do you think any man will want to marry me?"

"Of course."

"What man will marry a soiled dove?"

"You are not a prostitute. If a man refuses to marry a woman because she had an unfortunate incident in her past, he isn't husband material."

"Seems to me he'd have to be a special man to overlook something that seems to be so important to men."

"Wealthy men want to guarantee the heir to their fortune is *their* son. They purchase a virgin to breed not to love. Men should value women as something more than a baby maker. A man will love you for your humor, your talents, and all you have to offer."

"I don't think I could let a man touch me intimately after what Lyle did."

"Don't let what Lyle did destroy your chance at love."

"How can I forget what he did?"

"I don't know, but if it's like other bad experiences in life, you'll think about it less with time and replace it with beautiful memories."

"I hate Lyle for what he did, but I'm angry with my mother for not defending me." Tootie drove her fist into the pillow. "I don't want to hate my mother. I loved her, but I can't forgive her."

"You have to forgive to let go of the hate," Jess said. "Have you ever written your mother since leaving home?"

"No."

"Maybe you should. Tell her how you feel. And at the end, tell her you forgive her."

Tootie sat upright. "But I don't."

"It doesn't matter," Jess said. "By forgiving her, you place the responsibility on your mother. It's her problem, and you don't have to worry about it."

Tootie frowned. "Let me think about it."

Chapter Fourteen

Jess was nearly asleep when the door creaked. Someone was sneaking inside. She had placed Ed's gun on the lamp table by the bed and reached for it. She pulled back the hammer and the cylinder rotated. "Who is it?"

"Your husband." Morgan stepped into the low light from the fireplace coals. "Don't shoot."

Jess lowered the gun and eased the hammer down.

Morgan had left his rain poncho dripping by the door. The daily storms prevented any chance the Potomac River would calm enough to build a bridge and provide an escape route. Morgan slowly removed his belt and let it fall to the floor before collapsing in a chair. He leaned his elbows on the table and rubbed his eyes.

Jess climbed out of bed. She placed the gun next to the unlit lamp. "I heard you kept Buford and his cavalry at bay."

"No easy task. We reclaimed Hagerstown, but I warned Imboden and his officers that Buford will probably return at dawn. We need to be ready."

He was exhausted. "You're going back out?"

"At first light."

Jess removed the cast-iron pot from the fireplace. "Would you like some chicken and biscuits? I don't know how they'll taste after being over the coals for so long."

"Anything tastes good to a starving man."

She placed the pot on the table and removed the lid with a wadded towel. "I'll fetch a plate."

"Don't bother. All I need is a spoon."

He scraped the container clean and sighed. She should have been mad. He had kissed her without permission. He had left her breathless and disoriented, or she would have slapped his face. A waspish reprimand would remind him of his boundaries. But he nodded, his long lashes fluttering. Her words would be wasted tonight. "Give me your coat." Jess waited while he struggled out of the dirty jacket. "What did you do, roll around on the ground?"

"A cavalry rider attempted to cut me down. We wrestled in the mud."

"What's that on your shirt?" Blood stained the lower part.

"It's blood." His golden eyes were filled with pain. "It's not mine. I had no choice, Jess. It was me or him."

He'd killed a Union soldier. It wasn't his first and yet he appeared guilty. "You're a soldier. It's your job."

"I hate it." He clutched his head in his hands. "I bought into the fancy uniform and parades. I received a good education in exchange for selling my soul. I can't count the men I've killed, but I remember enough to be haunted by their cries of pain, the life going out in their eyes, their bodies crumpling to the ground. I can't forget them."

"It could happen to you," Jess reminded him. "It's the equalizer that makes it fair. It's not murder on the battlefield. It's survival."

"The one place where human life has no value.

Where the number of dead is a glorious victory. I've been lucky so far." He paused, studying her. "What happens when Gabriel calls my name?"

"Fate calls anyone's name, Morgan. Men have died in hallways of hotels." She had fired into the dark hall of the Mermaid's Mirth to rescue Blake. Buck Cassell had collapsed against the wall, bleeding from his gut, torn apart by a bullet she had fired.

His hand touched her cheek, and he caressed her with his gaze. "You want to tell me about it?"

"He was a bad man. He almost killed Blake."

"Then he deserved to die." Morgan struggled to remove his suspenders. He moved like an old man.

"What's wrong with you?"

He tugged his shirt free from his trousers. "A wagon fell on me."

"Why didn't you jump out of the way?"

"Then it would have fallen on the wounded men beneath it."

"Were any of them hurt?"

"No, I gave them enough time to escape."

"Take off your shirt." Jess opened her medical bag. "This is a liniment Ed's father prepared. It works wonders on sore muscles."

"Ed's father is a doctor?"

She uncorked the bottle. "No, he's a veterinarian."

Morgan stepped back. "Do I look like an animal?" He held up his hand. "Don't answer that."

Was he feeling guilty about stealing a kiss? "It smells."

Morgan grunted and groaned as he pulled the shirt over his head. His skin had turned black and blue in a wide strip that marked where the edge of the vehicle crashed against him. He had probably supported the wagon alone. Morgan's size was in his shoulders and upper back. Years of marching and fighting had left little fat remaining on his body. What had stayed was hard, sinewy muscle that rippled with every movement. He was bigger than any of her brothers-in-law and none of them were small men. "I hope I have enough."

He turned. His chest was equally toned. He sniffed the container. "That's nasty."

"It works." She poured some into her palm, worked it on her fingers, and rubbed it onto his back.

Morgan moaned.

"Am I hurting you?"

"It's hot but a good heat."

She blew against his skin. "Does that help?"

"Jess, I owe you an apology."

She corked the bottle and returned it to her medical bag. "What have you done?"

"The kiss." He waited for her reaction.

Jess had been furious and then confused by her lust and enjoyment. Her fingertips hummed from caressing his naked flesh. Or was it the liniment? Her emotions were warring inside. She needed time to sort them out. "It was just a kiss."

He sat in the chair. "That's worse than being gut shot."

Jess put her hands on her hips. "What are you upset about? I was the one naked. Did I bruise your inflated pride by failing to faint in your arms?" She clasped her hands together beside her cheek and softened her words. "Oh, darling, my heart flutters whenever you're near me."

"You could pretend you liked it."

"And I could tell the truth."

"Then tell him you liked it," Tootie hollered from the bed. "I'd like to get some sleep."

Jess put her hand on Morgan's chest when his arms pulled her close. "You will not manhandle me." She raised her voice. "And because Tootie is a terrible chaperone, there will be no kissing without my permission."

Morgan studied the thin nightgown she wore. "Didn't Ed sample a few things?"

She gasped in outrage. "There was no sampling."

"None?"

"A few kisses. Certainly none of the pawing and grabbing you did."

"I didn't have anything to hold onto except skin."

"You stole my towel." She put the pot and spoon in the dry sink and dumped water into the container to soak overnight.

"I returned your gun."

He was a contradiction in behavior. "Why did you do that?"

"In case we lost and you needed to protect yourself." Morgan frowned. "I've heard cavalry men are fond of their horses, but you could change a man's mind."

She returned to the table and jabbed her finger in his face. "Being compared to a horse is not flattering."

"You both have nice lines."

Jess put her hands on her hips and glared. "That is not an apology."

"I was going to my death, Jess."

"It would take more than Buford's men to kill you," she said.

Morgan rubbed his neck where she had held her knife against his throat. "You wanted to kill me."

"You kidnapped me."

"Then we're even," Morgan reasoned.

"I didn't succeed."

Morgan closed his eyes and yawned. She softened her tone. "Go to bed. You have to get up in a few hours, remember?"

"Then you're not mad?"

She jabbed him in the chest. "You promised to protect me. That means you don't startle me by barging in without knocking or stealing my towel, and if I give you permission to kiss me, it will be when I'm fully dressed."

"Do you have to remain dressed?"

She smacked his chest. The sound echoed in the cabin. "Morgan Mackinnon, you try my patience."

Morgan stood. "I try yours? Woman, you're standing in front of me in nothing but your nightgown with the fire behind you. You might as well be naked."

Jess examined her nightgown. The light filtered through the thin fabric. He was right. She dashed to the bed. "Remember, I have my gun."

"*Lass, a kiss oan yer bonnie lips woods be worth a bullet.*"

The deep Scottish brogue curled her toes, and she had to calm her breathing. Why did the deep rumblings of a man's voice make her tremble with anticipation? She gripped the covers tightly in her fists to keep from joining him in the small bed where the ropes creaked beneath his weight.

"*Guid nicht hen guidwife an' sweit dreams,*" Morgan called out in the dark.

More like nightmares.

****

It began as a murmur, a whisper on the morning breeze. "General Robert E. Lee is coming."

The rain had stopped momentarily, and civilians joined the soldiers as they lined the street to Hagerstown. Jess wore a dress from the trunk Donna had shared. It was a summer frock of blue and white gingham. She had found a matching bonnet and a lace parasol. Morgan offered his arm. "You look lovely, Mrs. Mackinnon."

Jess strolled along the boards someone had placed in the muddy streets to keep the ladies' gowns clean. "I don't know what all the fuss is about. Didn't Lee lose at Gettysburg?"

"Bite your tongue," he said. "Look around. You can tell your Ohio boys we're not beat, not now, not ever."

They would fight until the last man was standing. But that meant a great deal of men would die before the end came.

"He's coming!" someone shouted in the distance.

Those who could stand, joined the crowd gathering to greet the commander of the Confederate army as he led his troops into town. The Ohio boys complained about the incompetency of their own commanders. They were cowards or incompetent fools. They had wasted opportunities for a quick end to the war. Meade had given them their first taste of a major victory. But for every Union loss, there had been a Confederate victory. This loss was seen as a minor setback.

The man in a gray pristine uniform had to be Lee. He took pride in his appearance, and everything about him spoke of a competent soldier and leader. His hair and beard were white, but he didn't appear old or frail.

Lee rode Traveler, a beautiful light gray horse that stepped high as they passed the walls of men, cheering his arrival. The troops loved him. They had lost thousands of men, and yet their spirits were as high as the victors'. Lee had maintained their confidence, and that was his greatest strength. The men would follow him where he led, even into the pits of hell.

Although cavalry from both sides had fought at nearby Hagerstown, Lee had ridden through the town unmolested. It added to his mystique. Unlike Meade and the Union generals before him, Lee was decisive. When he discovered the river was impassable, he ordered the men to build breastworks. They would make a stand with the river behind them if necessary.

The celebrating was replaced by work. Morgan was reunited with his regiment and worked alongside them to build the defenses. Jess donned an old work dress and helped with the wounded who had arrived with the army.

She found a crutch for Tootie who was beginning to walk short distances inside the cabin or to a chair on the porch. Each day Morgan expected Meade and his men to attack. J.E.B. Stuart patrolled the area with his Confederate cavalry. He repelled Buford at Boonsboro but had to retreat to Funkstown when Union infantry arrived. They fought July 10 at Funkstown, and Buford retreated to Beaver Creek. It was a cat and mouse struggle while both sides waited for Meade and the Army of the Potomac to arrive.

Maybe it was the lull before the storm that made Jess forget she was a woman surrounded by thousands of men. There was no pump in the cabin, and she was fetching water from the well in front of the church when three men surrounded her and blocked her path. One was a sergeant and the other two were privates. Their uniforms were homemade, gray in color, and worn thin in most places. They sported beards, and by the way one private scratched, a nest for fleas.

"Now aren't you a pretty young thing," the sergeant remarked, pulling the scarf from her head. "I bet you could make the hours pass for me and my friends."

"If you're bored, your commanding officer can find tasks to keep you busy." Jess cradled the bucket in her arms. She had left Ed's revolver in the cabin. She judged the distance. Could she outrun the men? In her younger years, she had beat the boys in foot races back home in Darrow Falls, but these were grown men. If they caught her, they would want to claim their prize.

"Why don't you dip your fingertips into the water and wet my parched lips?" The sergeant moved closer and puckered. One of the privates elbowed the other and snickered. Did they think their brazen words would be met with bashful giggles?

"You look hot and tired." Jess hoisted the bucket. "You need to cool off." She threw the bucket of water at the sergeant and took off with her skirt in both hands. If she reached the cabin, she would use Ed's gun no matter what the consequences. It was better to die in a gun battle than suffer rape at the hands of the three monsters pursuing her.

Their voices screeched behind her, cursing her as they shortened the distance between them. She shouted for people to get out of the way as her feet raced on the hard dirt road. They had to know what was happening, but no one interceded on her behalf. A few men urged the three to hurry and catch her. Were they insane? When did attacking a woman become entertainment?

One man blocked her path, and she pushed him, but his action had slowed her enough that she could hear the boots of her pursuers pounding in pursuit. The pack of men hunted her down like ravenous wolves. She dared not look back and slow her pace. The cabin was visible in the distance, but could she close the distance before they caught her?

"Grab her!" the sergeant ordered. Someone tugged on her skirt and the basting stitches to the bodice pulled apart. He grabbed her sleeve, and it ripped at the shoulder seam. She screamed and slapped at the arms reaching and clawing. Her hair tumbled out of the loose chignon at the base of her neck and tumbled in a wild wave of curls that blinded her. They were upon her. She spun around to fight them off and landed her boot against one man's shin. She turned to escape but hit something hard and unyielding. Strong arms held her in a vise-like grip. She was trapped. A sob escaped her parched throat.

"We claim her, Major," the sergeant spoke.

Major? Jess brushed her hair from her eyes and followed the double row of buttons upward on the gray material of her captor. Morgan wasn't smiling. Fire flamed in his golden eyes. She embraced him, tears of relief flooding her face. "Morgan."

He examined her ruined sleeve. "Someone tore my wife's dress."

"Wife?" The private turned to the sergeant. "We didn't know she was your wife, Major."

"We didn't know she was anybody's wife," the other private said. "She had no escort."

Jess wiped her face with her sleeve and turned to face the men. Morgan kept his hand on her bare shoulder. "Does my wife require a guard wherever she goes? I was under the impression Southern men were gentlemen. I see we have a few exceptions."

"You can't fault us for having a bit of fun," the sergeant defended. "We meant her no harm."

"Who are you?"

"Sergeant Will Starr from Texas." He spat a stream of tobacco juice at Morgan's shiny boots. His hand rested on the ivory handle of his revolver hanging on his hip.

"Those are the men who have been harassing the women in town," Donna shouted as she approached from the cabin. Tootie was standing on the porch. "Scaring the girls and taking food from the women that's meant for the sick and wounded."

"It seems this isn't your first offense," Morgan said.

"What are you going to do with us?"

"As an officer, I could have you tied to a wagon wheel and whipped like the dogs you are."

"You can't do that to a man," Will said.

"What were you going to do to me if you caught me?" Jess demanded.

"We might have stolen a kiss. What harm is there in that?" Will asked.

Morgan's fist connected with his face, and Will stumbled backward. One of the privates helped him rise from the ground. "No one kisses my wife but me, and even I ask permission first."

160

Jess had calmed her breathing to a normal rate. She had been terrified of what could have happened, but Morgan's presence restored her courage. She looked at Donna and the other women. "You need to respect women instead of scaring and chasing them through the streets."

"We meant no harm," Will said.

"Your definition of no harm doesn't match mine," Jess said. "Women are respected where I come from. I don't have to be afraid to walk down the street."

"I didn't know you were a lady," Will said. "I'll remember to tip my hat the next time we pass."

"You're mocking me," Jess said. "You need a lesson in humiliation."

"Your man is double my size."

Jess pointed at the leather holster strapped to his thigh. "You have a fancy gun. Do you consider yourself a good shot?"

His hand rested on the revolver. "I'm one of the best."

Jess stepped forward away from Morgan. "Then I challenge you to a shooting contest. If you lose, you apologize to all the women in town and treat them with gentlemanly manners from now on."

"And when I win?"

"I'll bake you a pie."

Will grinned at his two companions. "I take it the major considers himself a good shot."

"Only one way to find out," Morgan said.

Jess put her hand on Morgan's arm but faced Will. "You're not shooting against the major. That wouldn't be humbling." Jess pointed to herself. "You're shooting against me."

Will laughed. "I'm not shooting against a woman."

"Afraid?"

He guffawed. "Of you?"

"Then you agree." Jess extended her hand.

"I like blueberry pie." Will spat into his hand and offered it. Jess spat in hers and shook.

Will looked around. "Where are we going to hold this shooting contest?"

"The breastworks my men built are high," Morgan said. "You can shoot against them."

"You can't take her place, Major," Will said.

Morgan leaned in close. "Are you sure you don't want me to challenge him?"

"You weren't the one chased down in the street like prey. I need to show him I'm a worthy opponent." Jess placed her hand against his chest. "Don't you think I can beat him?"

The corner of his mouth lifted slightly. "If you say you can, then I believe you."

Will twirled his fancy gun. "You're about to find out how good I am."

Chapter Fifteen

Word spread of the shooting contest. Tootie insisted upon joining them so Jess placed a quilt in a wheelbarrow, and Morgan pushed her to the breastworks. The women of town gathered on one side of the shooting alley while the soldiers grouped on the opposite side. A few men took bets. More than pie was riding on the outcome.

Captain Otis Baker was in charge of officiating. Will had his fancy gun, and Jess had Ed's revolver. Each had three loaded cylinders, one in the gun and two spares.

Six tin cups were lined up on a board perched on posts in the ground in front of the breastworks.

Will tipped his hat. "Ladies first."

Jess had changed into a plain work dress. She wore her floppy hat to keep the sun out of her eyes. She took a stance in the dirt, her leather boots shoulder width apart with her right foot slightly forward. She gripped her gun with both hands, the left around the handle and the right overlapping the left in a double grip and raised her arms to shoulder height, her gaze down the barrel.

"Don't forget to cock the hammer, little lady," someone shouted from the crowd. Others laughed.

Morgan waved at them. "Quiet."

Jess shifted her weight slightly forward, her arms tense to steady her frame. She cocked the hammer,

163

aimed down the barrel, took in a breath, exhaled slightly, and held it. The gun remained motionless in her steady hands. She squeezed the trigger. The first cup jumped from the board and sailed into the air. She fired five more times, sending each cup into the air.

"Six out of six," Otis announced.

Jess removed the empty cylinder. The men had gone quiet, but the women erupted in a cheer.

Morgan handed her a loaded cylinder. "Ed teach you how to shoot?"

"He taught me how to hunt. Jake taught me how to shoot. Mostly snakes on the towpath."

"Cousin Jake who worked on your grandfather's boat, the *Irish Rose*," Morgan said. "Killed at Antietam."

He had remembered the details of her life.

Otis placed six cups on the board. "Your turn, Sergeant."

Will stared from Jess to Morgan. "This is some sort of trick. No woman can shoot a gun like that."

Morgan grinned. "Are you going to cede?"

Will stepped to the line.

"You can do it, Will!" one of his companions shouted.

He raised his arm in a single hand stance and squeezed the first shot. The cup flew off the board followed by five more. Will turned and waved to the crowd. "See, I told you I was the best shot."

"My baby sister could hit the cups from this distance," Jess said. "Why don't we step back to a respectable distance?"

Otis moved the crowd back and marked the firing line. Cups were lined up on the board.

Jess nodded at Will. "You can go first this time, Sergeant."

"Let me show you how it's done, little lady." He emptied his gun. Five cups flew from the board, but one remained. "My gun must have misfired."

"No," Otis said. "You were high and to the right." Otis replaced the cups and examined the logs behind the target. "I found your lead ball." He dug it out. "Five hits, one miss."

"She'll never hit all six targets." Will wiped his brow with his dirty kerchief. "Not from this distance."

Jess needed to hit all six cups. Five cups meant she would have to shoot again, and Ed's revolver was heavy. Fatigue would make her arms shake. Her aim would suffer the longer the competition continued. She shook her arms to relax and took her stance. She double-checked the position of her feet, arms, and grip to guarantee they were correct.

"Hurry up or the war will be over," someone called from the crowd of men.

The laughter made her relax. Five cups flew off the board. She paused, took an extra breath, and squeezed the trigger. No cups remained.

"Six hits," Otis announced. "Mrs. Mackinnon is the winner."

The men stood in shock, but the women clapped and cheered. Donna approached Will. "You may say your apologies, and to prove there are no hard feelings, I baked you a pie." She lifted a basket.

"It's called humble pie!" Tootie shouted from her seat in the wheelbarrow.

"It's blueberry," Donna said.

Will turned to Jess and removed his hat. "I

apologize for any behavior on my part that caused you distress, Mrs. Mackinnon."

"I accept your apology on behalf of all the women of the town." She planted a kiss on his cheek. A few Rebel yells escaped from the crowd.

"Now what are we goin' to do for entertainment?" one of the soldiers asked.

"Can one of your men play the fiddle?" Donna asked.

"Only one good tune," Will said. "*Dixie*."

Morgan bowed and offered his hand. "Mrs. Mackinnon?" His hand encircled her waist and his other grasped hers as he led her around the open area where dirt had been removed to build the breastworks. The flat surface was packed and provided a large dance floor.

Jess nodded at the fiddler. "Couldn't he play something else?"

"We are Southerners."

"The ladies are not," she reminded him.

"Great tune." When he finished, he signaled to the fiddler and other musicians who had joined him to form a small band. "Let's have a country dance or a reel."

Otis stood on a raised platform and called for the ladies to form a circle. The men stood in a circle outside them. He explained the series of steps. When completed, the men would advance to their right and repeat the steps with a different lady partner.

Morgan and Jess began as partners but were soon parted. They completed the set and danced several more before excusing themselves. "Confederate soldiers dancing with Union ladies," Morgan said. "I would never have believed it."

They found Will with an empty pie tin. "You ate

the entire pie yourself?"

"I had some help." The two privates had berry stains on their uniforms. "Did you teach your wife how to shoot, Major?"

"No, I can't take credit for my wife's talents."

"Or my vices," Jess added. She clapped as the band played a march. "I would love to get my hands on that fiddle."

"All you need to do is ask."

Jess tucked the fiddle under her chin and ran the bow over the strings. "It has a sweet sound." She played a mournful Irish tune. Tears were hastily wiped away when she finished.

"Let's have something to cheer the crowd," Morgan suggested.

"How about *When Johnny Comes Marching Home*?"

It was a lively tune that both sides claimed. The men marched about, and the women twirled to match the words.

When the stars appeared in the sky, fires were lit. Morgan sat beside Jess on a log and wrapped a blanket around her shoulders. "Blake and I would sit by the fire talking about our futures. We never mentioned war."

One of the men sang a hymn. Jess joined in, singing harmony like she did with her sisters. Morgan took the bass part. They sang several more songs before parting company. Morgan handed Jess her haversack with her gun and looked around for Tootie.

"Donna asked Will to push her home hours ago," Jess said. "She missed a lovely night."

"Good food, fine music, and excellent company." Morgan tucked her arm in the crook of his elbow.

She wanted to forget the suffering and death that haunted her. The dancing and singing had been a pleasant respite, and she wasn't ready to return to reality. "If it wasn't for this awful war," Jess said. "It looms over everything good in this life, threatening to destroy any chance at happiness."

"Let's not think about the war." Morgan sat on the bench in front of the cabin and pulled her onto his lap. "How about we canoodle under the stars?"

He was teasing, but her heart thumped in her chest. This wasn't Ed, who blushed with every kiss. And she had no chaperone to remind them they weren't truly married. She settled on his hard thighs and reached around his neck with her arms, her lips brushing his cheek. "You have permission to kiss me."

He said nothing. His body remained unresponsive. Was he shocked by her bold invitation? It was dark in the shadows of the porch, and she couldn't read his face. She struggled to stand. "Maybe you don't want to canoodle."

"Not likely." His arms trapped her, cradling her in his grasp as he leaned in close, his mouth hovering above hers.

Jess expected his kiss to be hard and demanding like before, but Morgan exercised a different tactic. He nibbled on her lower lip, whetting her appetite. He brushed tender flesh, teasing her desire for more. She wanted to surrender, but there was no future for them. She curled her fingers in his bushy hair to fight the growing need within her. She moaned, and he captured it as his mouth crushed hers.

A cough interrupted them. Morgan broke the kiss but held Jess firmly on his lap. It was Otis. "Major, we have orders to report to the breastworks."

"Let me say goodnight to my wife."

"I'll meet you there, sir."

Jess slid off his lap. "You don't think he saw?"

"It's dark."

Jess checked the buttons on her dress. Two had become unbuttoned. "I don't want him to think poorly of me."

"Hardly, my dear." Morgan patted her behind when she turned to enter the cabin. "An affectionate wife is the envy of other men."

****

Morgan spent the night with his men, but his thoughts were with Jess. A willing kiss had given him a taste of what her body could promise and unleashed a hunger that could not be satiated. Even though she was his wife in name only, they were playing a serious game of seduction and gratification.

He couldn't marry her. Not with a battle looming. If the Confederate army withdrew, he wouldn't see her until the end of the war. What if the fire they had stoked cooled with time like her love for Ed?

"Impressive sight," Otis interrupted his thoughts.

Morgan looked at their defenses. The Confederate soldiers had six miles of breastworks in place on high ground with guns strategically located to defend the line no matter where the Union army attacked. Ewell's Corps was in command of the west end about a mile and half southwest of Hagerstown. They would be in charge of protecting the only road to Williamsport. Now all they had to do was wait.

"Major Mackinnon."

It was Theo. The corporal saluted and handed him

an envelope. "I'm to wait for your reply, sir."

Morgan tore open the missive and read it. "Is this for Mrs. Mackinnon as well?"

"Yes, sir."

"Tell the colonel we would be honored to join him for supper tonight."

Theo saluted and turned to Otis. "You are invited as well, Captain."

Otis waited until Theo had left. "Perhaps you should tell your wife about the invitation."

Morgan hesitated to return to the cabin. But passion had a way of cooling in the daylight hours, and Tootie would be present. "I won't be long."

"Take as much time as you need," Otis said.

Perhaps the captain had seen something last night. "I hope as an officer and a gentleman, you will practice discretion with anything you may have seen last night, Captain."

"Of course, sir. But if I ever marry, I may write you for advice."

Morgan laughed and headed home. He wasn't the instructor. He wiped his boots on the scraper by the cabin door and knocked. Tootie called out, and he entered.

His sister occupied the rocking chair where she was knitting socks. Jess was preparing soup at the fireplace. She turned and smiled. Had he imagined last night? He had expected her to be outraged about taking advantage of the dark. He removed his hat and sat at the table.

"I was hoping you would come home for dinner." She placed a bowl in front of him and dipped her finger in it, tasting the liquid. "It's not too hot."

The spoon shook in his fingers as she licked her lips.

Jess sliced a loaf of bread. "Do you want some butter on it?"

Why was everything she said coated in tantalizing visions of lovemaking? He concentrated on her face. Her huge eyes penetrated into a man's soul. They were slanted in a way that reminded him of a cat, especially with the green color. But his favorite feature was her mouth, well-formed, full, and begging to be kissed.

She reached for the crock of butter, and he inhaled the scent of vanilla in her hair as the flaxen locks fell in a wave of curls across his line of vision. "I like your hair unbraided."

She straightened and smiled. "I washed it." She played with a curl. "It dries quicker loose."

He bit into the creamy butter coating his bread. "Colonel Chauncy LaDonte has invited us to dine with him tonight."

A queer smile played on her lips. "Chauncy?"

"It's a respectable name for a man."

"And little girls." She waved toward Tootie. "Is your sister invited?"

"Oh, no!" Tootie cried. "I prefer my knitting to dining with a bunch of officers and sitting on a hard chair. Please make my excuses."

Morgan didn't have the heart to tell her she hadn't been included in the invitation. Jess was frantically tossing items out of the Shultz trunk. "Did you lose something?"

"I need to find something to wear."

Morgan chuckled. "I'll call at six. Be prompt. The colonel doesn't like to be kept waiting."

Chapter Sixteen

It had been a long time since Jess had dressed for a fancy dinner. Tootie had helped lace the corset over her sheer chemise and lace trimmed bloomers. She'd added the corset cover and crinoline. She hadn't worn any crinoline on the trip. It was too uncomfortable for the long ride, but Donna had lent one. She tied it in place, and Tootie helped to drop the petticoat and silk gown over her head and arrange them on the stiff frame.

She stepped into the slippers and gathered her gloves, fan, and pull-string purse. She stared at her reflection in the small mirror on the wall. Her hair was pulled high and cascaded in flowing curls around her face and down her back. She barely recognized the tomboy who had handled the masculine roles on the farm because she had no brother. "How do I look?"

"I know a better judge than me." Tootie opened the door, and Morgan, who had been waiting outside, entered.

Morgan had cleaned his uniform and polished his boots. He had his hat in his hand and nearly dropped it.

Jess didn't need Morgan to say anything. She could see his approval in his smoldering golden eyes. She smoothed the silk lace trimming the wide-cut bodice that exposed a creamy expanse of skin and bare shoulders. Tall and thin, Jess had filled out with curves that had been more an annoyance than a blessing for her active lifestyle.

"I better take my gun," Morgan growled.

"It's dinner not a raid," Jess said. "Remember we're married. You should be familiar with my body and bored with it."

"I'd have to be dead first." He continued to stare as she gathered her belongings. She handed him her shawl. "Do you mind?"

He arranged the lacy fabric on her shoulders and crossed the ends in front, covering her chest.

Jess tugged on her white gloves and a corner of the shawl slipped off her shoulder. Morgan rearranged the covering.

Tootie waved. "Enjoy your dinner."

Jess hesitated by the door. "Are you sure you don't want to come?"

"Donna is bringing beef stew," Tootie said. "Better than any army food."

Morgan opened the door and offered his arm. Jess ran her hand along Morgan's bare cheek. He'd shaved and tamed his curls as much as the heat and humidity would allow. "I didn't realize you were hiding a handsome face under all that hair."

Morgan rubbed his chin. "It already itches."

She clung to his arm as she navigated the narrow boards to avoid the mud.

"This may not be entirely a social call," Morgan warned. "Colonel LaDonte was pretty mad about me searching for Tootie and not joining the wagon train right away. He threatened to demote me to captain."

"At least he's polite enough to feed you before demanding your stars."

"You may have to sew my captain bars back on."

"Maybe I can charm him into saving me a task with needle and thread."

"I doubt any man will be able to patch together a comprehensive conversation with you wearing that dress."

"A few yards of silk can conquer officers?"

"It's nae th' fabric, mah bonnie lass. It's whit th' goon isnae coverin'." His gaze lingered on her breasts. "You're like an onion."

"A what?"

"Onion. You peel a layer off an onion and discover another. A nurse, a fighter, a friend to a lonely girl, a sharpshooter, a fiddler, and the most beautiful woman in the world."

"Your flattery has gone too far. I know I'm not the *most* beautiful woman in the world."

"To me you are."

She recognized that look. She had seen it in Blake's eyes when he looked at her sister, Cole. When had Morgan Mackinnon fallen in love with her? And why didn't it terrify her?

The boards disappeared, and Jess hesitated to venture into the muddy swamp that had once been a road. "I should have worn my boots."

Morgan swept her into his arms against her initial protest. "Be careful my crinoline doesn't swing upward and expose all my secrets."

"You should worry more about a pink rosebud escaping." He nodded at her bodice.

Jess tugged on the edge of her gown. "Maybe the décolletage is too daring."

"I'll warn you if flowers begin to bloom."

"You can't stare at my bosom all night."

His grin broadened. "Then why did you wear it if you didn't want my attention?"

"I wanted to look pretty."

A group of soldiers greeted them. "Major. Mrs. Mackinnon."

She glanced over his shoulder at the strangers. "How do they know me?"

"You're the talk of camp, Mrs. Mackinnon. A few married men have given me advice."

Jess searched his face. "What sort of advice?"

"It seems they don't think I've properly trained you as a submissive wife."

Jess looked around. "Who are these men and where can I find them?"

"Then there are those who are under the impression you are in camp because you want to have a baby. Do you know there are several positions recommended for the breeding of a child?"

She shook her finger. "There will be no breeding."

"Aren't you curious about what they said?"

"I've seen drawings."

"In medical journals?"

"No. My older sisters shared some of their experiences when Cole married Blake."

Morgan stumbled, and Jess clung to his neck. "Blake didn't know what to do?"

"Cole is expecting a baby. I think he figured it out. Besides, it was for her education more than his. The Beecher women may be innocent before the wedding night, but we're eager students in the marriage bed."

Morgan nearly dropped her. She clung to his neck until he regained his balance. "Are you all right?"

He took a deep breath and pointed to the walled

tent. "We're here."

Morgan introduced Jess to Colonel LaDonte, and Chauncy made introductions and seated Jess at his right hand. Morgan sat across from her. Theo served fresh fish, fried potatoes, and coleslaw. He wore the coat she had mended. "Thank you for packing the basket for our trip, Theo."

"I knew you would be hungry, Miss Jessie."

Morgan grunted. Was he still angry that Theo had nearly allowed her to escape? Jess placed her napkin on her lap. "It's such a pleasure to finally meet you, Colonel. I've heard so much about you."

Morgan's eyebrow shot up. A man of few words, his facial expression spoke loud and clear. She met his inquiring gaze. "Not from you. From my sister, Jennifer."

"Miss Jenny," Chauncy said with tender affection. "I heard she married Logan Pierce."

"They're grateful you spared his life."

"I can't believe how much you resemble your sister," he said. "You're prettier if that's possible."

"My sister may change the name of her daughter when I tell her that." Jess sipped the wine. She had never acquired a taste for the bitterness of alcohol, but coffee and tea were rare in Southern camps.

"Daughter?"

Jess smiled as she recalled her niece. "Chauncy Theodora Pierce. She's eight months old and beautiful."

Chauncy laughed. "Theo, we have a namesake."

Theo poured more wine into Morgan's glass. "What's a namesake?"

"Miss Jenny named her baby girl after you and me. Chauncy Theodora."

Theo grinned. "I never had nobody named for me."

"It's a great honor to have a namesake," Chauncy said.

Morgan raised his glass. "You must have made quite an impression on Miss Jenny."

"I helped her find her husband."

Jess glanced at Morgan. "My sisters and I don't forget those who help us in a time of need."

Chauncy covered her hand with his. "I should have listened to her when she warned me about the Cassell brothers."

"What did they do?"

"They shot the colonel," Theo said.

Jess examined Chauncy with a nurse's eye. Most soldiers were thin from long marches and lack of proper food, but Chauncy had a raspiness to his voice that betrayed his near-death experience. "Why?"

"I was going to have them hanged for attempting to steal the regiment's payroll. They overpowered their guards and stole two horses. I was in a hospital for nearly a year recovering. If I ever meet those two again, I'll settle that score."

"You only have to worry about Clyde. Buck Cassell is dead," Jess said.

"Are you sure? Those two have been reported dead before."

Jess swallowed. What would they think about her role in Buck's death? "Last fall he was shot and died at the Mermaid's Mirth while trying to rob Blake Ellsworth."

"Morgan and I were talking about Blake Ellsworth before the withdrawal," Chauncy said. "I was telling him how Blake delivered Theo's coat."

Theo stepped forward. "Miss Jenny made this coat, and Miss Jessie sewed on the buttons and mended my sleeve." He showed the repair to Otis.

"You're a lucky man to have two special ladies care for you," Otis said.

"Didn't you say Blake attended West Point with you?" Chauncy stroked his mustache. "Maybe you should recruit him. We could use more officers."

"He's a captain in Meade's Twelfth Corps."

"Our adversary," Chauncy said. "Too bad."

"We're lucky Mrs. Mackinnon is on our side," Otis said. "You should have seen her best Will Starr in the shooting match."

"I remember Miss Jenny mentioned a sister who won a five-dollar gold piece in a shooting contest," Chauncy said. "Was that you?"

"Guilty."

"I didn't know Morgan was married, let alone to a sharpshooter," Otis said. "You were quite a surprise."

"As much of a surprise as Tootie?"

"I should explain," Morgan said.

Jess turned to Chauncy. "Morgan wrote me Tootie had arrived in camp and needed a place to stay. I traveled to Gettysburg to take her with me. She was lucky I arrived when I did. The poor girl had been shot and left on the field."

"Why did Tootie disguise herself as a soldier?" Otis asked.

"Tootie disguised her femininity but as a civilian," Jess interrupted. "Some men may think it's a crime for a woman to wear men's clothing, but I've found it to be practical at times."

"You've disguised yourself as a man?" Otis asked.

"My sister and I wanted to help the wounded, and the only woman allowed on the battlefield a year ago was Clara Barton."

"Roe Greystone told Theo how much you've helped at the church. He's making preparations for more wounded."

Jess laid her fork on the table and dabbed at her mouth. "Why?"

"Our scouts have informed us Meade has arrived and has his forces in position," Chauncy said. "We expect him to attack tomorrow."

"Another battle." Her appetite was gone.

"I'm sorry to distress you, Mrs. Mackinnon," Chauncy said. "The river is low enough for the men to build a pontoon boat bridge. We'll be able to evacuate the wounded if the rain holds off and we can curb Meade's advance."

Jess smiled. "That's good news."

Theo served dessert, and the conversation turned toward the battle if Meade attacked as expected. The Confederate forces had the advantage with the high ground and well-built defenses. The losses could be high on the Union side.

The men sounded excited. How could they look forward to another fight? She had seen one battle, but that had been enough to recognize the futility of two forces attempting to kill each other. Hot tears brimmed on her lower eyelids, and she stood. She didn't want the men to catch her crying.

Morgan was by her side, his hand cradling her elbow. "I didn't realize it was so late. We have a busy day tomorrow, gentlemen. I hope you'll excuse us."

"For all the men present, I want to thank you for

gracing us with your presence. What a pleasure and honor it has been to meet you," Chauncy said. "Please give your sister my fondest regards, and thank her for naming her daughter after Theo and me."

Jess hugged Chauncy. Then she hugged Theo, and because she couldn't think of any reason not to, she hugged Otis. "Be careful tomorrow." She meant it. She had friends on both sides of the conflict now.

They paused at the mud, and Morgan lifted her in his arms. "Is there any way to avoid a battle tomorrow?"

"We'll fight if we have to defend ourselves, but Lee is no risk taker. If the boats are ready in time, we'll cross."

"I'm sick of the killing."

"The sight of blood doesn't make you queasy. Who shot Buck Cassell?"

Jess refused to answer.

"I've killed too many men to judge you. What happened?"

Jess had never talked about it, not even with her sisters. "Buck and Clyde had taken over the Mermaid's Mirth while we were at Antietam," Jess said. "When we returned, they hit Blake over the head and beat him to make him reveal the location of his gold. Cole and I shot blindly into the hallway. Buck was hit in the gut. He died in the hallway while Clyde escaped."

"The hallway of the Mermaid's Mirth. You mentioned that before," Morgan said. "How do you know your shot killed him?"

"I don't. It's the only thing that keeps me from being a murderer."

"Some men deserve to die."

"Isn't all life valuable?"

"When people use the word all, alarm bells should go off," Morgan said. "People are too different to group in neat little categories. One man steals out of greed while another steals to feed his starving family. Do they deserve the same punishment? Our laws need to be flexible to provide justice for individuals. I know you well enough to say with confidence if you killed a man, he deserved it."

Jess rested her head against his shoulder. "Thank you. I couldn't share my fears with Cole. I didn't want her to bear the burden, but now it doesn't feel so heavy."

"As you have noted on occasion, I have broad shoulders, big enough to bear both our troubles."

"Remind me why I didn't like you when we met."

"You didn't like me?" Morgan's voice was playful. "I was under the impression you were enamored of my charms."

"I could have done without the filthy gag."

"Too bad I didn't search you sooner. I can still feel the blade of your knife against my throat."

"It was the dull side."

His laughter echoed in the darkness. He carried her to the cabin and placed her on the ground to open the door.

Tootie was in bed, snoring. "She's loud for a little girl."

"She also snatches all the covers."

"You could sleep in my bed tonight."

"Morgan!"

"I have to report to my men and wait with them."

"For the battle." Jess fought the urge to cry. She

turned her back. "Before you leave, could you unhook my dress? I doubt if I can wake Tootie to do it."

Morgan studied the gown.

Jess looked over her shoulder. "What's wrong?"

"How do I unhook it?"

She faced him. "You've never undressed a woman?"

"I'm a soldier not a lady's maid."

She turned away. "Start at the top. Pinch the edges together and the hook should slide out of the eye."

"Why don't you have buttons?"

"A formal gown uses hooks and eyes."

He unhooked the gown as Jess held the front firmly in place. He reached the waist. "You're unhooked."

Jess stepped behind the screen and finished undressing.

Morgan gathered his weapons. "Do you want me to extinguish the light?"

"No." Jess tied her robe over her nightgown and emerged from behind the screen.

Morgan stood near the table. He was attaching his scabbard for his sword to his belt. He looked up, his gaze catching hers. "If we never see each other again…"

"Don't say the words." Jess ran to him and placed her hand over his lips. "Say a quick prayer."

He grinned but nodded. "*Dae Ah daur believe yoo've groon tender feelings fur me?*"

"Kiss me before I remember I'm an abolitionist."

His mouth crushed hers with a fierceness and desperation to hold onto the precious moment.

Jess clung. Nothing would be the same after tomorrow.

Chapter Seventeen

Jess spent a restless night and woke on July 13 to silence. Soldiers passing the cabin informed her Meade was in position, his men dug into trenches. The Southern soldiers were ready for an attack.

Jess reported to the church to help prepare the wounded for the trip across the pontoon boat bridge.

"The cavalry has only seen Union scouting parties," Roe said. "That should give us time to evacuate the wounded. I believe Lee could withdraw the army during the night."

"He would run away from a fight?"

"Lee won't attack after Gettysburg, and if Meade won't attack, it's a stalemate. Better to take the men into Virginia and fight on home ground."

Jess replaced dirty bandages and dosed the men with laudanum before the stretcher bearers loaded the wagons with the wounded. The men were in better condition to endure the long trip. They thanked Jess and the women of town who had fed and cared for them.

As the church emptied, the women of town reclaimed its sacred walls, scrubbing the floors and furnishings of any sign of the wounded.

Roe extended his hand to Jess. "Thank you for all your help."

Roe had experienced more surgeries and medical ailments in the past months than most country doctors took a lifetime to master. But like the Ohio boys, her feelings were sisterly toward Roe. How could her attraction to men be so vastly different? Morgan had captured her heart but would her love for him fade as her love for Ed had ebbed with time and distance?

War would keep them apart. It might destroy any chance at happiness. Morgan was no longer the enemy. The war was.

Jess joined Tootie in the cabin and fixed supper. Theo knocked and asked for Morgan's storage chest. He was packing supplies for the evacuation. Roe had been right about Lee. He had given the order to cross the pontoon boat during the night. If Meade decided to attack tomorrow, he would find the enemy gone.

Morgan arrived after dark. "Why aren't you dressed to go, Tootie?"

"I can't return to the Confederate army," Tootie said. "Everyone knows I'm a woman."

"I'll take care of you."

"I don't want to go."

"What are you going to do?"

Jess stood. "She's going to Washington City with me."

"Why wasn't I consulted?"

"We're discussing it now."

"I won't have her living off your charity."

"It's not charity," Jess said. "I've offered her a job at Blake's hotel, the Mermaid's Mirth."

Morgan ran his fingers through his thick hair. "Is this what you want?"

"I'll have a place to live and a job. It's the answer to my prayers."

"She'll be safe there," Jess said. "After the war,

you can find her. The hotel is in Washington City on Maryland Avenue on the other side of the Long Bridge."

Morgan pointed to the crutch Tootie used. "How can she work when she can barely walk?"

"She's improving every day," Jess said. "The ladies of town will let us stay here until Tootie is ready to travel. She won't get better if she goes with the army."

"If she's well enough, she could return to the store in Richmond."

"No!" both women said in unison. Tootie bowed her head. "I can't go back there, Morgan. It isn't safe for me."

His voice was hard, demanding. "Why not?"

Tootie spoke in a rush. "Lyle hit me when I broke an expensive vase."

Morgan balled his hands into fists. "I'll teach him to hit a girl!"

Jess touched his arm. "Let her come with me. When the war is over, you can be reunited." *We can be reunited.*

Morgan pulled Tootie against his chest and kissed her forehead. "I love you." She cried. "I wish I could stay, but the last place I want to spend the war is in a prison camp. Nothing but starvation and disease. I'd rather take my chances on the battlefield."

"We made sandwiches for you." Tootie shoved them into his haversack.

Morgan's gaze locked on Jess. "The Union army will arrive soon. Do you have your gun?"

"The Ohio boys are my friends."

"Unsavory types exist in both armies. Keep your

gun under your skirt and don't let any stinkin' polecat take it." Morgan's grin widened. "He might fall in love with you."

It was the closest he had come to a declaration. She didn't expect more. She loved him, but it was futile. Love would wither and die with time. She desperately wished it could be otherwise.

Morgan slung the pack over his shoulder. "I'd like to take something else with me."

"We packed everything you could possibly need," Tootie said.

He turned to Jess and hesitated. "I want your photograph. The one Ed carried."

Jess retrieved her haversack from the corner and dumped the contents on the table. Their fingers touched when they went to grab it. He stroked her hand before tucking the photograph in an inside pocket of his coat. "There's one more thing I need to take."

He needed to leave. She didn't want him to see her bawl. "What's that?"

"This is where I take back my name, Mrs. Mackinnon." He stepped closer. "But before I do." He jerked her tightly against his chest, his mouth poised above hers. She went limp in his arms. All she could hear was their heartbeats pounding together in an accelerated rhythm. He lingered above her, waiting. "May I?"

This could be the last time they saw each other, the last time they touched. A moan escaped, and she offered her lips. He feasted on them, and she refused to let him starve.

A shout outside the door broke them apart. Morgan removed a letter from his coat and placed it on the table. "When you see Blake, tell him if God is merciful, I hope to see him when this damn war is over." He headed for the door. It slammed shut.

She hadn't told him she loved him and ran after him, yanking open the door. But he had disappeared into the darkness. Jess burst into tears.

****

Jess sat on the bench in front of the cabin as the Union army arrived. The Ohio boys stared as if she were a ghost. Jess waved, stood, and walked toward them. "I baked some bread."

The boys whooped and headed inside without waiting to be dismissed. Blake wasn't so easily won over. "If I wasn't relieved to see you alive, I'd spank you for disappearing." He slapped his dusty hat against his thigh. "Sid nearly had a heart attack when you turned up missing."

"It's nice seeing you, too, Blake." She led the way inside.

"What happened?"

"Your friend, Morgan Mackinnon captured me."

"The bloody hell! Where is he? I'll kill him."

"There's been enough killing." Jess introduced Tootie, who was resting on a cushion in her rocking chair. The boys were slathering the bread with strawberry jam. "You're too late. Morgan and the Confederate army crossed during the night into West Virginia."

"Meade hesitated." Blake shook his head as he grabbed a slice of bread. "He could have attacked yesterday. We were ready, but he sent out scouts to do reconnaissance. The war would have been over if he hadn't waited. They couldn't have escaped with the

187

river behind them."

"They wouldn't have surrendered without a fight," Jess said. "Have you seen their breastworks? This time they would have been in the trenches with barricades to protect them, and you would have been in the open, ripe for slaughtering."

Ethan stopped eating. "Whoa, cousin. Whose side are you on?"

"I want you to stay alive," Jess said. "I'm tired of burying good men and watching others torn apart or butchered by doctors. I'm sick of it. Do you hear me?" Her voice trembled and tears clouded her vision.

Blake pulled her against this chest. "No more talk of war, boys."

Harry offered Tootie some bread. "How did you and Jess meet?"

Jess and Tootie had agreed her presence among Confederate troops didn't need to be shared. Someone in the Union might want to make her a prisoner even though she was a woman. "I was wounded in the crossfire at Gettysburg."

"By a Rebel?"

"Hard to say. A stray bullet ricocheted off a tombstone on Cemetery Hill."

The implication hung in the air. One of them might have shot Tootie.

"You're Theresa Mackinnon," Blake pointed. "Your hair was in braids."

They stared at her short hair.

"She had a fever," Jess explained. "I had to cut her hair."

They didn't challenge her story. Some suffragettes bobbed their hair so it wasn't unusual for some women to wear it short.

"The women of the town will provide food and any help to the Union, too," Jess added.

"Whose place is this?"

"Mrs. Shultz is letting us stay here until we return to Washington City."

"Jessica offered me a job at the Mermaid's Mirth," Tootie said.

Blake raised a dark eyebrow. "Has business been good enough for extra workers?"

"All the rooms are filled, and with Colleen not able to work, we could use another helper."

"When are you returning?"

"Depends on how long you boys are staying."

"The Rebs didn't take my horses and wagon, did they?"

Jess laughed at his distress. "They're in the lean-to by the chicken coop, all rested for the ride back home. Morgan said Romulus and Remus were fine horses."

"Morgan wouldn't know a draft horse from a mule."

Jess withdrew a letter from her skirt pocket. "Morgan left this note for you."

Blake tore open the missive and read it aloud. *"Blake, old friend,*

Congratulations on your marriage. If Colleen is anything like her sister, I know you'll be happy."

"What?" Jess interrupted. She should have read the letter before giving it to Blake. He gave her a look, one of suspicion. "Nothing happened," she claimed.

"I appreciate you allowing me to borrow your team of horses. We had our blacksmith reshod them for the long trip home. We'll probably beat you there as

slow as Meade moves his army.

Morgan."

Blake crumpled the note. "That arrogant Scotsman. Who does he think he is criticizing our commander?"

"You said Meade was slow or you would have attacked yesterday."

"I can say that because I'm in Meade's army," Blake said. "No Reb can insult him and certainly not Morgan Mackinnon."

"I don't know how Meade beat Lee at Gettysburg," Jess said. "He didn't look beaten when he arrived here."

"Did you meet General Robert E. Lee?" Zach asked.

"Yes, he was everything you would expect." Jess clapped her hands. "He rode Traveler into camp like a king. You should meet him sometime."

"Yes, let's invite him to the Mermaid's Mirth for drinks." Blake's voice was thick with sarcasm.

"I don't believe he drinks alcohol," Tootie said.

Blake scowled.

"It does seem rude not to invite him," Jess added. "After all, soldiers have been squatting at Arlington House since the war started."

Blake paced. "And I suppose we should return his home and property after the war is over."

"I think he would expect it if they win," Tootie said.

Blake threw up his hands. "What side are you on?"

"I was raised in Richmond, don't you remember?"

Blake pointed at Jess. "You're lucky I'm in love with your sister."

Ethan laughed. "She's teasing. Jessie always said the most outrageous things."

Maybe they were outrageous because no one would believe the truth. "We have the bed, but you boys could sleep on the floor, and Blake can have the single bed. Morgan slept there."

"Under the same roof? We'll sleep outside."

The boys groaned.

Blake pulled her aside. "Did Morgan do anything I should be aware of?"

"What do you mean?" Was she blushing?

"He's a big oaf when it comes to women. Did he compromise you?"

"Tootie served as chaperone. And I had my knife and gun to remind Morgan to be a gentleman."

"I'm surprised you didn't have to use them."

"I had the edge of my knife against his throat once," Jess said. "That was warning enough."

"And I was worried about *you*." He released a laugh. "We'll camp nearby. If you need anything, ask."

"There's plenty of room in the lean-to with Romulus and Remus."

"I'll check on them."

Tootie followed Jess outside and stared at all the Union soldiers moving into the camp the Confederates had vacated hours before. "Do you think we should lock the door?"

"The only difference from the soldiers on your side is the color of the uniform. At one time we were all Americans."

Chapter Eighteen

General Meade ordered the men to build breastworks on the Maryland side of the river while the Confederate built their defenses on West Virginia's side. They worked all day. Blake returned to the house without the boys.

"They have to stay in the breastworks, but Meade ought to know you can't attack from the trenches," Blake said. "Does he think Lee will cross the river and fight on Union soil again?"

Jess shrugged. "So they worked all day for nothing."

"They built a beautiful ditch."

When word arrived that Lee had abandoned the shores of the Potomac River, the Twelfth Corps was ordered south toward Sharpsburg, shadowing the Confederate army, ready to block any attack on the capital.

Jess and Tootie traveled with them instead of traveling alone to Frederick and on to Washington City. Ethan drove Romulus and Remus with Jess beside him, her eyes the only thing visible as they choked on the dust raised by the marching men. Tootie rode in the back on a stretcher padded with a quilt on a thick layer of straw to help prevent her hip from hurting.

As they traveled south along Hagerstown Turnpike, the surroundings grew familiar. "Where are we?"

"Nearing Sharpsburg."

Antietam. She grabbed Ethan's arm. "Stop!"

Ethan pulled on the reins. They were in front of Dunker Church. The small square building had been a field hospital. Bullet holes marred the walls, and the roof had been damaged by artillery. After the battle the wounded had been lined up along the turnpike, torn and bleeding bodies in a row. Some waited for surgery inside the church. Other were piled into ambulances and transported to hospitals, leaving a trail of blood dripping through the floorboards. Then there were those who were given opium and water, waiting for death. Sid had been one of the wounded, waiting along the side of the road for his turn to have his useless shattered foot removed. Jess pointed to a withered cornfield on the opposite side. "That's where Cousin Jake was killed."

Ethan removed his kepi. "They call the Seventh Ohio the roosters. Remember how Jake could crow?"

"I think about all the summers we spent on Grandpa's canal boat together," Jess said. "He made each day an adventure."

"He taught me how to tie knots, and he taught you how to play the fiddle," Ethan recalled.

"No one realizes the price of war until you break it down to the names and faces of those who made the ultimate sacrifice. The future became sadder when Jake died." Tears burned a hot trail down her cheeks. "Sometimes you forget, but then a remark or a gesture reminds you of what you've lost, and the pain is as real as the first time. It never goes away completely."

Ethan wiped his tears with his dusty sleeve, leaving marks across his sunburned face. "I want to kill all those dirty Rebs."

"That's not the answer, Ethan." Jess grabbed her canteen, poured some water on a kerchief, and washed her face. "Being with the enemy, I learned how much we're alike. When the war is over, we're going to have to make peace with the fact that we've killed. We're going to have to live with what we've done. We're going to have to be friends."

"Not in my lifetime."

Jess offered the damp kerchief. "Then the war will never be over."

Ethan cleaned his face. "I hope you don't think less of me for bawling."

"I'd worry if you didn't cry." She took a drink from her canteen and offered it to him.

Blake joined them. "I remember the church being bigger."

"This place haunts my dreams." Jess pointed to the battered cornfield opposite the church. The farmer hadn't plowed or planted this year's crop. The wounded had called for water, begging for death. "That's where Jake fell."

Jess jumped to the ground and stepped gingerly into the field. She took a few steps and stopped. The wind rustled the broken stalks of corn, whistling a warning through the shattered shafts almost like a voice. A shoe was half buried in the dirt. The ground contained artifacts of the battle. Jake's remains were buried at home in Darrow Falls, but his presence seemed to remain. She shivered and headed back to the wagon. "Are we spending the night here?"

"No, we're heading south to Harper's Ferry." Blake helped her climb to the seat. "I plan to put the horses and wagon on the train. You and Tootie can return to Washington City."

"What will the army do?"

"We'll continue to shadow Lee."

When they reached Harper's Ferry, soldiers were celebrating. Ethan stopped the wagon near the depot and unhitched the team. Blake shared the news that had been transmitted from the West. "General Ulysses S. Grant won at Vicksburg. After nearly three years of losses, the Union can claim two major victories." Blake waved his hat in the air and led a cheer from the regiment.

Tootie joined Jess on the depot platform. "General Lee won't give up easily."

The men in gray worshipped Lee. It would require more than a couple of victories to break Lee or his army. But today the Union celebrated its wins.

Ethan loaded their belongings in the same freight car with the horses. The wagon was placed on a flat car. Jess exchanged hugs with the boys and said goodbye. It could be for the last time, but she refused to entertain her fears. She nodded toward Blake. "Take care of the captain."

Blake purchased tickets and handed Jess two letters, both addressed to Cole. "Take care of my wife and baby."

"She's in good hands. Jem is the best midwife I know."

"I don't know what our orders will be, but if I can, I'll come home to her as soon as possible."

****

When Jess and Tootie arrived in Washington City, she asked a couple of soldiers to hitch Romulus and

Remus to the wagon and load their belongings. They were happy to comply. Jess helped Tootie climb onto the bench seat where a blanket added some cushion.

"Is that you Miss Jessica?" It was Sid. He hobbled toward her, his brows tied in a knot as he frowned.

Jess swallowed, bracing for the onslaught of reprimands. Sid was no relative, but his long history with the Beecher sisters had given him authority to berate them.

He climbed aboard and took the reins. "Captain Ellsworth sent a telegram informing us you were returning home. I've been checking every train. I hope you had a lovely trip." He spoke calmly and evenly, but a tremor revealed his barely controlled anger.

"It was nice, thank you."

He raised his fist and shook it. "What did you mean wandering off on a battlefield?" Others looked in their direction, but he didn't lower his voice. "We thought you'd been killed."

Her sisters could charm him out of any temper or disagreement, but Jess resorted to straightforward reasoning. "I was delivering supplies to the boys."

"On a battlefield without a truce?" Sid demanded. "You're no novice during a conflict."

"Maybe if we had gone into the cornfields at Antietam before the truce, Jake would be alive." She hadn't meant to say the words. Anger tumbled out from inner turmoil she had suppressed. Jake's body hadn't bloated or darkened like those killed the previous day of the battle or those who had lain on the field through the heat. Jake had died near dawn after being in the field without care all night. If only they had reached him sooner. If only... "We stopped at Antietam. I

196

showed Ethan where Jake died." Tears blurred her vision, and she searched for a handkerchief.

"I better take you home." Sid's voice was low and soothing. "Your sisters are waiting for you."

"I'm sorry everyone worried." Jess dried her tears. "I sent a letter."

"A few lines without any mention of where you were or why."

Morgan had censored any mention of the location of the Confederate army. She shrugged.

"Don't think they'll let you off without a proper chastising, Miss Jessica. Captain Ellsworth's telegram only arrived two days ago. Your sisters have been fretting since they received that one letter you'd written."

Sid made the turn onto Pennsylvania Avenue and made his way through the heavy traffic, the horses' hooves echoing on the uneven cobblestones. He maneuvered the wagon around to stop in front of Pierce House.

Jess gathered her belongings from the back of the wagon, including a crutch. Sid helped Tootie to the ground, and she hobbled toward the front door. Sid carried the trunk that had belonged to Donna Shultz.

The door of the former boardinghouse flew open, and Jem hurried down the steps. Her dark red hair reminded Jess of Morgan, and she took a breath to steady her heart. Cole stood in the doorway, her advanced pregnancy preventing her from making a public appearance.

Jem hugged her so tightly, she could barely breathe. "You're alive!"

"Not if you squeeze all the air out of me."

"Bring her inside so I can whip her with the rug beater," Cole shouted from the doorway.

"Fine way to welcome me after being captured."

"What?" All the color drained from Jem's face. "Blake didn't give many details. He sent a telegram saying you were at Harper's Ferry and would return home as soon as possible on the train."

"And I did."

"But you said you were captured," Jem said.

"I was more a guest of the Confederacy." Jess handed Jem her basket and helped Tootie up the stairs. Sid followed with the trunk.

Cole pulled her as close as her rounded belly would allow and whispered, "Did they violate you?"

"They were Southern gentlemen."

Cole brushed back her ginger curls and stared. "How did you defend yourself against the entire Rebel army?"

"I had a champion. This is his sister, Tootie Mackinnon."

"Tootie?"

"I knocked my teeth out when I was little and whistled when I spoke. My brother, Morgan, called me Tootie."

"Mackinnon?" Cole repeated. "Why is that name familiar?"

"Morgan Mackinnon is Blake's friend from West Point."

"Mac?"

"The same." She put her arm around Tootie's waist. "We need to put her to bed. She's recovering from a gunshot."

"A soldier shot her?" Sid demanded. "Those dirty

Rebs."

"Oh, it wasn't the Confederates who shot me," Tootie said. "It was the Union soldiers."

"None of our boys would shoot a woman," Sid defended.

"I'm sure it was an accident," Tootie said. "It was dark, and I was wandering around the cemetery."

"What were you doing that for?"

"I was worried about Morgan. He had been fighting at Culp's Hill, and I had a dream he was in trouble. I was lucky the bullet ricocheted off one of the stones, or I'd be dead for sure. I was in the cemetery all night with nothing but a bogle to keep me company."

Sid wrinkled his brow. "Bogle?"

"A boggart in Ireland," Jess said. "A mischievous spirit."

"Morgan found me, but I was in too much pain to move," Tootie said. "He commandeered the wagon and Jess to nurse me."

Jess put her arm around Tootie. "If I hadn't helped her, she might have died."

Sid studied her. "Where were you shot?"

Tootie blushed. "In the cemetery."

Jess frowned at Sid for asking a personal question.

"Do you need medical care?" Jem asked.

"No," Jess said. "I took care of her in Gettysburg."

"Then why didn't Morgan let you go once you took care of Tootie?" Cole asked. "Aren't there any Rebel doctors?"

"Not for women," Tootie said. "I was dressed as a boy, and it was embarrassing."

"This story is full of holes, if you ask me," Sid said. "Where have you been all this time?"

"The wounded had left the battlefield, and we had to travel through an awful storm to catch them. By the time we did, we were in Williamsport," Jess said. "The pontoon boat bridge was destroyed, and they couldn't build one until the water receded. I sent a message."

"It didn't say anything about Williamsport," Cole said. "It didn't say much at all."

"Morgan wouldn't let me send any messages that might warn the Union about their precarious position," Jess defended. "By the time Meade attacked, the Rebels were across the river. I waited for the Ohio boys to show up, and they took Tootie and me to Harper's Ferry to board the train."

"*Humf*," Sid snorted. "You never were good at lying, Miss Jessica. You were kidnapped by them villains and tortured. And I was responsible. It is a futile endeavor to keep you women out of trouble. See these gray hairs." He plucked a few hairs from his receding hairline. "I'm a young man, but you ladies are aging me before my time."

"I'm sorry for causing you worry, Sid. Blake already reprimanded me."

"Don't think that's going to let you off the hook." Sid pointed at Tootie. "And don't think I'm not keeping my eye on you, missy. I'll wager you're here to spy."

"Tootie is not a spy." Jess put her hands on her hips. "I promised Tootie a job at the Mermaid's Mirth. She has nowhere else to go."

"We could use more help," Cole said. "This baby is taking its time to arrive, and I don't know how long it will take me to recover."

"I'm telling you, she can't be trusted," Sid said.

Jess stood with her hands on her hips. She was

done explaining herself. "I believe you should take Romulus and Remus to the Mermaid's Mirth. They'll be happy to return to familiar surroundings."

Sid's wooden leg thumped on the steps as he headed for the wagon.

Jess put her arm around Tootie's waist, but she hesitated to climb the stairs. "I don't think I can make those steps."

"I have a sick room off the kitchen," Jem said. "Why don't we put you in there for now?"

"We'll take you to the Mermaid's Mirth tomorrow," Jess said. "You can have a room on the main floor."

Once Tootie was settled in bed, the three sisters gathered around the kitchen table. Jess placed the basket from her trip in the middle. "You were right about this basket. We never went hungry. It is officially magical with a little help from Theo Jameson."

Jem stopped unpacking the basket. "Theo?"

"I met Theo and Colonel Chauncy LaDonte in Williamsport. They were honored to have Chauncy Theodora named after them."

Jem's hand went to her heart. "How is the colonel?"

"He was shot by the Cassell brothers," Jess said. "I told him he wouldn't have to worry about Buck Cassell anymore."

"Too bad Clyde escaped," Cole said. "I was sure I hit him."

"You hit him?" Jess demanded. "I thought I hit him. I know I'm the one who killed Buck."

"I fired at him, too," Cole said. "I could have killed him."

Jem raised her hands. "You two are the most morbid creatures arguing about who killed Buck Cassell."

They turned on her. "You liked Buck Cassell?"

"Heaven's no," Jem said. "That brute deserved to die, but if Clyde finds out you killed him, he might come after you. I wouldn't brag about it."

Jess nodded. "We'll share the credit and speak no more of either Cassell brother."

Jem finished making sandwiches. "Let's eat in the parlor."

Cole lowered herself on the sofa next to Jess. "Now that we're alone, tell us what really happened."

"I did."

"We're your sisters," Cole reminded her. "I want to hear details. What is Mac like?"

"He's sneaky." If they wanted to hear a story, she'd tell one. "After I delivered supplies to the boys at Culp's Hill, I was driving back to the Baltimore Pike. Morgan set a trap by curling up along the side of the road and pretending to be wounded. When I knelt to help, he grabbed me and stuck a dirty rag in my mouth so I couldn't scream."

Jem gasped. "Blake calls this man his friend?"

"Oh, he's a villainous sort," Jess said. "He tied my hands and tossed me in the back of the wagon, but I cut the ropes with my knife. When I threatened him, he wrestled the blade from me. Nearly cut my throat in the struggle."

"Mac sounds like an awful brute," Jem said. "And he's Tootie's brother?"

"She's nothing like him," Jess said. "He's a huge Scotsman with wild red hair and eyes like a hawk."

"What's wrong with red hair?" both sisters demanded.

Jess had to turn away to hide her smile. "Then I overheard they were retreating from Gettysburg. Morgan said I couldn't leave and warn the Union."

Jem gasped. "He did kidnap you. How awful."

"He must have changed since Blake knew him," Cole said. "He always talked fondly of Mac."

"War can change men," Jem said.

"What about Ed's gun?" Cole asked. "Didn't you try to escape?"

Jess lowered her eyes. "He found it."

Cole's eyes widened. "You wear your gun under your skirt."

Jess pulled her arms into her sides. "He pinned me on his legs and wrestled it from me. Then he tossed me to the ground."

Jem gasped. "Sounds like a detestable chap."

"The worst."

Cole studied her. "But handsome I bet."

Jess smiled and sighed. "Terribly."

Jem gathered the dishes. "You liked this Mackinnon brute?"

Jess waved her hand in the air. "He was tolerable."

"Did he take advantage of the situation?" Cole asked.

"At every opportunity."

Jem gasped. "Jessica Sterling Beecher, I hope you haven't done anything to embarrass the family."

Jess sighed. "Unfortunately, no."

"It's not fair." Cole rubbed her belly. "You had a marvelous adventure and left me at home."

Jem stood with the tray. "Was this all a tall tale?"

Cole laughed. "We told Jess to tell us a story, and she spun a yarn. Did Morgan Mackinnon kidnap you, or did you volunteer to fall into his big strong arms?"

"Everything happened as I said." Jess searched her pocket. "Your husband says hello, and if he had found you in the back of the wagon, he would have tanned your hide." She handed the letters to Cole. "He sends his love."

Cole ripped open the missives. "How did he look?"

"Madder than a hornet when he saw me sitting on the porch in Williamsport waiting for them to ride into town."

"No," Cole said. "Was he much changed?"

"More somber, but thousands were killed at Gettysburg." Jess twisted the ring on her finger and removed it. "Did you hear about Ed?"

Cole looked up from her reading. "Sid said he died on July 3." She grabbed the ring and examined it. "It's much nicer than the laurel root ring he made you."

"He gave the ring to me before he died. I didn't have the heart to tell him I didn't want to marry him, so I put it on my finger. This is the first time I've taken it off."

Cole returned the ring.

Jem put her arm around Jess. "Logan made it easier for me to love again, but you never forget the special people in your life. I love Logan, but I loved Ben, too."

Ben Collins had been killed at Bull Run, making Jem a widow. Then Paxton Ravenswood, Jake Donovan, and Ed Herbruck had died.

Ed's image had faded, but Morgan's face was sharp. She had fought any feelings for the man, knowing his fate would be the same as the others. How could she fight against a war that devoured lives with an insatiable appetite?

Chapter Nineteen

Tootie was moved to the Mermaid's Mirth, and Jess split her time between the hotel and Pierce House. Logan moved another bed into Cole's room as her due date neared. Jess was on duty to alert Jem if her midwife skills were needed.

Jess woke with a start. The room was dark, but someone was calling her name. It was Cole. "What's wrong?"

"My water broke."

Jess lit a lantern on the nightstand by her bed. She grabbed her robe. "Any pains?"

"Cramps. Do they count?"

"I'll fetch Jem." Jess hurried to the bedroom shared by Jem and Logan and rapped on the wooden door.

"What is it?" Logan growled.

"I need Jem."

"Is it Cole?"

"Her water broke."

Jem appeared at the door. "Give me a minute to dress."

Jess didn't wait. She joined Cole, who was standing by the bed, her gown clinging to her in wet folds. She gripped the bed post and grimaced. "Agh!"

Jem arrived with a handful of towels and her medical bag. "How do you feel?"

"I'm sorry Jess woke you. I feel fine."

"Sometimes it takes hours for the first baby."

Cole grabbed the bed post and groaned as another contraction moved across her abdomen.

"And sometimes it doesn't." Jem unpacked her bag. "Breathe," she reminded her sister.

"That wasn't a cramp."

Cole was shivering. "Let's remove that wet gown." They changed her nightgown and wrapped a blanket around her. Jess put socks on her feet as Cole sat in the rocking chair.

Jess stood. "I'll change the bed."

Cole's cries stopped her. She gripped the arms of the rocker and bent forward as another contraction moved along her body.

"Breathe," Jem ordered. "Breathe through the pain." She looked at her pocket watch when the contraction ceased. "Five minutes. I'm going to boil water. Spread a sheet on the floor and make her a bed."

"On the floor?" Jess asked.

"The floor works better for delivery. Once the baby is born, we can gather the sheets and wash them. And we can put Colleen in a nice clean bed." She glanced toward the rumpled bed. "After you change the wet sheets."

Jess and Cole had helped with a few baby deliveries, but Jem was the midwife. They didn't argue with her instructions. The soft feather mattress was more comfortable but would make pushing and delivery difficult.

Jess spread the sheet on the floor and stacked several pillows against the wall. "The bed is ready."

"Don't lie down yet," Jem said. "Not until the contractions are closer. Walk around, squat, rock, or do whatever you need to handle the pain."

Jess stayed by Cole's side with each contraction. The first couple of hours were routine. The pain peaked and ebbed, and Cole rested between the contractions. By dawn the contractions were closer and more intense.

"Let's place her on the floor," Jem instructed. "Lie on your side if it's more comfortable." She handed her a pillow, and Cole cushioned her body against the floor.

"Breathe," Jess reminded her sister as another contraction began.

Jem examined her. "We're getting close. I'm going downstairs to fetch the hot water." She draped a blanket over Cole's legs. "Keep warm so your legs don't cramp."

Cole glanced toward the window. "It's morning."

Jess opened the window more to allow a breeze to enter. "It's a beautiful day to be born." Heavy footsteps echoed in the hallway. "Logan?"

It was Blake. He paused in the doorway. "I arrived in Alexandria this morning and wrangled a pass."

Cole was in the middle of a contraction. "I'm going to kill you."

Jess waved Blake in. "She doesn't mean it. Ignore anything she says until the baby is born."

"The baby is coming?"

"Didn't Jem tell you?"

"I passed her in the foyer. She said to go upstairs."

"Take off your coat. You can help."

Blake's gray eyes widened. "Don't fathers wait downstairs?"

"Not in this family." Cole panted. "You put this baby in me, and you can help take it out."

Blake removed his hat, gloves, belt, and captain's

coat and hung them on a peg by the door.

Jem returned with a kettle and pitcher. "Everyone washes their hands," she ordered. "First rule of midwifing; everything that touches the mother or baby is clean."

"What about me?" Cole asked as everyone washed their hands.

"You're the patient. We'll take care of you." Jem knelt by Cole's feet.

Blake dried off his hands. "Where do you want me?"

"Sit against the wall behind Colleen and let her lean against you." He moved behind his wife and straddled her body. Jem handed him a wet cloth. "Wipe her brow."

Another contraction began, and Cole screamed as the pain became more intense. She grabbed Blake's arm and squeezed. She took a deep breath as her contraction eased. "How much worse will it get?"

Jem exchanged a look of worry with Jess. "Let's see how far along you are." Cole had her legs tight against her body, her feet braced against the floor. Jem knelt and moved her nightgown higher out of the way. Her hands moved around her belly and checked her internally. "I can feel his head."

Cole screamed with the next contraction.

"Breathe!" Jem reminded her. "Blow out, breathe in. Slow and steady. Don't push. Not yet."

Jess replaced the bloody towel with a clean one. "It won't be long now."

Sweat dripped from Cole's face. Her breathing was ragged, short gasps as she struggled with the building labor pains. Her legs shook with fatigue. "I don't know how much more I can take." As soon as the words were out, another labor pain began.

"We're there," Jem said. "Push. Blake, roll forward and help her push."

Both husband and wife bore down. Jess waited for the baby, but the contraction passed and Cole leaned back against Blake.

"Take a few deep breathes and get ready to push," Jem said.

Cole grunted and rolled forward with Blake behind her.

"I'm being ripped in two," Cole screamed.

A head appeared and then as Cole relaxed, it disappeared.

"One more time," Jem said. "Bear down with all you've got."

Cole gripped her knees, and Blake shadowed her body. Jem had her fingers around the baby's neck as she turned the baby and eased one shoulder out. The entire baby followed. "Relax, Mama."

Cole panted, falling back against her husband. "What is it?"

"A boy," Jess announced as he let out a wail.

Tears fell from Cole's eyes. "You have a son."

Jess placed the baby on Cole's belly. He flayed his arms and legs, his eyes staring at his parents, who returned his curious looks.

Blake pointed at a white substance on his skin. "What is he covered with?"

"Vernix." Cole gently rubbed in the white substance. Her action soothed his cries.

"It keeps his skin moist," Jess said. "After all, he's been floating in water for nine months."

Jem examined the afterbirth and tied off the umbilical cord. It took Jess two tries with the scissors to cut through the slippery thick cord, but mother was severed from son.

Jem washed the blood off Cole's body and prepared a pad of cloth hooked to a belt to gather her flow. "Why don't we put you in the bed, and you can feed him?"

Jess took the baby, and Blake helped Cole to her feet. "Take off her nightgown."

"Me?"

"Don't tell me you've never removed her clothes," Jess said.

Blake reddened. "Not in front of others."

"We're her sisters," Jess said. "We've seen her naked."

"Maybe Blake shouldn't see me...like this," Cole turned. "Close your eyes."

"You're beautiful." Blake pulled the gown over her head. Jem handed him a clean nursing gown, and he dressed his wife. Once she was settled in bed, Jess returned the baby.

Cole stroked his cheek, and he latched on to her nipple. She gasped. "That's stronger than I expected."

Blake knelt by the bed. "I'm glad I didn't miss this." He brushed Cole's hair back from her face and kissed her brow. "I love you."

"What are you going to name the baby?" Jess asked.

"Jacob Loren Ellsworth," they said in unison.

The boy would honor both sides of the family, Blake's father and their cousin Jake Donovan.

"How long will you be able to stay?" Cole asked.

Laura Freeman

"I don't know. We're waiting for orders."

Jem gathered her supplies and pulled Jess toward the door. "Let's leave them alone."

****

Jess had lost her bed at Pierce House, but she had another at Mermaid's Mirth. Ethan, Harry, and Zach were relaxing in the parlor, sharing their latest tales with Sid and her.

"All that marching and we ended right back at the Rappahannock where we started," Zach complained. "I hate Virginia."

"They gave us papers from Ohio, and we read about those Copperheads who want the North to reconcile with the South," Ethan said. "Don't they know we're going to win this war?"

Tootie hobbled in and sat on the sofa next to Jess.

"Hush," Sid warned. "Don't say anything in front of the S-P-Y."

"Tootie is not a spy." Jess frowned. "And she can spell as well as you." She turned to the boys. "Where do you think they'll send you?"

"Someone said New York," Zach said. "When did Lee invade New York?"

"What do you think, Sid?" Harry asked. "You know everything going on in the war."

"I think Lincoln is worried about more riots in New York City," Sid said. "They moved the draft to August 19 after all those earlier riots."

"Why were they rioting?" Tootie asked.

"The poor were angry that rich men can pay three hundred dollars for a substitute," Sid said. "But I don't understand why they attacked poor blacks. They should have attacked the rich men who were avoiding the

212

fight."

"They attacked innocent people?" Jess looked at the boys. "Why?"

Ethan shrugged. "Bullies pick on easy prey."

"I wonder what kind of soldier a bought man will be," Harry said. "I doubt any amount of money can buy courage."

"We're going to find ourselves alone on the battlefield while those hired men high-tail it back North," Zach added.

"Not if they hang them for desertion," Harry said. They had witnessed the hanging at Leesburg. Sid and Jess exchanged knowing glances.

"New York ought to be a nice change from Virginia," Sid said. "When do you leave?"

"We're waiting on a ship," Ethan said. "Wherever we're going, it'll be first class."

While they waited for orders, Jess and the boys toured the city. Jess had visited the monuments and buildings the previous year with Ed, Art, and Blake. Their tour ended when news of the *S.S. Baltic* was ready for them to board.

Blake said goodbye to Cole and his son. The boys hitched Romulus and Remus to the wagon, and Jess traveled along. She would drive the wagon home.

"Isn't Sid driving?" Blake asked.

"He insisted upon accompanying Tootie to the market. He won't let her out of his sight."

"He says he thinks she's a spy," Harry added. "I think he likes her. Have you seen how he blushes whenever she says something to him?"

"Sid and Tootie?" Jess shook her head. Sid was old. No, he was only twenty-eight. He appeared older because most of the soldiers were young like Harry, Ethan, and Zach. She had been so busy helping with the baby and running errands, she hadn't paid much attention to Tootie. She was walking without a crutch, and when she stumbled, Sid always seemed to be close by to catch her. Had she missed a blossoming romance under her nose? Tootie had reacted in fear to the one-legged soldier, but his constant chatter about the unending bits of knowledge he stored in his brain had won over her trepidation. But romance?

"Tootie enjoys baiting him. She always throws the name of a Southern officer at him when he brags about one from the North," Ethan said. "They're like two children fighting."

"She takes after Mac then," Blake said. "He was always up for a challenge."

Jess silently agreed. She had attempted to beat him, but he had met every attack with a counter move. Had it been a game to him? Had he forgotten her? She had expected memories of Morgan would fade with time. She could barely remember Ed, and she had known him all her life. But recollections of Morgan intensified with time. Her skin tingled with memories of his touch, her lips burned from his kisses, and her body vibrated when she was alone in the dark, desperately seeking release from the torture his absence ignited.

Blake drove the team to Alexandria with Jess at his side. "You said Mac was promoted to major."

"After the battle at Gettysburg. I sewed the stars on his collar."

His black eyebrows shot up. "You did?"

"Tootie was in no condition to do it."

"I feel guilty about her injury. It could have been

one of my men who shot her."

"No one is to blame during a war," Jess said. "Life isn't normal. Young men die, and a girl walking through a cemetery is shot. A woman driving a wagon is kidnapped by a big, loud Scotsman whose best friend is married to her sister. It doesn't make any sense. It hurts to think about it. We put one foot in front of the other and hope the nightmare ends soon."

When they reached the dock, Jess stared at the *S.S. Baltic*. The huge ship had a side-wheel, a smokestack, and two large sailing masts.

"It'll transport sixteen-hundred men to New York," Blake said. "It looks like it could handle about anything."

"Sure beats riding in a boxcar," Ethan said.

"I rented an officer's cabin on the upper deck for twelve dollars," Blake said.

"Twelve!" Jess shook her head. "For one room? We're going to have to raise the rates at the Mermaid's Mirth."

Chapter Twenty

Morgan was on a reconnaissance mission. He'd been ordered by Lee through Chauncy to find out where the Twelfth Corps had gone. Normally positioned opposite them on the Rappahannock River, they had marched off and hadn't returned for a week.

He peered through his field glasses as the Union soldiers boarded the *S.S. Baltic*. A familiar wagon waited by the dock. He focused on the driver. It was Jess. She wore a green dress with white trim and a bonnet of matching green material. Three young men were gathered around her. Blake was patting his horses. He helped her down and everyone hugged and kissed her. He'd never been jealous before, but the sight of other men saying goodbye to Jess made him think of his own bittersweet farewell.

When he joined the Rebel gunners at the battery near Kettle Bottoms on the Virginia shore of the Potomac, they talked about a sitting duck. The *S.S. Baltic* had run aground on a sandbar.

"We could blow it apart," the one gunner said.

"Give those boys in blue angel wings."

"You're to do nothing," Morgan ordered. "Lee wants those boys to leave town."

"We can make them leave permanently."

"No. Those are members of the Twelfth Corps on that tub. The longer they're stuck, the better for us."

"What do you mean, sir?"

"The Twelfth has been a thorn in our side since the beginning of the war. Now they're out of commission. Lee has been waiting for confirmation of their departure. You blow them out of the water, and you eliminate Lee's element of surprise."

"What's he planning to do?"

"When are you privy to the general's plans? All you have to do is let those boys pass unmolested."

Morgan had been ordered to confirm the departure of the Twelfth. He figured that meant they were to reach their destination. At least that's how he would explain his actions. No one had to know his best friend was on that ship. The guns could kill a few men, but if the ship sank, the men trapped below would drown. Blake owed him twice for sparing his life.

He talked to the commanding officer and told him Lee wanted the Twelfth Corps to reach New York. His men weren't to fire upon them. He waited around to make sure none of the men disobeyed. It was four days before they finally moved the ship off the sandbar and out to sea. They didn't have to shoot the men. They probably were cooked in their sun-baked quarters. Hell would have been kinder. Before leaving the area, he sent a letter to Tootie. Inside was another letter to Jess.

Without the threat of the Twelfth Corps, Lee sent Longstreet's First Corps south by train to assist General Braxton Bragg against Union General William Rosecrans' Army of the Cumberland. By driving the Union army out of the Deep South, Lee would make amends for losing in Pennsylvania.

****

After Sid examined the letter addressed to Tootie,

he handed it to Jess. "I told you she was a spy."

"I'm not opening her letter." Jess gave it to Tootie, who disappeared in her room. Jess stayed nearby, bumping into Sid, who was keeping a vigilant watch.

Tootie joined them and thrust the letter into Sid's hand. "Here, you old buzzard. Read it."

While Sid read the letter, Tootie slipped another letter to Jess, who hid it in her pocket.

"Dear Tootie,

I hope you are not a burden to others at the Mermaid's Mirth."

Sid looked up. "How does he know you're here?"

"I told him she would work at Blake's hotel," Jess said.

"You should keep your head down when Lee attacks Washington City."

Sid waved the letter in Tootie's face. "He's going to attack." He pointed at Jess. "What did I tell you? She's probably sneaking men into town."

"I'll go look under the beds." Jess hurried upstairs to her bedroom and ripped open Morgan's letter.

"Darling Jess,

I won't talk about the war. We won't betray our loyalties. You've made my life bearable and yet unbearable. I long to see you, touch your face, and kiss your lips, yet time drags by slowly without you. I'm afraid we will have to marry when the war ends. I talked about you endlessly to those who met you. It would be cruel to tell them the truth. That we were strangers drawn together by a war. If nothing else good comes from this conflict, that will be enough for me.

Your devoted husband,
Morgan"

"Husband," she repeated aloud. "You took back your name, Morgan Mackinnon."

As she reread his words, her anger rose. He only mentioned marriage to spare his men hurt feelings. Had she read too much into Morgan's actions? Meeting her was enough?

His kisses had stirred embers of love that during their separation had flamed into a burning desire. The Scotsman had taken possession of her soul, and he was content to have *met*? She crumpled the letter.

****

The leaves turned color in mid-September and nights cooled for comfortable sleeping. Jess and Cole sat on the porch of the Mermaid's Mirth. Cole rocked Jake to sleep for his afternoon nap.

"Was it worth all the pain to have a baby?"

Cole kissed her son's head. "What pain?"

"The pain from that big boy you're holding," Jess reminded her.

"Papa always said if something comes too easy, you don't value it."

"Then babies ought to be the most valuable thing on Earth."

Cole stared at the street. Jess turned. A soldier was nearly running along the street. "What is it?"

"Blake!" She handed Jake off and ran down the steps. Blake took her into his arms and kissed her.

Jess had never been jealous of her sister until now. She wanted a husband, someone to hold her, someone to love her. She stared at Jake. Someone to be the father of her children.

Cole dragged Blake to the porch. "Watch Jake for me."

Laura Freeman

"Don't I get to see my son?" he demanded.

"Take a look!" Blake glanced at the baby before Cole pulled him inside and up the stairs to the bedroom she occupied.

Three familiar figures, Ethan, Harry, and Zach, joined her on the porch. They stared at Jake. "Is he bald?"

"His dark hair fell out. Cole thinks he's going to have red hair."

Ethan ran his fingers through his ginger locks. "Like the Donovan clan."

"I think he'll look like Jake."

"Can't go wrong with that," Ethan added.

"What are you boys doing here? I thought you were at the camp by the Rapidan River?"

"We received orders to report to the Bealeton Station. Being so close, we couldn't leave without saying goodbye."

"Bealeton Station? Where is that?"

"A little south of Warrenton."

Had they gotten lost? "You boys can be hanged for desertion."

"Blake ordered us to hitch up the team," Harry said. "We'll reach the depot in time for departure."

"Where are they sending you?"

"West," Zach said.

Jess relaxed. "You won't be fighting Lee?"

"Unless he visits Tennessee," Harry said.

"Tennessee." Jess looked up at the second-floor room where Blake and Cole were making love. Blake had returned home, probably without orders, to say goodbye. It would be a long time before Cole saw her husband again. "Take your time hitching Romulus and

220

Remus. It'll give me time to pack some food for your trip."

"Thank you, Miss Jessica." Zach tipped his kepi.

Jess hurried inside. The bed creaked above her. Did Cole know they had only a little time together? Why hadn't she taken advantage of the time she had with Morgan? She went to the kitchen where Amber, the former slave, cooked for guests. Her twin daughters, Tia and Mia, were ironing the sheets they had washed the previous day.

"I need some sandwiches and any fresh fruit for the boys. They're leaving soon."

Amber looked down the hallway. "What boys?"

"Ethan, Harry, and Zach. Blake is upstairs." A bed creaked.

The girls giggled. "Hush," Amber warned.

"They have to eat on the run," Jess said. "The boys are hitching the team now."

Amber looked at Jake. "Did Captain Ellsworth see his son?"

"A peek." Jess stroked his soft cheek. "He doesn't know how precious you are."

Amber placed a large basket on the table to pack for the trip. Jess measured Jake against the basket. "Do you have another one?"

"Miss Colleen and the baby going with them?"

It would give Blake time to spend with him. She took Jake and the basket upstairs to the nursery. She lined the basket with a blanket and wrapped Jake against any cool weather. As soon as the noise quieted in the bedroom next door, Jess knocked. "The team is ready. Cole and I are going with you. We'll drive the team back."

Cole squealed. Blake was outnumbered.

Jess gathered her belongings from her room and returned to the kitchen where Amber had a basket of food ready. She carried both baskets to the front porch.

"Let me take that for you, Miss Jessica." Zach looked at the basket's contents. "Hey, this has a baby in it."

"I'll take that." Blake strode through the front door and took the basket with his son. He stared back with big blue eyes. "You did a good job, Mrs. Ellsworth."

Cole gathered a shawl around her shoulders and leaned against her husband. "I like to think you helped."

Ethan drove the team, and Jess joined him on the seat while the others rode in the back. Blake held Cole in his arms as they stared at the child their love had created. They were a perfect family, but so much could happen to destroy their happiness. She didn't dare dream about having a family of her own.

"Save some food for me," Ethan yelled back at Zach and Harry, who had begun eating.

"What happened in New York," Jess asked.

"Nothing. By the time we docked, any riots were over," Ethan said. "Miracle we were alive after roasting below deck in the heat."

"I said you could join me in my cabin, although it wasn't much better without a breeze to be bought," Blake said.

"We didn't want the other men to call us girls."

"What's wrong with being a girl?" Jess demanded.

"Nothing if you are one."

"Why are they sending you west?" Jess asked.

"Reorganization," Blake said. "They're sending

222

what's left of the Eleventh Corps and the Twelfth Corps to help Major General William Rosecrans."

"I bet it's because of Rosecrans' retreat," Harry said. "He could have used us when Longstreet's men attacked."

"It's like Lee knew we weren't around," Zach said.

Jess crossed her heart. "I didn't say anything and neither did Tootie. Sid keeps such a close eye on her, she couldn't breathe without him knowing it."

"She hasn't sent any correspondence to Mac?" Blake asked.

"She received one letter." Jess had burned Morgan's letter. "But he didn't say anything about where he was camping."

"He's with Lee across the Rapidan River. No matter where we roam, we end up back at the same spot."

"You saw him?" Jess asked.

"No, but that big Scotsman wouldn't be hard to miss."

Fear clutched her heart. Morgan was a big target.

Cole gripped Blake's arm. "How long will you remain in Tennessee?"

Blake stared at his wife. "Any time is too long."

They stopped the wagon outside Bealeton. The entire area was crowded with men from the Eleventh and Twelfth Corps. Blake sent Harry and Zach to find the Twenty-ninth Ohio regiment and report back.

"They have thirty trains with twenty cars each to transport the two corps," Harry said. "They're packing thirty soldiers to a freight car, and I mean packing."

"When a train pulls up, a regiment boards," Zach said. "They store the gear on one end and pick a spot to sit. There are benches along the walls and down the center but not enough for everyone. Some of the men are riding on top. Once they're full, the train leaves."

As trains departed, room opened up for the team to edge closer. It was the Twenty-ninth Ohio Volunteer Infantry's turn to board. Ethan helped Jess down from the wagon. Another goodbye. She hugged him, and he kissed her. She gave Ethan, Harry, and Zach a hug. They took their belongings and what remained of the food and headed for their fellow soldiers.

While the non-commissioned soldiers crowded into the cars, the officers were assigned one of their own. Blake waited, his arm around Cole, his son cradled in his other arm.

Some familiar soldiers scrambled onto the roof.

"Don't fall off," Jess yelled at Ethan, Harry, and Zach.

Ethan waved. "We'll say hello to Ohio for you."

It was Blake who explained his remark. "The train will pass through Ohio and Kentucky to reach Chattanooga, Tennessee. That's where the Rebs chased Rosecrans. All the way from Chickamauga. We lost so much ground. We probably won't fight until spring."

"Tennessee is so far away," Cole said. Jess couldn't help overhearing their tearful farewell. "I won't see you until the war is over."

"Maybe I'll get a pass to come home during the winter months," he said. "I'll write as soon as I arrive in Chattanooga."

Cole smiled and waved until the train was out of sight. Then she burst into tears. Jess comforted her then joined her in tears. "I hate this war."

Chapter Twenty-One

Time was measured by the weeks between letters from Blake. Cole shared them with everyone on Sunday afternoons in the parlor at the Mermaid's Mirth. Logan and Jem along with their niece, eight-year-old Deidre, and daughter, eleven-month-old Chauncy, gathered in the parlor to listen to the latest news received in October.

Tootie served refreshments and lingered.

Sid frowned. "You should take a seat." He gave up his chair.

"You're not going to call her a spy and make her leave the room?" Jess asked.

"Nothing she hears from Tennessee is going to help her," Sid said.

Cole rattled her pages and read.

"The train took us through Zanesville and Xenia before we stopped at Columbus."

"That's the capitol of Ohio," Sid explained to Tootie.

Cole frowned at her letter being interrupted.

"A few of the men missed the train to Indianapolis, but I made sure our regiment boarded in time. We traveled through Kentucky to Nashville. It was like passing through a lush garden to a crumbling city of ruins. War in the West has laid waste to the cities. I asked about my hotel in Memphis, the Lucky Gambler,

and a man told me it was nothing but rubble. I'm glad I sold it, for more than one reason."

The sale had brought Blake to Ohio where he had met Cole.

In mid-October President Lincoln relieved Rosecrans of his command, Logan informed them. Ulysses S. Grant took command of the Military Division of the Mississippi and replaced Rosecrans with General George Thomas as commander of the Army of the Cumberland.

Rumors spread in Washington City about a big build-up in Tennessee, and Sid tracked the troop movements for them on a map they kept in Blake's office.

November arrived, and they gathered for another letter from Blake. Jess shared a few letters from the boys, but they had little to say. She read a few lines from Ethan.

"We're building little huts with fireplaces to winter in Normandy," Jess read. *"We've been ordered to guard the Nashville and Chattanooga Railroad. It's like watching water freeze."*

"I would think they'd be grateful they don't have to march or fight," Jem said.

"Boredom makes them think of home," Logan said.

Deidre coaxed Chauncy to take her first step, but she clung to Logan's knee.

Cole opened her letter from Blake.

"We celebrated election day," Cole read. *"Most everyone in the regiment voted for John Brough. No one wanted a Copperhead for governor of Ohio. The boys had a little too much to drink and are learning the hard way to control their appetites for whiskey. Too*

many young men are adding drunkenness to their vices. I'm determined three young men won't repeat their mistake."

"Drunk?" Jem demanded. "Martha Herbruck will have a cow."

"I'd like to see that." Harry's mother didn't believe in drinking, dancing, or womanizing and had kept her boys in line when they were at home. Harry sounded like he was sowing some wild oats.

"We're heading to Chattanooga tomorrow. The boys are reluctant to leave their shanties. Unguarded wood is stolen for another home or a fire. I will miss my room at the boarding house. It was small but more comfortable than the hard ground.

Kiss Jake for me.

All my love,
Blake"

Cole folded the missive and kissed her son's forehead as he slept on her shoulder. "I should never have fallen in love with a soldier." She crumbled the letter in her hands and burst into tears.

Jess put her arms around her and patted Jake's back. "We shouldn't have to worry about our loved ones dying. It isn't fair."

"You have Jake to comfort you," Jem reminded her.

Cole raised a tear-stained face. "I want my husband."

"Maybe I should join…" Logan began.

Jem cut him off. "Washington needs you. We need you," Jem added. "Would you abandon all of us? One more soldier won't make a difference in the war, but your death would destroy all our lives."

227

Jess agreed. Morgan had only pretended to be her husband, but the brief experience of marriage had been enough to convince her that Morgan was the man she wanted to spend the rest of her life with. But the war had destroyed any chance at happiness. He would die for a cause she could never champion. For that reason she didn't dare dream of any future. Someday she would forget him.

Amber entered the room.

"I thought you had gone home, Amber," Jess said. "Is something wrong?"

"I met a woman in our camp askin' about Missus Pierce. I brought her here."

Jem stood. "Who is she?"

Amber signaled to someone in the hallway, and a black woman appeared in the doorway. She was dressed for traveling with a bundle tied across her chest and back.

"Esther," Jem said. "Did you run away from the Silver Pheasant?"

"No ma'am. Miss Regina sent me to find you."

A little boy poked his head out from behind the woman's skirt. He was about two with blonde hair and big brown eyes.

Jess knelt to his level. "Hello. What's your name?"

"Speak up," Esther said.

"Jefferson."

"Jefferson Vandal," Esther said.

Esther pushed Jefferson forward, and Jess took his hand. She placed him on the floor near Deidre. She offered them lemonade and cinnamon cakes.

Jem made Esther sit beside her. "What are you doing here? Where's Reggie?"

Reggie had been married to Edward Vandal, a loyal Confederate and slave owner. He had traveled to Darrow Falls in 1860 searching for a runaway slave named Tess. Clyde and Buck Cassell were his hired chasers. When Jem was searching for news of Ben in 1861, she traveled to Richmond. Edward had forced her to go to his home and help Reggie, who had given birth to Jefferson but was bleeding to death. Esther was Reggie's personal maid. They had returned to Vandalia in western Virginia when Edward joined the Confederacy.

"Miss Regina died about two months ago," Esther said.

"How?"

"Miss Regina was weak after having her baby, and when that little girl died, she followed her to the grave."

"Where is Edward Vandal?"

"Don't know. Miss Regina hadn't received word from him since his last visit nearly a year ago. Before she died, she told me to take Jefferson to Washington City and find Missus Pierce."

Esther withdrew a letter from her pocket. "She told me to give you this."

Jem read the letter aloud.

"Dear Mrs. Pierce,

If you are receiving this letter, I have not recovered from my illness. After my baby was born, I never regained my strength, and when she died, I had no more fight in me. You saved me when Jefferson was born, and I never forgot your kindness. I want Jefferson to have a good home. I've written to your sister, Mrs. Montgomery, who has a son Jefferson's age. I know Tyler will help find my husband if he is still alive. It was safer to send Esther east to Washington City with other slaves. I'm asking you to take Jefferson to Ohio so Tyler and his wife can care for my boy until he finds Edward.

Sincerely,
Regina Vandal"

Jem folded the letter. "We were planning to go to Ohio for Christmas. We'll take Jefferson. If anyone can find Edward, Tyler can."

Tyler had remained out of the war initially because he was a Virginian by birth. Cory and their son were another reason, but more importantly, the widows and families of dead veterans relied on Tyler to obtain the pensions owed them. They had made the ultimate sacrifice with the life of a loved one, but it took a little prodding from a small-town lawyer to remind the government of the debt.

"How did you travel all the way from Vandalia?" Jess asked.

"We walked most of the way. Sometimes we rode."

"What are you going to do now?" Jess asked Esther.

"I'm going to look for work. I was a lady's maid for Miss Regina, but I can cook and clean. Do you know any place that would hire me?"

Jess looked at Cole. "The Pirate's Cove needs a cook."

"What is that?"

"It's an inn near Lake Erie."

"Is that the lake slaves cross to reach Canada?"

"It was, but there aren't any chasers in Ohio."

"If Mr. Lincoln loses this war, there will be."

Jess looked at Cole. Slavery. Sometimes they forgot why the war was being fought. Why friends and family had died.

"I plan to visit the inn when we travel to Ohio," Cole said. "You can go with us. If you like the place, you have a job."

"I'd like that."

"It'll give Jefferson time to know us," Jem added.

"I think Chauncy likes him," Deidre said. Chauncy reached for Jefferson, but he scooted away. Chauncy let go of Logan's knee and stepped toward the little boy.

"Look!" Deidre shouted.

Chauncy babbled something and grabbed a clump of Jefferson's straight blonde hair.

"Ouch!" Jefferson fell with the one-year-old girl tumbling on top.

Logan rescued his daughter and helped Jefferson. "She's a baby," he excused. "Are you all right, son?"

He stared at Logan. "Are you my daddy?"

Logan didn't answer. Cole burst into tears at his innocently spoken words. Jefferson hadn't seen his father in so long, he couldn't remember him. How would Jake know his father? These were precious years. Chauncy's first steps had been witnessed by Logan, but would Blake see his son walk?

Jess pulled the boy against her. "No, he isn't your daddy, but Uncle Tyler and Aunt Cory are going to take care of you. They have a little boy your age. His name is Sterling. I bet you're going to be best friends."

****

Jess pointed out the train window as they pulled into Darrow Falls. "There's our hometown." Jess smiled at Jefferson who stared at the snow-covered roof of the depot and the blanket of fresh snow on the ground. Snow in Washington City resembled slush and never lasted more than a few days. But in Ohio, layers piled upon previous snowfalls and remained until spring thaws. Jefferson was bundled in a matching hat, scarf, and mittens Jess had knitted. She had made friends with the little boy during the long train ride, but instead of comforting her, Jefferson reminded her of what she would never have. She was doomed to be a spinster. How could she marry any man when Morgan haunted her dreams?

Tyler Montgomery was waiting at the depot with the family wagon and a team of draft horses. Tyler was nearly as big as Morgan, and his winter coat added width to his broad shoulders. His dark hair was long, showing beneath his hat, and his pale blue eyes surveyed the visitors. Would he honor Reggie's dying request? Tyler had been raised in Vandalia, but he had never been friends with Edward, who was a few years older and bullied him. Their animosity increased when Tyler befriended Reggie, the woman Edward had chosen to marry.

He greeted everyone and studied Jefferson. "He's Edward's son. Looks exactly like him."

"He's not Edward," Jess reminded him.

Tyler smiled as he patted the boy's head. "I know. Besides, he's Reggie's son, too."

Tyler loaded the luggage into the wagon while Logan helped the women board. He introduced Esther to Tyler.

"You were Miss Olivia's boy," Esther said.

"I was."

"She was a kind lady."

Tyler paused in his work. "I appreciate you recalling her that way."

"No other way to remember her."

Tyler had shared his past with the Beecher family before marrying Cory. Miss Olivia had run the Dunking Witch, a whorehouse in Vandalia. Tyler had been raised by a Quaker couple to keep their relationship a secret, but Edward had discovered the truth and shared the information with Tyler's friends, resulting in a brawl. Tyler had broken Edward's nose and was sent to boarding school as a result. After graduating from Harvard, he had proposed to Reggie to prevent her from marrying Edward, but she had refused him. For all his faults, Reggie had loved Edward.

"I have some of Major Vandal's letters he wrote to Miss Regina," Esther said. "I don't know if they'll help you find him."

"Thank you," Tyler said. "It's hard enough to find missing Union soldiers, let alone a lost Confederate officer, but I'll do my best."

They turned away from the picturesque town with its Main Street shops and church steeple covered with a thick layer of snow and headed along River Road to the Beecher Farm. The large white farmhouse had porches on each side of a middle portico, an architectural style common in Northeast Ohio. Tyler stopped the team at a cleared walk leading to the nearest porch. Logan helped everyone out. The doors opened, and the women and children were ushered inside.

Jefferson clung to Jess, but she reassured him the strangers were friendly. Her younger sisters, Cass and Jules, chatted with the little boy as she removed his outer clothing.

Cass was fifteen and wearing long skirts. She had stopped wearing her dark hair in braids and was experimenting with different styles that emphasized her maturity. In the time they had been gone, Cass had transformed from a girl into a young woman.

Jules would finish school next year but was content being the baby with her strawberry curls and huge blue eyes. Gifted with the strongest singing voice in the family, she liked to show off.

Cory sat on the sofa in the front parlor. Her hair was dark like Cass but had red highlights. She held Sterling and waited to allow the toddlers to size each other up before being introduced. Jefferson was a couple months older, but Sterling was bigger in size.

Once everyone was settled, the boys were placed on the floor. Maureen Beecher gave each of the toddlers a tall spool with wooden rings of varying sizes stacked on it. Chauncy walked toward Jefferson and grabbed one of the rings Jefferson had removed from the spool.

"She's walking." Maureen clapped her hands.

"And she gets into everything," Jem warned. "Better put anything breakable up out of her reach, Mama."

Maureen disappeared and returned with a cloth doll. She waved it in her hand, and Chauncy walked to her, reaching for the doll. Maureen cuddled her granddaughter.

Sterling ran to his grandmother. "Mawma, up!"

"Someone is jealous." Cory smoothed her skirt over her slightly rounded belly. "I hope he doesn't resent the baby."

"Like you did when Jennifer was born?"

"I wasn't jealous. I always knew you loved me

234

best."

Jem threw a pillow at Cory.

"Hey, I'm with child," she reminded her.

"How did you do it, Mama?" Jess asked. "With six of us?"

"The farm kept you busy and out of trouble most of the time."

"It'll be nice to have you around to help with the chores," Jules said.

Tyler and Logan entered with a large trunk and several bags. "Where shall we put these?"

"Logan and Jennifer are in the guest room above Sterling's office. The girls are upstairs."

"Girls?" Jess and Cole echoed.

"I'm a married woman with a baby," Cole reminded her mother.

"Let me see Little Jake." Maureen removed his bonnet and stroked the soft growth of red hair. "Jake Donovan."

"Jake Ellsworth," Cole reminded her.

Maureen brushed away a tear. "Of course. Has Blake written lately?"

"No. I told Sid to forward any letters here if they arrive at the Mermaid's Mirth."

"I'm sure he'll write soon," Jess reassured her. She wasn't as optimistic about Morgan. Even Tootie hadn't received any letters from him.

"Esther and Jefferson will go home to Glen Knolls with us," Cory said.

Jess wasn't ready for her bond with Jefferson to be severed. "Maybe I should go with him."

"It's only for the night," Cory said. "We'll return tomorrow."

Children had never been important until now. They were an extension of the family, the next generation. Cory, Jem, and Cole had children to love, teach, and invest a future in. Jess had been gone from home fewer than two years, but she had changed. She had fallen in love, fallen out of love, and witnessed the death of two dear friends. But more importantly, she had met the man she wanted to spend the rest of her life with, but would her parents approve? He was a Rebel. And if he survived the war, there was no guarantee he would marry her. If she had fallen out of love with Ed, Morgan could fall out of love with her.

"Is that all right, Jess?" Cory asked.

She had been deep in thought. She nodded.

"Are you feeling well?" Maureen placed a motherly hand on her forehead.

She wasn't going to ruin everyone's holiday by brooding over a Scotsman who had forgotten her. She smiled at Jake who was perched on Maureen's hip, but her lip trembled as she fought back tears. *Morgan Mackinnon, I hate you.*

Chapter Twenty-Two

Sterling Beecher arrived from a medical call as the food was being placed on the table. Jess noted her father had more gray in his hair and moved slower. He kissed his wife and each daughter. He shook hands with Tyler and Logan and asked about their work. Although Maureen talked about the town activities and plans for the holiday, the men couldn't avoid the topic of war.

Sterling turned to Logan. "When the war ends, how do you think Lincoln will treat the South?"

"He wants reconciliation," Logan said. "But others want the South to pay for their treason."

"Tyler, you were raised in the South," Sterling said. "Do you think there can be peace between the two sides?"

"Only if we learn to compromise better," Tyler said. "This war is a result of two sides who believed they were right and refused to change."

"But slavery is wrong," Jess argued.

"Morally, yes, but the law made it legal," Tyler said.

Jess crossed her arms. "Now you're talking like a lawyer."

"That's why I can look at both sides," Tyler said. "Morally, slavery is wrong, but our law, our Constitution, made it legal. The Southern states claimed the right of the law to protect slavery."

"But wasn't Congress going to change the law?"

"Which is why they seceded, and this war began," Tyler said. "I've gone over this problem with different solutions. We offered to send the blacks to Africa. We offered compensation to the masters. We issued the Emancipation Proclamation. Slavery wasn't the problem."

Jess frowned. "How can that be?"

Tyler had everyone's attention. "Why does slavery exist?"

"Because it's evil." Jess had seen the former slaves crowding the streets of Washington City. She had seen their scarred backs, their crippled hands and feet. Esther had shared some of her experiences on the train ride. She sat beside her, listening to Tyler's words.

"You're thinking like an abolitionist," he said. "Think what will happen when slavery is abolished. What will the South look like?"

Jess looked around at the others. They seemed as puzzled as her. "I don't know. Won't the owners of the plantations have to pay the slaves?"

"With what?" Tyler demanded. "Farmers live or die according to the weather. A bad crop can send a farmer into bankruptcy. Slaves were used to pay off debts or obtain loans. Now, the banks would foreclose on the farms."

Logan leaned forward. "Do you have a solution I can share with the leaders of the country?"

Tyler leaned back, a grin on his face. "Why is the North prospering?"

Jess shook her head and looked to the others for an explanation.

"This is how my husband wins cases in court,"

Cory said. "Why is the North prospering, darling?"

"Who made your shoes? The material for your dress? The wagons?" Tyler prompted.

Cass ventured a guess. "Factories?"

He winked. "Industry. The South needs to change from an agricultural economy dependent on slave labor to a manufacturing one."

"We should have moved industry to the South years ago," Logan agreed. "Then we could have phased out slavery and trained a work force."

"Slaves will need jobs when they're freed," Tyler said. "Soldiers will need work as well. If Lincoln is reelected next year, he has the task of convincing businessmen to invest in the South."

Jess had seen the destruction of buildings and crops the war had caused in Virginia. "What if he doesn't?"

"From my experience, no jobs means poverty, and poverty means anger." Tyler looked at Logan.

"If the South doesn't admit defeat, it will fight every change the government makes," Logan said. "We'll be right back where we were before the war."

"And what about all the men who have died?" Jess demanded. "Will their deaths be for nothing?"

"Jessica Sterling Beecher," Maureen reprimanded. "All life is valued."

"Valued?" she demanded. "You haven't seen their bloated bodies on the battlefield twisted in pain before releasing their final breath. You haven't gripped the arms and legs, still warm, as the doctor severs the limbs to create an army of cripples." She raised her hands, palms up. "You haven't had your hands coated with the blood of thousands. If life is so valuable, why is there a war? Especially if we're right back where we started?"

Her cheeks were soaked with tears. She couldn't stop.

Her father was holding a glass to her lips. "Drink this."

She protested, but he poured the wine down her throat. Cole was by her side, stroking her hair. "Ed died in her arms. And she was with me at Antietam when we carried Jake's dead body out of the cornfield."

Their mother burst into tears, and all her daughters followed her example.

"I'm sorry," Jess apologized. "I didn't mean to upset everyone. I must be tired."

"Of course you are after such a long trip." Maureen helped her to her feet. "Let's put you to bed."

"I'm not a baby, Mama. I'll go lie down for a little while."

Jess stumbled and arms lifted her. "Morgan?"

"Who's Morgan?" Tyler asked as he lifted her. He carried her upstairs, and her sisters ministered to her, putting her to bed with a heated brick wrapped in a towel at her feet and a thick quilt to keep her warm.

"I think it's best we do not discuss the war anymore," Maureen spoke outside the door. "This is the holidays. A time for celebration."

"It's my fault," Tyler admitted. "I forgot how much Colleen and Jessica have seen. I can only imagine the horrors they've experienced."

"I know Logan must return to Washington City, but I think my girls should stay here for the winter," Sterling said. "They need the rest."

"I know Cory would appreciate having Jennifer nearby to help deliver her baby."

The next morning after Tyler and Cory arrived with the boys, Jess apologized for her behavior and to prove she was no longer suffering from hysteria, she suggested a trip into town for some last minute shopping.

"I'll take care of the grandchildren," Maureen volunteered.

Jess huddled beneath the heavy blanket, snuggling with her sisters in the back of the wagon as they passed the depot and entered town. The air was crisp, but everyone was bundled in warm coats and knitted hats and gloves. They had made these trips as girls, but it was the first time they were all together after going separate ways the past few years.

Jess pointed at the familiar sights in her hometown. Paula Stone's hotel on the corner of River and Main streets was a two-story building with an abundance of gingerbread trim painted a vivid red. The white drifts of snow and icicles provided natural decoration for the holiday season. Paula had added green cuttings to form wreaths on the doors and had decorated them with large red velvet ribbons.

The shops surrounding the town square were similarly decorated. They stopped at the Blacksmith shop opposite Paula's hotel. Noah St. Paul had been the blacksmith but had joined a black regiment earlier in the year. He was Tyler's half-brother, but only family were aware of his relationship. Tyler and Cory called on Noah's wife, Tess, who had been a slave of Edward Vandal. She had been Reggie's maid before Esther. They updated Tess about the news of Reggie's death and Jefferson living at Glen Knolls.

The men were given the task of carrying packages back to the wagon while the women divided up to do their shopping. Jess grabbed Cole's hand and dragged her across the square, following a path of well-worn footsteps to the Community Congregational Church on the north side of the square. The doors were decorated with wreaths made from twisted grape vines and decorated with holly. Jess pulled her past the church entrance.

"Where are we heading?"

"Next door to the cemetery."

Cole stopped. "After what happened at supper?"

"I have to prove I won't burst into tears every time I think about the war," Jess said.

"Who's going to stop me?" Cole asked. "My husband is in Tennessee. I don't know if I'll ever see him again."

"We have to be strong for each other," Jess said. "We've always been partners in our past adventures. This is one more."

They passed the church and entered the wrought-iron gate Noah had made for the cemetery. Jake's grave was easy to find. They had attended his funeral. Ed's stone took searching, but they found it near a tree. "Do you think their deaths are in vain? That nothing will change when the war ends?"

"We won't let that happen," Cole said.

"I was blubbering like a baby," Jess said.

"You need to blubber more often. You hide too many secrets, Jess. When are you going to tell Mama and Papa about Morgan Mackinnon?"

"There's nothing to tell."

"Either you let it out a little at a time, or it's all going to pour out like it did last night," Cole warned.

"How do I tell them I'm in love with a Southern soldier?"

"Then you *are* in love with him."

"I'm waiting to fall out of love with him like I did with Ed, but so far, I can't seem to forget him."

"I knew something was different when you returned," Cole said.

Jess pointed at another set of footprints leading to Ed's marker. "Who's been visiting Ed's grave?"

"Mama said Martha Herbruck visits every day."

"I should call on her."

They said a prayer for Jake and Ed and headed for a candy store on the east side of the square. "What is Morgan like?"

"He's a big, loud brute."

"Were you trembling in his arms?"

"What?" Jess stared at her sister. "Are you crazy? I told him…"

Cole laughed as they entered the store. "I bet he was the one trembling."

Cole had been teasing her. "Only when I held a knife to his throat."

"And I didn't think you knew how to flirt with a man," Cole said. "Did he work up the courage to kiss you?"

"More than once."

Cole bumped her hip, and their crinoline skirts swayed. "You hussy."

"Me, who kissed Blake in front of everyone, including Grandpa?"

"That was to distract him so I could throw his paper in the canal," Cole said.

"You were the one distracted." Jess laughed. "Why didn't someone tell us men could be so wonderful?"

"I had to sit through hours of poetry reading in our

243

parlor until I found the right one," Cole said.

"Don't remind me about all the hours I wasted chaperoning you."

They paid for their purchases and were giggling as they entered Marcus Wheeler's dry good store. Jem and Cass were examining some yard goods and looked up. "What's so funny?"

"Memories," Jess said. "We were recalling how Cole met Blake."

Marcus Wheeler pointed at Jem. "I remember when you and Mr. Pierce met right in this store."

"He claims we were introduced when my horse and buggy nearly ran him over in the road," Jem said.

"At least you didn't have to shoot him like Cory shot Tyler," Jess said.

"Or have the Cassell brothers shoot him," Cole added.

"Maybe we shouldn't talk about shooting and killing." Jem nodded toward Jess.

"I promise not to become hysterical," Jess said. "Besides, it seems to be a tradition in the Beecher family to meet the man of your dreams through violence."

"How does that make two people fall in love?" Cass asked.

Jess winked. "Maybe someday you'll find out."

"Mrs. Ellsworth." Marcus retrieved an envelope from the mail slots. "I have a letter for you. It was forwarded from Washington City."

Cole removed her gloves and tore open the missive. Jess waited while she read through the letter. She frowned. "They reenlisted."

"What?" Jess grabbed the letter and read the words.

"Cole darling,

We guarded prisoners at Lookout Mountain instead of fighting. We were lucky. The Seventh Ohio lost nearly all of its officers. We've been building roads and exploring the mountains and caves in the area. The boys are enjoying themselves. They reenlisted. Besides the four-hundred dollar federal bounty, there's the one-hundred-fifty dollar Ohio bounty and a thirty-day furlough. I had to decide before I could talk to you. I hope you understand. I couldn't leave the boys alone. We'll be in Cleveland after Christmas if the paperwork is approved. Do you think you could travel to your home in Darrow Falls? I'll send word when we arrive in Cleveland."

"He reenlisted," Cole repeated, tears glistening in her eyes. "His enlistment would have been over next year."

Jess put her arm around Cole. She was trembling. "It may still be over. The war can't last much longer." She returned her letter. "And he's coming home."

Jem and Cass crowded around, staring at the letter. "Why did he reenlist?" Cass asked.

"For the boys," Jess answered when Cole choked on a reply. "He won't leave Ethan, Harry, and Zach. He promised he'd take care of them."

****

Morgan huddled around the fire as he sipped on a hot cup of coffee. The rare brew was a special treat for the holidays. Some of the men had gone home with the promise of returning in the spring. He had no home. Lyle and his stepmother lived above the store in Richmond. It belonged to him, but he had no reason to return. Tootie was in Washington City. So was Jess.

She was home.

He'd enclosed a letter to Jess with the one to Tootie. Correspondence was difficult to send across the lines. He had written several times, but had the letters reached Mermaid's Mirth? He had received a short missive from Jess.

"Morgan,

Tootie is improving each day. She misses you. Blake arrived to help deliver his son, Jake. He and the Twenty-ninth Ohio have gone to Tennessee. I try to encourage Cole, but the distance means she may not see him until the war is over. She misses him terribly.

Jess"

Was she talking about Blake and her sister or them? Neither had promised undying devotion or spoken words of love. But his letters gave him a second chance. If only they reached her.

Morgan removed the photograph he kept in his breast pocket and stared at it by the light of the campfire. He was wearing out the edges of the cardboard it was mounted upon, but studying her lovely face gave him peace.

No matter how ugly the world became, Jess was a reminder of what beauty existed. Theo asked about Miss Jessie, and by proxy Colonel Chauncy was kept abreast of any information. He wished he had more to share. The Twenty-ninth Ohio had been given furlough. Jess was probably in Ohio visiting with her family and the young men in the regiment. Blake was spending time with his wife. Being alone during the holidays reminded him of how much he had taken for granted. The only friends he could claim were his fellow soldiers. He sipped his coffee. When would the war be over? But more importantly, what would he do when he was no longer a major in the army?

Chapter Twenty-Three

Pirate's Cove Inn was on the shore of Lake Erie and built to withstand the winds that traveled south from Canada across the water. Sailors and a few hardy souls stayed during the winter months. Esther began her duties as cook. She wasn't used to the cold, but the kitchen's fireplace and stove helped her adjust to the frigid air. An elderly couple had been hired by Blake when he bought the inn last year and were having trouble completing all the work required to run a business. Esther was a welcomed addition.

While Cole and Jess waited for news of the train carrying the soldiers, a blizzard struck the area. The freezing cold turned the lake to ice and winds raced along its surface making the air bitter, stealing the breath away from anyone unlucky to be outside.

Cole and Jess set out for the Cleveland depot in a wagon drawn by two mules. They trudged through the snowy landscape breaking a path through the drifts. Not many people had come out to welcome the men arriving, some after two years of fighting.

Jess barely had time to stop the wagon when Cole spotted Blake standing on the platform and scrambled down from the seat. She ran to him, calling his name. Blake turned, took her in his arms, and kissed her. His companions cheered.

The boys were in high spirits. They were home and

could forget about fighting, starving, and surviving the hardships of war.

Everyone climbed aboard the wagon. Jess joined the boys in the back so Blake could drive and Cole could sit beside him on the narrow seat.

"Are you sure you don't mind?" Cole asked.

Jess was huddled among the boys. "I have three bodies to keep me warm"—she laughed—"to your one."

"One is enough." She snuggled against her husband. "I'm sorry there weren't many people to welcome you home. The storm blew in suddenly."

"At least we have a warm place to stay. Those Ashtabula boys are walking home."

"The whole way?"

"Maybe someone will take pity on them and give them a ride. At least the army issued our winter coats." In addition, Blake had grown a beard. The boys had grown facial hair, but only Harry had managed a respectable mustache.

"We're spending tonight at the Pirate's Cove, and tomorrow we'll head home by train," Jess said.

"I have to report to Captain Myron Wright in Akron in a few days," Blake said. "He's been working on recruitment since November. I have to help him replace the soldiers who didn't reenlist and will be mustering out next year."

"They're going to regret it," Ethan said. "They won't be able to put those Johnny Rebs in their place."

"Once we reach our quota, I can enjoy the month home."

"Let's hope men are feeling patriotic," Cole said. "I want you all to myself."

Esther had dinner waiting for them. It had not taken her long to master the kitchen. She'd made fried chicken with cornbread dressing, potatoes, beans, beets, and hot rolls. She served pudding for dessert.

After dinner, Blake showed off Jake to the boys. "He's doubled in size."

Cole helped Jess clear the table, but her gaze wandered to her husband and son in the adjoining room.

"Spend time with the men in your life," Jess whispered. "I'll entertain the company."

"Three young men? I should chaperone."

"Chaperone?" Jess laughed. "I can handle these three."

Cole bumped her with her hip and removed her apron. She sauntered gracefully into the parlor, her movement attracting the attention of all the men. Cole had that effect on the opposite gender. She placed her hand on Blake's shoulder. A simple touch was enough to signal a night of lovemaking. "I think Jake is ready for bed." She glanced toward the staircase. "Why don't you carry him upstairs?"

Blake reacted as if a siren had called his name. He juggled Jake in his arms and followed Cole upstairs.

Jess shook her head. How did Cole do it? A look, a smile, an innocent word, and Blake followed her to the ends of the Earth. Would Morgan forsake bachelorhood, the Confederacy, or his men for her? Not hardly.

Jess took a tray of coffee and cake Esther had prepared and placed it on the small table in the parlor.

Ethan stared out the window. "Quite a storm out there."

"I hope it doesn't delay the train," Jess said.

"Everyone is anxious to see you."

Ethan glanced at the ceiling as the ropes in the bed creaked. "I feel bad about Blake reenlisting, but we couldn't quit with the job not done."

Jess poured the coffee. "How many men reenlisted?"

"More than three hundred in the regiment," Zach said. "We were mustered out and then sworn back in as the Twenty-ninth Ohio *Veteran* Volunteer Infantry." He pointed to the chevron on his sleeve. "We're veteran soldiers now."

It was a single stripe, but it meant a dedication to duty to the men who wore it.

"We didn't reenlist for the bounty even though some men did," Ethan said. "But it is a substantial amount of money."

"Enough for a down payment on a farm," Harry said.

"Ed always talked about buying a farm," Jess said. "Is that what you want, Harry?"

"If I finish my training as a veterinarian, I think I should have a place for animals."

"My grandfather could hire you to take care of his horses," Zach said. "We keep brood mares and raise the foals. I help with training the colts and fillies for saddles or pulling a carriage."

"Where does your grandfather live?"

"In Medina County." He looked outside. "There's no train from Darrow Falls to Ravenswood farm, and the coach will have trouble in the snow."

"You're welcome to stay at our home if you don't want to travel to Ravenswood," she suggested.

"I may for a few days. At least until the weather

clears."

"You can meet my ma and pa," Harry said.

"And my folks," Ethan added. "My father owns half the inn in Peninsula. Plenty of room."

"Aren't you three sick of each other yet?" Jess asked.

"We have more in common than anyone else we know," Harry said. "Don't get me wrong. I can't wait to see Ma and Pa and the others, but it's not the same. I've changed."

"You haven't been gone that long."

"Long enough," Harry said.

"I think the furlough home was the reason most of us reenlisted," Ethan said. "Even though we've only been gone a year, some of the men have been gone since the fighting began."

Men on both sides had been fighting since '61. Men like Morgan. "Will you return to Virginia soon?"

"I think we're part of the Army of the Cumberland now," Harry said. "Colonel Finch is in command with Lt. Colonel Edward Hayes second in command."

"So what is Tennessee like?" Jess asked.

"As different as night and day, cousin," Ethan said. "The rations in the Shenandoah Valley were grand compared to starving. We've been eating field corn, if you can believe that."

"Corn for animals? Isn't it hard?"

"Boil it long enough and you don't break your teeth on it," Zach said.

"It's such a gourmet feast, we have to fight the Rebs for it," Harry added.

"You shoot them over field corn?"

Ethan laughed. "Nah, we fight them with our fists

and some well-aimed taunts."

"When we aren't starving, they're working us to death," Zach said. "We have to cut down trees, split them, and lay the halves in a swamp to build a road."

"Don't they have any roads in Tennessee?"

"Not where we're going," Ethan said.

"What does Blake do?"

"He supervises." Harry grabbed the last cake.

"He doesn't help with the work?"

"Sure he does. More than any other officer," Ethan said. "They give him grief for it. He takes extra food and shares it with us on the sly."

"Why on the sly?"

"We don't want to be known as dandies," Ethan said. "Those scarecrows out west call us paper-collar white-gloved gentlemen for being in proper uniform."

"Don't they have to wear uniforms?"

"Their officers don't expect anything of them but to fight," Zach said. "The ragtag army Sherman dragged with him from Mississippi wears anything they like."

"You ought to see the headgear they pass off as military." Harry slapped his knee. "One man wears a coonskin cap. Thinks he's Daniel Boone."

"Geary believes in discipline and doesn't like the lack of proper dress among the western soldiers," Ethan said. "He has roll call every morning, and we have to wear our uniforms and kepis."

"We grumble, but discipline is important for an army," Zach said.

"After Ed and Art telling me how they wore rags most of the first year of their enlistment, I should be proud to have a new uniform," Harry said.

"You look handsome, Harry. As do all of you."

"We read that President Lincoln was at the dedication of Gettysburg Cemetery," Harry said. "He didn't make much of a speech though."

"He wasn't the main speaker, but what he said was beautiful." Jess retrieved a book from a table and removed a cutout from the newspaper. "I saved it."

"Read it, Miss Jessica," Harry urged.

Jess held the paper near the lantern to read the small print, but she had memorized most of the speech. *"Fourscore and seven years ago our fathers brought forth on this continent…"*

When she was done, Zach coughed to break the silence. "He's a fine speaker, President Lincoln. I hope to meet him someday."

"He's too soft," Harry said. "He's offering amnesty to all Southerners who take the loyalty oath."

"All soldiers are going to want to avoid being taken prisoner," Jess said. "The South isn't accepting any food from the North for our boys anymore. The women are upset about it."

"They'll starve the prisoners," Ethan said.

"We ought to do the same," Harry said.

She listened as they vented their anger over the decisions on both sides. Cousin Jake had warned her war had a tendency to become ugly. She never imagined how ugly.

When yawns replaced talk, Jess showed the boys their rooms and retired to her own bedroom. Jess added coals to a bed warmer and ran it over the sheets before crawling beneath the quilt. It would be nice to cuddle against a warm body, a husband who would comfort her during the nightmares that haunted her when memories of the battlefield and wounded men couldn't be forced from her thoughts.

What was Morgan doing on this cold winter's night? Did he have a woman in his bed to keep him warm? "He better not," Jess said to the empty room. She punched her pillow and settled against the mattress.

Chapter Twenty-Four

Jess was packing a basket for the trip to Akron when Cole strolled into the kitchen. No other word could describe her gait. She purred as she sipped a glass of warm milk.

"I'd say the cat is content," Jess said.

"Meow."

"Where's your baby?"

"Blake has taken possession. I doubt if he'll put him down long enough for me to change his diaper."

Blake strutted in with his son cradled in his arm. "Jake would like some bacon and eggs."

"Jake has eaten." Cole leaned against him and whispered something in his ear. He chuckled as he squeezed her.

"How many eggs would you like?" Jess asked.

"I'll cook," Cole volunteered.

"I do the cooking here," Esther said. "I don't want no other woman messing with my kitchen."

Cole winked at Jess. "Have you decided to stay?"

"I'll stay."

Esther remained at Pirate's Cove while the others traveled to Akron on the train. They pulled into Darrow Falls, expecting the depot to be deserted because of the cold weather, but the town folk were gathered on and around the depot platform and clapped as they exited the train along with local members of the Sixth Ohio battery who also were on furlough.

They sang *When Johnny Comes Marching Home* and escorted them to the Community Congregational Church on the Town Square where the rest of town had gathered. The soldiers and their families were given front row seats.

The mayor made a speech, the pastor prayed for the men's safety, and families took their loved ones home.

Ethan joined his brother Paddy and his parents, Padrick and Salome Donovan, who headed to Peninsula and Grandma CJs Inn. Harry joined his brothers John and Art, who visited Ed's grave next to the church before heading home to a homemade supper with his parents and sister.

The Beecher clan gathered at the farmhouse with Zach as their guest. It was crowded, but no one complained.

Toward evening Jem and Logan joined Tyler and Cory with their children and headed to Glen Knolls. It freed the bedroom above Sterling's office for Blake and Cole and allowed them privacy.

Jess joined Cass and Jules in the parlor to entertain Zach. His awkwardness was replaced by zeal when Cass shared her love of horses.

When Jules kept interrupting, Jess distracted her. "Hey, Juliet," Jess called. "I didn't tell you about the soldier I met. His name is Romeo."

Jules flew at her, but Jess only laughed. "I hate that story. No one can call me Juliet."

"I named you Juliet," Sterling said from his fireside chair. "You have to stop flying into a rage whenever someone teases you. *Romeo and Juliet* was written by

Shakespeare. No shame in being associated with it."

"The boys make fun of me."

"Those same boys will be calling on you Sunday afternoons," Cole said as she and Blake joined them. Maureen followed with Jake in her arms.

"I bet you have plenty of callers, Miss Cassie," Zach said.

"Not as nice as you."

"Don't worry, Jules," Jess comforted her. "You'll never meet Romeo. He's a Southerner."

"How did you meet him, Jessica?" Sterling poked at the fire.

Jess hadn't told her parents about being captured.

"Was that when Major Mackinnon kidnapped you?" Cole asked.

"Kidnapped?" Sterling looked at his daughters. "Why is this the first I'm hearing about this?"

Jess frowned at Cole.

She shrugged. "It's an exciting story."

"Do tell," Jules said. "I love a good story."

"Mackinnon," Sterling repeated. "Someone named Mackinnon wrote you." He withdrew a letter from his inside pocket. "Mr. Wheeler gave it to me when I was returning after checking on one of Mrs. Stone's sick tenants."

Jessica reached for the letter. She relaxed when she read the name. "It's from Tootie."

"Tootie?"

"She works at the Mermaid's Mirth."

"Then who is this Major Mackinnon?" Sterling asked.

"Tootie's brother," Jess answered. "And the man who captured me at Gettysburg."

"What?"

Jess cringed under her father's outburst. "I'm fine."

"I know you think I'm old and feeble and my heart won't take bad news, but I think I'm entitled to know when one of my daughters has been taken prisoner by the enemy."

"Morgan isn't the enemy." Jess waved at Blake. "He's Blake's best friend. They attended West Point together."

"He's a Union officer?"

Jess lowered her voice. "No."

"There are only two sides, Jessica. Which side does he belong to?"

"The Confederacy, but he doesn't own any slaves. Morgan's father owned a mercantile in Richmond, and Blake's father owned a hotel nearby." Jess took a deep breath. "His sister, Tootie, was wounded by one of the Ohio boys, and I took care of her."

"One of our boys shot a girl?"

"She was dressed as a man." Jessica waved her hand. "It happens, Papa. Clara Barton found a woman dressed as a soldier at Antietam."

"I read books for drama. I don't expect it in my own family."

"You can't expect us to sit around knitting socks all the time," Jess defended.

"It would be better than risking your lives on the battlefield."

"Men risk their lives, and someone has to help the wounded," Jess said.

"You raised fearless daughters, Dr. Beecher." Blake put his arm around Cole. "Or I wouldn't be alive today."

Maureen joined her husband by the fireplace. "Mothers and fathers worry no matter how old you become. Now that you have a son, you'll understand."

Blake studied Jake. "I have a feeling if he is anything like Mac and I were as boys, he's going to cause plenty of trouble."

Cole laughed. "You haven't heard all the stories about Jess and me."

"Neither have I," Sterling said. "And I consider that a blessing, but I want to hear more about Major Mackinnon."

"He's a loud-mouth, arrogant Scotsman," Jess said. "But I met Colonel Chancy LaDonte and Theo Jameson while at Williamsport. They're the men who helped Logan and Jem at Manassas, remember?"

"They shared a bit more detail than you are," Sterling said.

Cole pointed to the letter. "What does Tootie say?"

Jess silently thanked Cole for the diversion and tore open the letter. Another folded missive fell to the floor. It was from Morgan.

"My darling wife,"

Read it aloud," Sterling said.

Jess skipped the salutation.

"The winter is cold and lonely in Virginia. 1864 will surely be the last year of the war. The boys are cold and hungry and long for home. I heard the Ohio boys received furlough. I'm jealous beyond measure. Not because they have time away from the war, but because they will be spending it in your company. I miss our little cabin and the time we spent together as husband and wife."

"Husband and wife?" Sterling stood. "Are you

married to that man?"

"No, Papa. It was pretend."

"Do I have to worry about a pretend baby?"

"Papa! Tootie was with us. She was our chaperone."

"He courted you?"

Jess shook the letter in the air. "Do you want me to continue or not?"

Sterling sat down, and Maureen rubbed his back. "No man would take advantage of Jessica."

"Mama is right," Jess said. "I beat Will Starr in a shooting contest, and all the men had to be respectful toward the women in town."

Sterling looked around. "Who is Will Starr?"

"A Texas Confederate." Jess dismissed him and turned to her letter.

"Blake and I swore we would never marry, but if he can break his word, I can break mine. If I was to marry, you would be the first woman I'd ask."

"First? How many does he have on his list of brides?" Jess waved the letter toward the flames.

"Don't!" Cole snatched it from her hand. *"You're level-headed in a crisis and a fine woman with or without your clothes."*

Sterling confiscated the letter.

"He means nightgown," Jess lied. "He returned from Buford's raid and was all bruised from a wagon falling on him. I rubbed some of Doc Herbruck's liniment on his shoulders."

Maureen gasped. "In your nightgown?"

"It was dark, and he was facing the other way." Jess retrieved her letter and found where she had left off, scanning the words before she read.

"Colonel LaDonte sends his best as does Theo. I know I am bold in my writing. It's because this letter may never reach you. And no matter what your reaction, the pen allows me to say what I could not in person.

The men ask about you and beg to see your photograph."

"The one you gave to Ed?" Cole demanded.

Jess sighed. "He couldn't take it to heaven with him."

"I'd like to hear more," Sterling said. "Continue."

"I'm wearing the edges raw showing it to them. They say you put every other woman to shame. I have to agree. I study your picture, trying to recall every smile, every frown. You were spitting mad when I took your gun. You didn't need bullets to render me helpless. I may have captured you, but I've been your prisoner ever since we've met. You said you hated this war because of the dead and wounded. I hate it because it keeps us apart. If God is gracious to us, I pray we meet again when this awful thing is over.

Your devoted husband,
Morgan"

"If he's not your husband, why does he end the letter that way?" Sterling demanded.

"It's a joke, Papa. Like Romeo and Juliet, any romance with Morgan Mackinnon is a tragedy."

Cole put her arm around her waist. "If there wasn't a war, I'd think he'd make a lovely husband."

"He's not a bad fellow," Blake agreed. "Just joined the wrong side."

"It doesn't matter what we think," Maureen said. "Jessica has a level head on her shoulders. When

Morgan Mackinnon proposes, she'll know what answer to give him."

Her mother had more confidence in her abilities than she did. As long as the war continued, she had only one answer to marriage with Morgan.

The soldiers left Cleveland when their thirty days expired. The time had gone too quickly. Logan returned to Washington City and his work at the Treasury, but Jem, Cole, and Jess remained in Ohio, spending the winter with their family and waiting for the birth of Cory's daughter in March. They named her Olivia Regina Montgomery after Tyler's mother and Jefferson's dead mother.

Blake wrote that the Twenty-ninth Ohio was spending winter at Bridgeport, Alabama. Changes in the weather signaled the battles would soon resume. Cole shared the letters with Jess and the others.

"Cole darling,

Members of the white star division from Pennsylvania, New York, and New Jersey joined us. The first brigade under Charles Candy includes the Fifth, Seventh, Twenty-ninth, Sixty-sixth of Ohio and Twenty-eight and One-hundred-forty-seventh Pennsylvania. The Eleventh and Twelfth Corps are now the Twentieth Corps in the Army of the Cumberland. My address is 20th AC, Army of the Cumberland, 2nd Div., 1st Brigade."

Cass carefully wrote down the address. She had promised to write to the boys in the Twenty-ninth. Both Harry Herbruck and Zach Ravenswood shared a love of horses with Cass. It would be a race to see who won her heart. The attentions of the young men had finalized her transformation from a little girl to a young woman.

Cole continued to read.

"General Grant has been sent east, and General Bill Sherman is in charge of our western armies. The weather is warm here, and we are sending our heavy wool coats home for storage. Hopefully we will not need them for another winter. We play baseball during the day and play music at night to pass the time. Sherman is gathering a hundred-thousand men in three armies. About a quarter of the men are from Ohio. It won't be long before we march south.

All my love,

Blake"

Cole folded the letter. "I've neglected my duties long enough. We'll travel to Pirate's Cove, then Dutchman's Inn, and return to Mermaid's Mirth."

"That's the long way to Washington City," Jem said.

"Don't you dare complain," Cole sniveled. "You'll see your husband at the end of the trip. Who knows when I'll see Blake again?"

Jem looked at Papa. "May Cass join us? I was hoping to continue her training as a midwife."

Sterling turned his attention to Cass. "You were more interested in birthing animals than human babies."

"Not much difference," Cass said.

"Cory will need your help with the baby, and I need a nurse. Besides, Corporal Ravenswood and Corporal Herbruck know your address here in Darrow Falls. You won't receive letters any sooner in Washington City."

"Maybe I can visit next year," Cass said.

"The war better be over by then," Jess said.

"I don't want to visit the war. I want to visit the

Capitol and all the other sites."

"Yes, next year when the war is over we'll celebrate with everyone touring the city," Jess said. No one wanted to see the dying men and cripples who crowded the city, especially a fifteen-year-old girl.

They arrived in Washington City in April. Spring was no longer a time of flowers and birds singing. Spring sounded its presence with booming cannon and the death cries of men in mortal battle.

Blake had written that twenty-five-thousand Ohio sons were in the Army of the Ohio, Army of the Tennessee, and the Army of the Cumberland. They were divided into seventy-eight Ohio infantry regiments and a dozen Ohio artillery batteries and nearly a dozen cavalry outfits. Union General William Sherman was leading one-hundred-thousand men out of Chattanooga, Tennessee, to face Confederate General Joe Johnston's forces with Atlanta, Georgia, as the goal. Atlanta was the heart of the South with railroads connected to it from every important city in the Confederacy. Its capture would cripple the South.

Jess and Cole studied the map in Blake's office and moved the pins to mark the location of the Ohio boys.

In the East, Jess read the stories about Lieutenant General Ulysses S. Grant crossing the Rapidan River in Virginia to fight Lee and take possession of Richmond, the Southern capital.

"You met Lee," Cole said. "What is he like?"

"The men worship Bobby Lee," Jess said. "I hear Grant's men ridicule him. They call Grant a drunk."

"Maybe, but Sid says the U.S. stands for unconditional surrender. They won't laugh if he beats Lee."

Chapter Twenty-Five

Because Morgan was with General Lee, they followed the battles in the East as well. They were familiar with Chancellorsville where the Ohio boys had fought a year earlier. Fighting was going on nearby at a place called the Wilderness immediately below the Rapidan River. Clara Barton was traveling to the battlefield with supplies. They had loaded Blake's wagon with boxes of medical provisions they had collected from Ohio to help the wounded. Sid drove with Jess by his side. They traveled along the Germanna Plank Road and arrived the morning of May 6 at the Wilderness Tavern.

"You stay with me," Sid told her. "No wandering off."

"I learned my lesson," Jess said.

The armies of Lee and Grant had been fighting in the Wilderness woods all yesterday and had renewed attacks before dawn. The Wilderness was aptly named with thickets and trees preventing infantry from marching shoulder to shoulder. Soldiers crossed meandering streams and sank into marshy bogs. Men disappeared into the early morning mist as each side fought for a decisive victory.

Sid liked statistics and was betting the Union army with one-hundred-thousand more men than Lee's small force would prevail. Jess shook her head. Sid had never met Bobby Lee.

Ewell's Second Corps had been in the fight on the Confederate's left. Jess looked among the Rebel wounded for a certain Scotsman. She was giving a drink to a man when Sid hollered. He was driving the wagon toward her at a frantic pace and had to tug hard on the reins to stop Romulus and Remus. "What's wrong?"

"Git aboard! General James Longstreet arrived with his men, and they're pushing through the lines."

Jess barely raised her foot off the ground before Sid urged the team forward. Brush fires and smoke from the guns made it difficult to see and frightened the team. Sid took them behind the new Union lines where soldiers were digging in and building log breastworks.

Even though the Confederates were still outnumbered two to one, they pushed the Union forces back through the woods. With them, came the wounded.

The medical treatment on the field had become more efficient with pack horses loaded with medical supplies, field dressings, tourniquets, splints, and stretchers following every brigade. Ambulances had built-in lockers to carry medical supplies, lamps, folding tables, cots, blankets, bandages, sponges, tea, whiskey, and surgeon tools. Crates with chloroform in green glass bottles or the more portable tin canisters were essential for the amputations and surgeries that followed every battle. Soldiers were assigned hospital service. After treatment on the battlefield, the wounded were taken to a field hospital and transported by train to a division hospital.

Clara Barton was offering water to some of the

men resting in the shade outside the medical tent. Jess joined her with a bucket and ladle. A few of the men had burns from the fires. She gave them a mixture of alcohol and opium to ease the pain and wrapped the burns in linen strips soaked in water to offer some relief.

Jess jumped when a loud explosion echoed from the battlefield. "What's that?"

"Flames must have reached someone's cartridge box," the man with the burns said. "Now there's two of him."

"Was he alive?"

"He ain't now."

Jess fought the urge to vomit. How could men joke about such a horrific death? She excused herself and stood behind a tree, trying to calm her nerves. Her rest during the winter months had been a temporary respite. Now that she stood on the battlefield, she couldn't run from this fear that gripped her heart. A Rebel yell echoed from the field. They were attacking. Guns fired, and clouds of black powder filled the air. Was Morgan among the fighting men? Or was he among the dead? She tempered her hysteria and returned to her duties. The popping of the guns and the screams of the men ebbed as Rebels retreated.

"I'm betting he's dead," Sid said as he joined her.

Jess gasped, her hand going to her throat. "Morgan is dead?"

"Morgan? I was talking about Longstreet. He was shot in the throat. Must be why they stopped attacking."

How did she react? He was the enemy, and yet "Old Pete" was admired nearly as much as Lee by his men. "I'm sorry to hear that."

Sid frowned. "Did capture make you a turncoat?"

Sid viewed the world in black and white. Her experience in the Rebel camp had filled in the gray between the two sides. They were more alike than different. The North linked the issue of slavery to victory and sought total submission of the Southern army. The Southern soldier was defending his home from Northern invaders. Both sides considered their causes just. Slavery needed to end, but killing so many young men seemed barbaric for a country whose laws were debated in the Capitol not on battlefields.

"If we kill the good and decent men, it will leave the ruffians and scoundrels for our boys to face," Jess said. "They won't show any mercy."

Sid grunted, whether it was in approval or disagreement was anyone's guess. "Better eat something before the next attack."

By nightfall both sides had given up the battle, and everyone rested but those on the picket lines.

The wounded were stranded in enemy territory and without a truce couldn't be retrieved. Their cries of pain and thirst echoed throughout the night. Jess lay awake on straw and a blanket in the bed of the wagon. In the distant sky, the smoke snaked in upward spirals. Then the glow of flames sparked and flared above the dry limbs and grass. Brushfires ignited, and the wretched screams of the wounded abandoned on the battlefield penetrated the night air, their anguished cries of being burned alive too horrifying to bear. Jess covered her head with her arms and wept.

****

When she woke, it was dark and silent. Smoke, tainted with charred flesh, lingered on the rising mist.

She searched for Sid and found him having coffee with a group of men. "What's happening?"

"Nothing," Sid said. "Both sides aren't budging."

"What's General Meade going to do?" Jess asked.

A sergeant sipped his coffee. "Meade may be in charge of the Army of the Potomac, but Grant is general-in-chief, and the butcher likes to pile up bodies. I ain't going on one more bloody charge."

"I ain't good at math, but even if we outnumber them two to one, if we git killed or wounded twice as many, they is going to have the advantage come some point in time," a private added.

Grant was a different general from McDowell, McClellan, Pope, or Meade. He attacked. Lee didn't frighten him. Grant was pursuing Lee with no fear of the consequences, but at a deadly price.

"Richmond won't come to you," Sid said.

The sergeant finished his coffee. "Then we better return to our holes and wait for the order to charge. I hope you have plenty of bandages."

Jess pointed to men packing their gear and forming lines. "Where are they going, Sid?"

He grunted and hobbled toward the departing troops. It didn't take long for Sid to find the answer. Grant had ordered Meade's army to flank Lee's right. If Lee wasn't willing to fight in the Wilderness, Grant would pick a different location to confront the enemy.

"Any other general would have retreated after these past two days," Sid said. "Grant is going forward."

As soon as Lee's scouts discovered Grant's plans, he counter moved his forces. With the departure of the two armies, orderlies could retrieve the wounded, and the dead could be buried.

Jess retrieved her canteen and haversack with her medical supplies from the wagon. She followed the orderlies with their stretchers. She would apply a bandage to stop any bleeding, and they would transport the soldier to the field hospital. A senior doctor would determine if an amputation was necessary, and the younger doctors would begin the gruesome task of removing arms and legs.

Jess had accompanied her father on every call during her stay in Ohio, asking questions about procedures and treatments. He shared his medical knowledge freely, knowing she would use it on the battlefield. Although members of the Beecher family in New England were known for their religious zeal, Sterling was a man of science. He read papers by Louis Pasteur about bacteria and wine. He had shown them creek water with his microscope and concluded there was a world unseen that impacted humans. The concept of cleanliness was spreading to the army. Garbage was burned or buried, and tents were struck twice a week to prevent mildew and mold. Dirt was added to the sinks or outhouses every night. Reports of typhoid and dysentery were lower than in the past.

But cleanliness meant nothing during a battle. The carnage in the Wilderness was worse than Gettysburg. The wounded were scattered among the trees. When she found a soldier alive, she gave him water, treated any obvious wounds, and called to the stretcher bearers who carried him to an ambulance.

She had wandered deep into the trees and turned, fearing Sid's wrath. She was alone and searched for any recognizable landmarks. Water rushed over rocks. She was near the northern border of the battle where

271

Ewell's men had fought. Morgan had been here. Voices echoed in the distance, and she headed toward the sound. Her boots stirred ashes where the ground was blackened from fire. The brush and small trees were charred. A man leaned against a large fallen tree.

"Would you like some water?"

She stepped over the fire-marred trunk of the tree and discovered a burned corpse, its mouth agape in a scream, its flesh melted from the bones.

"Augh!" Disoriented, she ran in the opposite direction and tripped over a log. A Union soldier lay on the ground a short distance away. She warily approached. His face, or what was left, was covered in bugs feasting on the blood and fluids pooled in a gaping hole where his eye and nose had been located. Jess closed her eyes against the gruesome image and backed away. Her heel collided with something solid, and she stumbled.

She turned, expecting another grotesque corpse, but the man appeared whole. His chest rose and fell beneath a gray uniform. He was alive. One pant leg had been burned from fire. She tore what fabric remained and exposed an ugly burn above his boot on his knee and thigh.

His boot had saved his foot and lower leg from damage, but the burned skin around his knee was red and blistered. His other leg was barely touched.

She dampened a rag with water from her canteen and placed it across the burn. His body trembled. A bloody gash creased one side of his head and had severed his wide-brimmed hat. She gingerly removed what remained, tearing away dried blood caked in the man's long reddish-brown hair. His ginger beard was caked with black powder from biting open cartridges. She stared at the familiar face. "Morgan?"

The stars on his collar were the ones she had sewn. She wiped his brow where blood had seeped across his forehead and examined the head wound. It hadn't pierced the skull but had severed his scalp for several inches. Jess removed bandages from her haversack and wrapped his head. She searched for other wounds and found blood staining his coat. She unbuttoned his gray jacket and probed the wound on the side of his chest. She felt for a hole in the back. The bullet had passed through his body.

He needed immediate medical care, but Confederate soldiers were made to wait. Also, he'd be taken to a hospital and under guard where she couldn't visit him. Then if he recovered, he'd be shipped off to a prison camp for the rest of the war because Grant had halted all prisoner exchanges in April.

Jess turned. The dead Union soldier was a bulky man but shorter than Morgan. She could rip the pants and no one would be the wiser. It might work. She stood and searched for any other people in the woods. The voices she had heard earlier were closer. She'd have to act fast.

Jess removed Morgan's belt, coat, boots, and trousers and bandaged his chest and leg wounds. She searched the pockets of his tattered uniform and found her photograph along with his pocket watch and placed them in her haversack.

After stripping the Union soldier, she dressed Morgan in the blue uniform. She placed Morgan's uniform on the dead soldier. Morgan had large feet so she shoved his boots back on and replaced the dead

273

man's brogans. Beads of sweat dripped from her face, not from the heat, but from fear. Once the exchange was complete, she stared at Morgan. Had she done the right thing?

She found a letter in the Union uniform Morgan was now wearing. It was addressed to Corporal Eric Prior. "I hope you don't mind being demoted." Jess stood and shouted for the stretcher bearers.

They loaded Morgan, and she followed, directing them to take him to her wagon.

Sid wasn't around. Two men were already loaded across the walls. She covered Morgan with a blanket.

"He don't look like he's going to make it," one of the men remarked.

Sid escorted two bearers with their final passenger. They loaded him on the floorboards next to Morgan. "I guess we can head back to Washington City." He peered into her eyes. "You don't look well, Miss Jessica."

"It's the heat," she excused, sipping from her canteen.

He helped her board. Jess glanced at the patients in the wagon. Some groaned in pain, but Morgan remained quiet. She had dressed his wounds as best as she could, but was it enough? He'd suffered three injuries. How would Tootie take his death? "Let's go home, Sid. We can't do any more here."

When they arrived at the Mermaid's Mirth, Sid and Thomas, the hotel manager, carried the first patient into the hotel. Tootie joined Jess by the back of the wagon.

"Don't say anything." Jess pointed at the unconscious man. "It's Morgan."

"Why is he wearing a Union uniform?"

"I exchanged his clothes with a dead man."

"They'll hang him as a spy."

Jess grabbed her arm. "Do you want to save his life or have him die in a hospital with the other Rebel prisoners?"

Tootie squealed. "What if Sid finds out?"

"Sid has never seen your brother." She turned as Sid and Thomas returned. "Hush."

The men carried Morgan upstairs. "This one's name is Corporal Eric Prior." Jess waved the letter she had found in his coat. "Better put him in a separate room. He may not make it."

Sid struggled to carry him up the stairs. "Heavy fellow."

"Don't drop him," Tootie shouted when Sid adjusted the load.

"Your shrieking don't help my concentration."

Tootie crossed her arms. "I'm surprised you can walk and talk at the same time."

"Tootie," Jess said. "That was rude."

"She has no manners," Sid said. "That's what comes of a woman being alone. They get uppity."

"Better than having a man browbeating me."

Tootie had arrived at Mermaid's Mirth shy and scarred by Lyle's assault, but she had gained a tongue, even if it wasn't a sweet and complimentary one.

Jess and Tootie followed the same routine as the hospitals. They placed personal items in a labeled bag and stored them. Uniforms too worn to salvage, were cut off. Jess placed a blanket over each soldier's groin, and Sid and Thomas removed the clothing from the three men in the one room.

"I'll fetch water to bathe them." Tootie headed

downstairs.

"I'll do the bathing," Sid shouted after her. "And don't fill the bucket too full or you won't be able to carry it."

Jess went to Morgan's room and cut away the Union trousers.

Tootie entered and closed the door. "Should you undress him?"

"I already did once," Jess defended. "He's wearing undergarments."

"Sid will have a fit if he thinks we've seen a naked man."

"I don't know what's gotten into him," Jess said. "Was he this bad over the winter?"

"Worse. He followed me everywhere. Sometimes, I caught him staring at me. It's unnerving. And I can't do anything right. He's always telling me how to do the simplest of tasks."

"Sounds like you've learned to stand up plenty."

"I'm not afraid of Sid." She paused. "I never thought I'd say that about a man after what Lyle did. It's because Sid is utterly harmless. All bluff and bluster and no action."

"Sid adopted us as much as we adopted him," Jess said.

Together they managed to remove the Union jacket and Morgan's bloody shirt.

Tootie gave Jess a blanket to cover his groin. "Did you give him something to sleep?"

"No." She stared at his torn body. How much damage could a man endure? "I think he's unconscious from the head wound."

"Aren't most head wounds fatal?"

Jess brushed back the thick curls overlapping the bandage on Morgan's head. "Not when the thick skull belongs to a stubborn Scotsman."

Tootie giggled. "Eric Prior isn't a Scotsman."

"Maybe Eric's mother was from Scotland."

Sid interrupted their discussion of Eric's ancestry. He lifted a bucket of water. "Does he need a bath?"

Tootie stared into the bucket. "Not with that filthy water. Did you wash the three men next door with the same bucket?"

"It was clean when I started."

She grabbed the bucket. "They'll have to be washed again."

Sid stared as Tootie walked down the hall. "That woman needs to know her place."

"She's right, Sid. You can't wash all the men with the same water."

"Don't let her know that. She points out my every flaw."

"You need to try to get along with her, Sid. She works here."

"I worked here long before she charmed her way in with her face full of freckles and bobbed hair."

"She's young, Sid, and she's been through a lot."

"She don't want pity, and I don't give it." Sid hobbled down the hall and grabbed the buckets from Tootie. "You shouldn't have carried two."

"I have two arms to carry two buckets." She took one. "You can use that one to rewash the men in the other room."

He followed Tootie into Morgan's room. "You and Miss Jessica can't wash this man."

"He's unconscious," Jess said. "He won't care."

"It isn't proper. Neither one of you is married."

"All the interesting parts are covered," Jess said. Sid reddened, and Tootie snickered. It was enough to chase him from the room.

Jess poured some of the water into a basin. "I want clean water to wash his wounds."

"Where should I start?" Tootie asked.

"His feet. Infantry soldiers never take care of their feet."

Chapter Twenty-Six

Jess had to soak the soiled bandage on his head to remove it. A bullet had creased the side of his head and left a wide gap in his scalp. "I need to cut his hair to stitch his head wound." Jess retrieved her scissors and began snipping the curls from Morgan's head.

"He's awfully vain about his hair," Tootie warned. "He's going to call you Delilah when he sees it all gone."

"Just like him to liken himself to Samson. He's not that strong." Her gaze strayed to the bare shoulders and chest above the blanket. His muscles were sculptured into hardened masses, each one distinct from the next, rolling from chest to shoulder and on to bicep in a continuous flow of sinew and strength. He couldn't die.

Jess snipped more hair, tossing the locks into a chamber pot. She took a straight razor and shaved the remaining hair from around the wound and trimmed the edges of the skin parted by the uneven gash. She ran her fingertips along his head, searching for any breaks, but his thick skull was intact. When Jess cleansed the wound with alcohol, Morgan jerked and cried out in pain but didn't wake. She added some laudanum powder to the gash and stitched the torn edges together. He would have an ugly scar but his thick hair would cover it. Once it grew back.

She examined his chest and discovered several

bruises, scrapes, and small cuts. She gently inserted a porcelain ball probe into the bullet wound and removed fabric remnants with her tweezers. She cleaned the holes with alcohol and bandaged them. She would stitch the gashes later if no signs of infection showed. His knee and leg were swollen with clear-filled blisters surrounded by angry red skin.

"Is he going to lose his leg?" Tootie asked.

"Have you ever burned yourself on the stove or at a fire?"

"Not like that."

"It will take more than a week for the blisters to heal, but they need to remain intact. Torn blisters can fester." She gently bandaged the leg and knee. There was nothing more to do but wait. "I'll finish washing him. You better help Sid."

Tootie placed her hand on Morgan's chest. "He has a strong heartbeat."

Jess washed him, cleaning any gash she found, and covered him with the blanket. He hadn't stirred since the battlefield. "Please don't die."

Cole stood in the doorway with Jake on her hip. "Sid said this man might not make it. Do you want me to send for the doctor?"

Jess nodded. "He hasn't regained consciousness."

Cole examined the long hair on one side. "Did you cut his hair?"

"I had to for the stitches."

"You might want to cut the other side so it matches."

"He does look like a wild Scotsman."

"Scotsman?" Cole stared at her sister. "What have you done, Jess?"

She couldn't keep a secret from her. "It's Morgan Mackinnon."

"No, no. You can't have him here. Sid already is suspicious of Tootie. What will he do when he finds out her Rebel brother is under this roof?"

"I took care of that. His name is Eric Prior. He's a corporal in the Union army."

"That would make him a spy. Do you want him to hang?"

"Do you think Blake would want his best friend to die in a prisoner-of-war camp?"

Cole shook her ginger curls. "What are we going to do with him when he's well?"

She had said *we*. Cole was her partner as always. She grinned. "He could take the oath."

"Not if he's anything like Blake." Cole sniffled. "He'll want to fight to the end. It won't matter that he has a wife and a child he's hardly seen. Not to mention the three hotels he expects me to manage in his absence." She turned toward the window. "I promised him I'd be strong, but I didn't think the war would go on for so long."

Jess put her arm around her shoulders. "I promised to help. We're partners, and we know how to keep secrets."

"I couldn't make it without you, Jess." Cole pulled her close. "How did you come up with the name Eric Prior?"

"The dead Union soldier I took the clothes off had a letter addressed to him."

"You undressed a stranger?"

"He was dead, and I put Morgan's clothes on him. I wasn't going to leave him naked in the woods."

Cole studied Morgan. "He reminds me of Jake."

Morgan Mackinnon resembled their cousin in size and coloring. The baby reacted to hearing his name. "He can stay," Cole said.

Jess gathered her scissors and razor blade. "If I'm going to cut all his hair off, I better shave him, too."

"Do you know how to shave a man?"

"Can't be that hard."

"That's what you said about shearing sheep." Cole paused in the doorway. "Yell if you need bandages."

Jess nicked Morgan's face a few times but was satisfied with her first shaving experience.

Tootie showed her the nightshirt she had worn when wounded. "Look what I found in the trunk Donna gave us." She stared at Morgan. "What did you do to him?"

"I shaved him."

"With a sickle?"

Jess frowned. "His face has complex angles. At least I didn't cut his throat."

They dressed him in his nightshirt and placed socks on his feet. Then they covered him with the blanket.

Jess snuck into the room late at night and maintained a vigil in the rocker by Morgan's bed. His raspy breathing worried her, but his silence was more frightening. What if he never woke up?

****

Morgan's head throbbed. The last thing he remembered was the battle. They had marched through the swamps and trees to attack the Federal lines. The Blue Coats ran, and they pursued, dodging the brush that had burned earlier. He was rushing forward around a tree when he was shot in the chest. He'd stumbled and fell on scorched ground. The hot embers burned through his wool trousers. He rolled away and struggled to stand only to be knocked down by another shot. His head screamed, and his leg burned. He tried kicking off the blanket, but it was tucked tight. "Help! I'm burning to death!"

"Morgan!"

He opened his eyes at the sound of his name, but everything was blurry shadows. His head hurt to focus. Hands held him as he struggled. "You're fine. You're having a nightmare."

"Jess? What are you doing in the Wilderness?"

"You're at the Mermaid's Mirth. I found you in the woods and brought you here."

A roof was over his head, and walls surrounded him, but they spun in a swirl. He closed his eyes and reopened them, focusing on Jess. "Why are there two of you?"

She lit a candle and rejoined him. She moved her hand across his field of vision. "How many fingers do you see?"

"Four."

"You have double vision." She sighed. "Must be from the head wound."

"I don't mind two of you." He moved, but she held him down.

"You need to rest."

"My leg is burning."

"You have blisters from a fire. It's important you don't open them."

"It's hot."

"I'll place a cold towel on the burn. That should help."

She pulled the blanket back from his leg and added a wet cloth.

"I wish the room would stop spinning so I could see you clearly."

"At least you're not a blubbering idiot."

"Why would you say that?"

"We didn't know how the head wound would affect you."

"We? Has the doctor seen me?"

"Yes, but he wasn't any help. He said to make you comfortable and order a coffin."

"Then I'm going to die."

"The doctor is wrong."

"Even if I do survive, I'll spend the rest of the war in a prisoner-of-war camp."

"Only Tootie, Cole, and I know who you are. Everyone else thinks you're Corporal Eric Prior."

"Who?"

She repeated his identity.

"Corporal? I attended West Point to be a corporal?"

"You've never been to West Point. You're a volunteer in the Union army."

"Union? What have you done, Jess?"

"I found you on the battlefield near the dead corporal. I switched your uniforms so they wouldn't take you to a prison hospital to die."

"I have to get out of here before you get into trouble." He searched the room. "Where are my clothes?"

"The real Eric Prior is wearing them."

"I had personal items in my…"

"I have your watch and my photograph."

Morgan scratched his head and discovered the thick curls were gone. "What did you do to my hair?" His face was naked. "And my beard?"

"I had to shave your hair to stitch the gash in your head. Once I started shaving off your locks, I had to finish the job."

"Fetch me a mirror. I want to see."

"With your double vision, it'll be all blurry."

"What aren't you telling me? Hand me a mirror!"

"You don't have to shout." Jess returned with the mirror but held it out of his reach. "I shaved your beard to help disguise you." She handed him the mirror. "We didn't want you to be recognized."

"Hell!" Morgan swore. "Did you have to make me look so ugly?"

"You don't look ugly." Jess took the mirror. "But no acquaintance or spy is going to recognize you."

"Was the corporal ugly?"

"I don't know. He didn't have much of a face left."

Morgan hadn't seen Jess in nearly a year, and he was yelling. Was he an idiot? "Thank you."

"You're welcome. And for the record, I think you have a handsome face even if it is a bit swollen and scratched in a few places."

"What if Eric Prior has friends who come looking for him?"

"The Union army is moving south."

"South? Then we lost at the Wilderness."

"The Union had more casualties, but Grant isn't retreating."

Morgan rose to his elbows. "I have to return to my men."

"You're not going anywhere for weeks," Jess said.

"And you can stay in Washington City if you take the oath."

"Hell, no."

"Think about it," Jess said. "In the meantime, be careful you don't say much to Sid." She returned the mirror to the dresser. "He may be out of the army, but he's pure soldier. Everything is by the book. If he found out who you were, he'd insist you head for prison."

"Who is Sid?" he repeated slowly.

"He drove me to Gettysburg." She paused. "Boy, was he mad about me wandering off alone."

"I'll talk to him."

"No, you will not." Jess arranged his covers. "You know nothing about Sid, Gettysburg, or Tootie."

Morgan reached for her and had to wave his hand a little to contact her body. "It doesn't matter." His hand rested against her hip, and he slid it upward, tracing the curve of her waist. "I remember this."

"None of that." Jess removed his hand. "Eric Prior and I have never met. Remember who you are, Corporal."

"Can the corporal get something to eat?"

"I think there's some biscuits left from supper last night. I'll fetch them."

Morgan listened to the soft footsteps as Jess left. He was helpless in his current condition and in enemy territory. He should have been afraid, but Jess would keep him safe. The fate of a fierce Rebel Scotsman rested in the delicate hand of an abolitionist nurse. He found a gash on his neck. Had she shaved him with her knife?

When Jess returned, he gobbled the honey covered biscuits. The apple cider soothed his parched throat.

She wiped his mouth. "Get some sleep."

He looked toward the rocking chair where she had draped a quilt. "You sleeping there?"

"Now that I know you're not going to die, I'll return to my own room."

He grabbed for her, missed, and then connected to her wrist. "We could share this bed."

"Careful, Corporal. You forget who you are."

"Jess, it's been nearly a year since we said goodbye."

"Ten months." She kissed him.

He savored her lips upon his and sighed when she pulled away. "Must you leave?"

"If they find me in your bedroom in my nightgown, you'll face an altar instead of a hangman's noose."

His head pounded, his body ached, but Jess had provided medicine with her lips to send him into a restful sleep.

****

Tootie served his breakfast. She barely limped, and her hair had grown long enough to arrange in a small bun at the nape of her neck. She was smiling, something he hadn't seen when she was at camp. She moved a small table near the bed and placed the tray on it. "How are you feeling?"

"Like a hornet's nest has taken up residence in my head." He reached for the spoon and caught empty air.

"Miss Jessica said you were seeing double." She placed the spoon in his hand. "Can you find the bowl?"

It took him a few minutes to determine which one was real. He missed his mouth a few times before he closed his eyes and trusted instinct to locate his lips.

"At least you won't starve," Tootie said.

"This taste like paste."

"It's oatmeal."

"Oats?" He dropped the bowl. "That's horse food."

"Not this kind." She retrieved the bowl. "It's good for sick men."

A thud echoed across the wooden floor. A man with a wooden leg and dressed in civilian clothes paused in the doorway. "I see our patient is awake."

"Who are you?" Morgan demanded.

"Sid Wilson. Former sergeant in the Seventh Ohio. I'm in charge of the wounded, Corporal."

He'd almost forgotten his false identity. "I guess you outrank me," Morgan said.

"Good. You understand who's in charge here."

Tootie wiped Morgan's mouth with her apron.

"Hey, no need to treat the man like a baby," Sid hollered. "Don't you have other chores to do than spoon feed this man?"

"I'm feeding myself," Morgan corrected. "And who are you to order her about?"

Tootie placed her hand on Morgan's shoulder. "Ignore the one-legged blowhard." She gathered the tray. "He doesn't have anything better to do than stick his nose in everyone else's business."

Tootie carried the tray past Sid. "Don't talk his ear off. He needs to rest."

Morgan didn't want to talk, especially to double images of Sid. He settled his pounding head against the pillow and closed his eyes. Sid's steady thud, thud echoed down the hall.

Chapter Twenty-Seven

When Morgan woke, the sun was high in the sky evident by the short squares of light on the floor. The brightness hurt his eyes. "Jess!"

A red-headed woman entered and closed the door. "Stop shouting. What do you want?"

"Who are you?"

"Colleen Ellsworth."

He focused the two images but failed to form one. "You're Blake's wife?"

"Yes." She spun in a circle. "Do I meet your expectations?"

"All I can see is a colorful blur. How much did Blake tell you about me?"

"Your father ran a store in Richmond near his father's hotel. You went to boarding school together and attended West Point before Blake dropped out."

"His father died. The last time I saw him was at the funeral."

"He said you were close."

"Thick as thieves growing up. We were always getting into trouble."

"Trouble?" Cole laughed. "Jess and I were too sly to get caught."

He laughed at her boast but knew Jess too well to dismiss her words.

Jess leaned against the door jamb. "I'm glad you're

having fun."

Cole passed her on the way out. "I like him."

Morgan followed the blur entering the room. "I like your sisters."

"Sisters? You've only met one."

"I'm still seeing double."

"Any pain?"

"Besides the buzzing in my head and the burning in my leg, it hurts to breathe."

"You need to rest and let your body heal."

"Then what?"

"Then we'll talk."

A face to face talk? Had her affection for him faded as it did for Ed?

****

Morgan slowly recovered. He alternated between sleeping and eating. The skin around his knee was an angry red, and large blisters rose in bubbles in a line where fire had scorched the skin. He showed no signs of infection, but the ache in his chest from the bullet wound kept him in bed. His double vision hadn't faded, but he managed to feed himself with a few tries. Jess was gathering his dishes when Sid and Thomas carried a bed frame into his room.

"What's that for?" Morgan asked.

"You're going to have company," Sid said. "We have wounded arriving from Spotsylvania Court House."

Spotsylvania was a few miles south of the Wilderness. "Another battle so soon?"

"Grant isn't retreating no matter how many bodies he piles up," Sid said. "The Army of the Potomac and the Army of Northern Virginia are going to keep fighting until Lee surrenders."

Morgan grasped the change in tactics of warfare. Normally the Union army retreated, and men had time to recover from a battle. But Spotsylvania had followed on the heels of the Wilderness battle. Sid had told him General James Longstreet had been wounded in the neck at the Wilderness, but "Old Pete" had survived. J.E.B. Stuart was not so lucky. The generals who had led the Confederacy to numerous victories were dying on the battlefield, shifting the leadership to less talented men.

Two men shared Morgan's room as they waited to be discharged and go home. Morgan didn't want to ask questions, but they were eager to share news of the battle.

"We arrived May 8, and the Rebels were building fieldworks. Grant gave the order to attack, but you can't beat men dug in holes," declared a man who had lost his eye.

"I don't know how they expect us to fight in a rainstorm. We were gathered at a farm, trying to find a dry spot. We were given the order to attack after four o'clock. The thick mist reminded me of the Wilderness. Grant ordered brigade after brigade to attack an angle in the Confederate line. We could barely stand in the blood-soaked mud."

"How did you lose your eye?" Morgan asked.

"We had to resort to bayonets and hand-to-hand fighting when our powder got wet. A Reb gouged my eye with a knife. He would have finished me off but a cannon blast tore him apart. Bodies were piled that high in one place." He raised his arm above his head. "I'm grateful I'm not one of them."

How had his men fared in the battle? "Who won?"

"We lost more men, but the next day the Rebs left their breastworks and moved south," said the one-armed man. "The stretcher bearers had no trouble finding me. Nothing was left of the land but tree stumps and blast holes."

Morgan's knee was sore and stiff, but he began walking around, bumping into objects once in a while, but managing to maneuver the second floor. Every step took him closer to returning to his men.

Sid obtained a Union uniform, but Morgan refused to wear it. "I could be shot as a spy in that," he told Jess. She altered some linen trousers to fit him and explained to Sid that the wool irritated Morgan's sensitive skin.

Grant and Lee were playing a cat and mouse game toward Richmond. News arrived of a battle near Cold Harbor ten miles northeast of the Confederate capital. The fighting began the last day of May and continued into June. Thousands of wounded soldiers arrived from the battlefield. Even Sid was shocked by the numbers. Union losses doubled the Confederate losses in dead and wounded.

"The Rebs built the grandest barricades I've ever seen," said a man who had lost his foot. "They had logs buried in the earth and artillery at every angle of their zig-zag lines." He showed Morgan a journal with his name and birth place written on a page.

Morgan pointed to the mutilated journal. "Why are the other pages torn out?"

"We were going to die," he said. "The other men wanted paper to write their names on so they could be identified after the fight."

"How many of them survived?"

"You're looking at him." He wiped his arm across a tear streaked face. "That's not the worst part. Neither side would call a truce. I crawled off, but for three days and nights, the wounded lay on the battlefield crying out for water or a gun to end their lives. The cries grew weaker and then silent. By the time they searched for any survivors, there were only a handful. At least two-hundred wounded men died on the field."

"How could they leave wounded men to die? Their own men?" Jess clenched her fists. "Blake and the boys are lucky they're out West. Sherman wouldn't commit such obscenities."

Morgan wasn't foolish enough to believe a loss at Cold Harbor would deter Grant from his goal. Although he saw double, the dual images were blending together. The hornet's nest in his head had quieted to a low humming. The chest wound left him short of breath if he did too much, but it was time to challenge himself. He headed for the stairs. He'd push himself as much as Grant was pushing Lee.

****

Morgan was seated in the front parlor with Jess, Cole, and Jake. He was attempting to stack Jake's square blocks one on top of the other and struggling to align the blurs. Ten-month-old Jake laughed at his efforts. When he did manage to stack four or five, Jake knocked them down, and Morgan started over again.

Cole had opened the mail and read a letter from Blake. *"We arrived at Rocky Face Ridge."*

Morgan struggled to rise from the floor.

Cole paused her reading. "Don't you want to hear about Blake?"

He looked from Cole to Jess. "What if Sid finds out?"

"Stay," Cole said. "It would be different if Blake was in Virginia, but you're fighting in different arenas."

"I'd like to hear it." Morgan sat on the sofa next to Jess. Jake crawled up his leg. He lifted the boy onto his lap. "He's wet."

"Probably from all the laughing you encouraged."

Jess retrieved a diaper from a stack she had folded and changed Jake. "Go ahead, we're listening."

"We arrived at Rocky Face Ridge. The cliffs were steep and the passage so narrow we had to pass through single file. I didn't like the looks of things, but we were ordered to make a ruckus. We could see the Rebels on top, the sunlight reflecting off their guns. It was a turkey shoot, and we were the turkeys. The Pennsylvania boys fled, but Geary ordered a second attack."

"Geary was the general who ordered the Ohio boys away from Culp's Hill," Jess said. "I don't think they like him."

"You don't have to like a general, but you have to obey him," Morgan said.

Cole resumed her reading.

"The Rebs threw rocks and old wagon parts at us. We couldn't fire back without being an easy target, so I kept the boys back under the outcroppings. They took their turns shooting. We fought for more than four hours. Ran out of water before the ammunition was gone. A few of us stayed at the top while the others climbed down. It was a fool's errand, but we survived. The boys are excited to see Atlanta.

I long to see you and Jake.

> *All my love,*
> *Blake"*

"Ake!" Jake clapped his hands.

"Dada," Morgan corrected as he bounced the boy on his lap.

Cole crumbled the letter. "Sid said the Seventh Ohio's three-year enlistment is up, and they're going home. He's at the train depot saying farewell."

"Maybe Blake shouldn't have re-enlisted," Jess said.

Cole snatched Jake from Morgan. "Why can't you admit you made a mistake and call it quits?"

"Once war starts, it's out of our hands," Morgan said. "The fight is between Grant and Lee now. And it looks like neither one is going to yield."

Cole cuddled her son in her arms. "I'm going to put him down for a nap."

Morgan tossed the blocks into a basket as Jess retrieved those Jake had knocked under the sofa. "Your sister is angry with me."

"It's not you. It's the war. We're left here taking care of the home, business, and children, wondering if you'll return."

"I don't want you to worry about me."

"It's too late for that." She slapped his shoulder. "You're a part of my life now whether I want it or not. You haunt my dreams."

Morgan pinned her to the floor. She trembled beneath his fingertips, her breathing ragged as her heart beat accelerated. "You're still in love with me."

She futilely attempted to shrug free from his grasp. "Get off me, Eric Prior, before someone walks in and catches you molesting me."

The sound of Sid's peg leg echoed in the hall. Morgan stole a kiss, lingering when Jess responded, moaning when he parted. He rolled off Jess seconds before Sid entered. He waved the newspaper at them. "Grant crossed the James River. He's going to take Petersburg."

"Petersburg?" Morgan looked at Jess. "But Richmond is the capital."

"That'll be his next stop," Sid said. "The war will be over soon."

Jess grabbed the basket of blocks. "I have to tell Cole."

Morgan remained on the floor. Even if Grant took Richmond, Blake was in Georgia fighting Confederate General Joe Johnston. "You shouldn't get her hopes up."

Jess paused and turned to Morgan. "You think the Rebs are going to beat us?"

"No, but Lee will dig in. They already have fortifications at the Dimmock Line."

"You sure know how to put a damper on good news," Sid said.

"I'm a realist."

Sid looked at the ceiling. "It's been months since Mrs. Ellsworth saw her husband. She could use a little hope."

****

By the middle of June neither side had won a decisive battle and dug in for a siege of the city.

"There's no rush for you to return to your men now," Jess said. "They aren't going anywhere."

Morgan's vision had cleared enough for him to walk around without bumping into furniture, and the short walks had become longer as his knee healed. The bullet wounds in his chest left his breathing ragged when he did too much, but his strength was returning. He would remain long enough to recover completely from his injuries before he snuck into Richmond.

Blake's next letter was filled with news the Union army was pushing the Rebel forces deeper into Georgia. They had to look on the map for places called Pine Knob, Kennesaw Mountain, and Marietta where the boys were stuck in the trenches, fighting rain, mud, and mosquitos.

"I make the boys drink Quinine mixed in their canteens to prevent the fevers, and they've stayed out of the medical tents. Others aren't so lucky. The Twenty-ninth Ohio has fewer than two-hundred men."

Cole looked at the others gathered in the parlor. "How can they continue to fight with only two-hundred men?"

"You put one foot in front of the other and keep marching," Morgan said. "Because every step takes you closer to ending the war and returning home."

"Why leave home in the first place?"

"It makes home that much sweeter," Morgan said. "When this war is over, my wife won't have to worry about me seeking adventure anywhere outside her arms."

"You're married, Corporal?" Sid asked.

Morgan hesitated. "No, but a soldier knows a wife is more than a housekeeper or mother of his children. She's the peace after the storm."

Jess frowned. "You're full of blarney, Corporal Prior."

He needed to dispel her doubts. "It's the memories

of a wife or sweetheart that keep a man marching through the rain and mud. It keeps him warm during the cold nights alone. It makes him fight to stay alive."

****

Jess showed Morgan around Washington City, sharing the sites such as the Capitol's enlarged halls, the Patent Office, and Treasury Department where Logan Pierce worked.

Next door was the White House. Lincoln was away at Fort Stevens, but they admired the Executive Mansion and the statue of Thomas Jefferson in the center of the circular drive.

"It's not working, Jess."

"What do you mean?"

"Your plan to show me the Union government in order to sway my decision to take the oath."

"If you're going to lose the war, why not take the oath?"

Morgan had debated the decision since his arrival. He believed in the Union and the United States of America, but he believed in Virginia and had taken a vow to defend her.

"Because when your side is losing, that's when they need you the most." He looked at the White House. "I can't abandon my men. It might be different if I wasn't an officer, but I promised to keep them alive, to look out for their welfare. It is one thing to be in prison, but to sit out the war and abandon my men... I can't."

He put his hands on her shoulders. "I don't blame you for being mad. If I was a smart man, I'd stay here, pretending to be Eric Prior, but the bullet across my skull must have made me stupid in the head."

****

In July Jubal Early's Confederate cavalry was threatening Washington City with several Virginia infantry regiments. One of them was Morgan's regiment. He wouldn't have to travel all the way to Richmond to join his men.

Morgan examined his belongings. He'd been gathering supplies knowing he would soon depart. His vision had returned to normal, his leg was healed, and he could take deep breaths without his chest hurting. The only reason he remained was Jess. She had erected a wall between them and treated him like any other patient. He couldn't return to war with the chasm of unspoken words between them.

The door opened and Jess entered. "Were you planning to say goodbye before you sneak off?"

Morgan looked at his supplies. "Saying goodbye is why I'm still here."

Jess took a deep breath. "Then let's get it over with, and I'll drive you out of town."

"I know you're angry…"

"Angry! I'm furious," Jess said. "I didn't save your life so you could throw it away. Join your men, but don't expect me to search the battlefields for your remains, Morgan Mackinnon. I'm done with you. I won't have my heart broken like Blake has broken Cole's. It's not fair."

He pulled her against his chest. She pushed and fought, but he held her tight, refusing to ease his grip until her sobs quieted.

"I love you." He whispered the words before kissing the tears from her face. "Believe me when I say leaving you is the most difficult choice I've had to make. Every morning I listen for your footsteps as you approach my room. I study your face, hoping to memorize every lovely feature. I envy the poets as I stumble over words to express my feelings. And as I lay in my bed at night, it's torture knowing you are so close. My arms ache to hold you, to touch your skin, and stroke your hair."

She lifted her chin, her gaze locked on his. "Kiss me. Kiss me goodbye."

Chapter Twenty-Eight

Morgan joined Jess at the bottom of the steps. She had packed food, claiming a picnic. Sid and Tootie were at the market, and Cole was napping. It was easier to pass through Union picket lines during the day. "I hope I can find my men. Jubal Early is playing a cat and mouse game with the Union cavalry all over the Shenandoah Valley."

"You could become a prisoner of the Union cavalry if you find the wrong side," Jess said. "I'll take you as far as Arlington."

"What?"

"Romulus and Remus need some exercise."

"I better hitch them up."

Jess followed with her basket.

Morgan pushed open the barn doors, and they entered the cool darkness. The horses were in their stalls. He rubbed the nose of Romulus before heading toward the wagon. He froze. Sid and Tootie were sitting on the tack box in an embrace.

Morgan's booming voice broke the silence. "What's going on here?"

Tootie broke away from Sid and stood. "It's not what you think," she pleaded.

Morgan swore. "You dirty old man. I'll teach you to take advantage of a young girl."

"This is none of your business, Corporal."

Tootie stepped between Morgan and Sid. "There's nothing to worry about."

"You were canoodling in the barn."

"It's honorable on my part," Sid said. "I want to marry her."

"What?" Sid and Tootie had been courting. He hadn't been following her because he believed she was a spy. He'd been following her around like a man in love.

"Oh, Tootie, congratulations," Jess said.

Before Jess could hug her, Tootie turned on Sid. "What do you mean you want to marry me?"

"I'm in love with you, girl." Sid struggled to kneel on his good knee. "Will you marry me, Tootie Mackinnon?"

"Get up, get up!" Tootie burst into tears and ran out the door toward the house.

"I guess that's a no," Morgan said.

Jess jabbed him in the ribs. "Can't you see he's hurting?"

Sid limped toward the door, but Jess stopped him. "I'll talk to her."

"I don't understand." Sid looked at his peg leg. "Is it because I lost my leg?"

"No, Sid. That isn't it." Jess looked at the two men. "Behave."

"Nice pair of horses," Morgan remarked to Sid. The bossy ex-sergeant would make an odd brother-in-law. "Women can have different reasons for not wanting to marry a man."

"I love her," Sid confessed.

"How can that be? You're always arguing."

"We believe in speaking our minds. Sometimes it's

noisy, but we know where the other stands that way. She said she loved me. I don't understand why she won't marry me."

Sid was a thorn in his side waiting for him to mess up, but the man was in anguish. He loved his sister. "I'll check on the women." Morgan headed for the hotel.

Tootie's room was on the main floor. She was crying. Morgan knocked.

Jess opened the door. "Come in."

"Don't worry, Tootie." Morgan offered her a kerchief. "You don't have to marry that old blowhard if you don't want to."

"But I do want to marry him," Tootie said. "I love him."

Morgan sat on the edge of the bed. "Then why didn't you say yes?"

Jess placed her hand on Morgan's shoulder. "Listen. Don't say a word."

****

Tootie sat, her back more rigid than the parlor chair. "I can't tell him without you."

Jess took her hand and stood beside her. "No matter what he says, you'll always have a job at the Mermaid's Mirth. Sid can find work elsewhere."

Tootie sniveled. "Where's Morgan?"

"He's fetching Sid."

"Do you think I'm making a mistake?"

"No. You won't marry Sid without telling him, so if he won't marry you after you tell him, you've lost nothing."

"I've lost his friendship."

"If Sid judges you for something you had no control over, he's not your friend or mine."

Morgan remained when they arrived. He stood on the other side of Tootie. Sid sat opposite Tootie, his hands on his knees. They remained silent as Tootie shared her story. Sid's face darkened, and his fingers curled into fists.

"I'll understand if you don't want to marry me," Tootie said. "It was one time. Then I ran away from home to get away from him, but some men…"

Sid grasped her hands. "I'm glad you told me, but I know who to blame. Your stepfather will answer to me if we ever meet. But his villainous act doesn't change what I feel for you, Tootie. I know I'm not much to look at and working in a hotel is hard, but I'd be a good husband. I don't drink, I'd never raise my hand to you, and I'd be faithful to the grave."

"I know, Sid. That's why I wanted you to know everything."

"Will you marry me, Tootie Mackinnon?"

"It's Theresa."

"Theresa? Who started calling you Tootie?"

"That was my brother, Morgan." Tootie kept her eyes on Sid. "When I lost my front teeth, I whistled like a train. Toot, toot."

"I think Theresa is a fine name. Theresa Wilson, if you'll agree to it."

Tootie nodded.

****

Cole and Jess helped Tootie dress for her wedding. Jem handled the decorations for the parlor where the wedding would take place, and Amber and her daughters prepared food for the guests. The wedding dress was pink with a length of plaid wrapped around her waist.

"Is this the Mackinnon plaid?" Jess examined the red material with a narrow green pattern of large squares.

"Yes, Morgan will wear a kilt from the plaid."

Cole stopped fussing with Tootie's hair. "Morgan is wearing a kilt?"

"It's tradition to wear the family colors for weddings," Tootie defended.

"How are you going to explain Morgan giving you away without telling Sid he's your brother?" Jess demanded.

"I told him my father would have wanted a traditional highlander wedding, and Eric Prior was the only one willing to wear a kilt." Tootie giggled. "It was your idea to say Eric's mother was from Scotland."

Jess agreed with her logic, and asking Morgan to give her away had delayed his departure. But instead of being clearer about her future, she was more confused. "When are you going to tell Sid the truth about Morgan?"

"Not until Morgan is safely gone from Washington City. I don't want to test Sid's loyalty to the Union by waving a Rebel in-law under his nose and asking him to lie." Tootie gulped air. "I hope he can forgive me for deceiving him."

"If Sid can forgive me for wandering off at Gettysburg, he can forgive you for having Morgan as a brother."

Tootie showed Jess two envelopes. "I wrote my mother. I made two copies. One for the mail. One for Morgan to deliver in person when he returns to Richmond."

"Richmond?" Cole asked. "Aren't his men with

Early?"

"He'll never catch them," Jess said. "And he has business in Richmond."

Tootie grabbed Jess. "Does he plan to leave tomorrow?"

"He figures Sid will be busy on his honeymoon."

Tootie blushed. "Will you go with him?"

"I'll take him to a train station far enough away to avoid too many Union soldiers."

"He loves you, Jess," Tootie said. "The preacher can perform two ceremonies as easily as one."

"Your brother has trouble bending his knee to propose." Jess looked at Cole. "Besides, having a husband away at war is more trouble than it's worth."

"Is that what you think?" Cole demanded.

"I've heard you crying at night."

"Yes, I've cried, fretted, and prayed," Cole said. "But I wouldn't trade the pain for the months of joy marriage provided. It's like childbirth. You forget the pain after you hold the babe in your arms. When Blake is returned to me, I'll forget all the suffering. But we made vows to love one another, and I'll keep those vows no matter how much they hurt."

"War is a cruel mistress. What if Morgan doesn't return to me?"

"When have you been a coward, Jess?"

She had been afraid of losing Morgan to the war. She had admitted defeat before the contest was over. Coward. Never.

Jem poked her head in the doorway. "We're ready downstairs. Better hurry. Sid is so nervous, he'll faint if he has to wait much longer."

Jess handed Tootie her bouquet. "I'll fetch

Morgan."

****

Morgan had his back to her when she entered his room. When he turned, her knees went weak. The white linen shirt emphasized his broad shoulders. The pleated kilt was gathered at his waist with a leather belt. The kilt left his knees bare. One leg was an angry red from the burn, but the color would fade in time. His short hair curled in a rusty brown crown. He was the most handsome man she had ever seen or would, whether in an enemy uniform, a highlander kilt, or naked. Her heart had remained true. No matter how hard she had quelled her feelings for Morgan, her love had grown instead of faded.

"*Huvnae ye ever seen a Scotsman in a kilt?*" His wide mouth turned upward, and his golden eyes sparkled with mischief. "*If yoo're wonderin' what's under th' kilt, I'll lit ye peek.*"

He was teasing, but the question had piqued her curiosity. She was ready for marriage. "You look so handsome. I wish it were our wedding."

"You'd marry me knowing I plan to leave?"

She nodded. He wrapped his arms around her and kissed her. She clung to his shoulders, drawing hope from his lips. "You fell out of love with Ed. You could fall out of love with me."

"No. Cole said I would know when the man I should marry entered my life. I don't have any doubts, Morgan." They broke apart at the sound of footsteps in the hall.

Morgan looked at his kilt. "*Swatch whit yoo've dain, lass. Yoo've ruined mah pleats.*"

Jess turned as the door opened. Tootie entered and

twirled to display her gown. "I'm ready if you are."

"You look beautiful, Tootie."

"Thank you, Morgan. I feel beautiful."

Morgan put on his coat. "Are you sure you want to marry that one-legged powder keg?"

Tootie smiled, her face lighting up at his remark. "He's all bluster and bluff, but that's why I love him. Isn't it a wonderful mystery how we leave one place and travel to another where we meet the one person we're meant to be with for the rest of our lives? I never would have found Sid if I had remained in Richmond." Tootie smoothed her gown. "Now give me a kiss, and we'll say our goodbyes."

Morgan kissed Tootie. "I love you, Theresa."

"Take care of yourself, Morgan." She looked at Jess. "Mine won't be the only heart broken if you don't return."

Tootie turned to Jess. "You saved my life, and you've been a sister to me. You gave me strength to face my past, and now I have a future." She hugged her tightly. "I love you, Jessica."

Jess went down the stairs first. When Tootie entered the parlor, all eyes were on the bride except for Jess. She stared at the man escorting his sister. Morgan's gaze never left hers.

After the ceremony, Morgan made a toast. After eating, everyone escorted the couple to their carriage and sent them off on their honeymoon.

"The deed is done," Morgan said. "They're man and wife."

"With all the rights and privileges thereof," Jess added.

Morgan leaned close, his voice a whisper. "Would

one night be enough if we were given no more?"

Cole's words had echoed in her mind. The war was beating her with her fear of the unknown. She was sure of her love. "Yes," Jess said.

"Then marry me, Jessica Beecher, and we'll fight this war together."

Jess grabbed Cole's arm. "Where's the preacher?"

"Eating cake."

"We have another wedding for him to perform."

****

Jess listened to the thump, thump of Morgan's heart as she rested against his chest. Strong and steady. They had stolen naps between making love. Each time more exquisite than the last as they discovered how to pleasure one another. She stroked the smooth skin of Morgan's chest, memorizing every contour, tracing the scars that marred the perfection beneath her fingertips. He belonged to her. She wore no ring, but he had promised her his mother's wedding band once he retrieved it from the Richmond store. More than gold bound them together, but it was a fragile tie.

It was nearly dawn, and they would leave for Virginia. He would return to the Confederacy, and she would wait, wondering if her husband would return. His hand roamed across her naked body. He was awake. There was time to join as husband and wife one last time.

Morgan whispered Gaelic words of love as his hands stirred her desire, and his body molded with hers in the darkness, urging her passion to climb in a rhythmic beat. The gentle pulsing increased to a frantic pounding until the tension left her on the edge of a precipice, waiting for the exquisite moment of freefall when her body gasped with pleasure and cries of fulfillment echoed in the bed chamber.

****

Morgan hitched Romulus and Remus and drove the wagon south to a small train station in Virginia. He wore civilian clothes but kept a revolver tucked beneath his coat. A wide-brimmed floppy hat covered his head. Most military men had whiskers, and he was clean shaven to aid his disguise as an injured veteran. Once aboard the train, he would travel by rail as close to Richmond as possible and walk the remaining miles.

"Do you think Lyle is in Richmond?"

"I'm betting on it."

"Are you going to kill him?"

"Tootie asked me not to. She didn't want his blood on my hands." Morgan lifted his palms. "Like there isn't enough blood on them from this war."

"War or not, a man like Lyle should pay for what he's done," Jess said. "But a woman dare not go to court to charge a man for rape. Her name is ruined whether the jury of men believe her or not. You have to seek justice for her."

"I have a way to avenge Tootie and make a greedy man like Lyle suffer," Morgan said. "I won't have to kill him."

Morgan helped Jess to the ground and checked his watch. "The train is running late."

Jess put her arms around his waist, inhaling the manly scent that would soon be only a memory. She made a helpless plea. "Take me with you, Morgan. I could cut my hair, dress in men's clothing."

"Too many of my men would recognize that pretty face no matter how you disguised it. Stay at the

310

Mermaid's Mirth. It'll be a weight off my heart to know you're safe during these dark hours."

"When the war is over, you'll return to Mermaid's Mirth." It was a statement.

"I worry you won't want me to return to you if the war stretches into more years."

"I don't care if you're legless, armless, blind, and dumb. Promise you'll return to me."

"*Lass, 'at doesnae lae much tae brin' ye.*"

"It leaves the most important part." Jess placed her hand on his chest. "Your heart." He kissed her, and the lightning shot through her the way it strikes a tree. "Maybe you should bring back your lips, too."

His mouth widened. "*I'll return if only tae gie ye th' chance tae spit in mah yak an' curse mah nam fur bein' a rockit.*"

She snuggled against him. "You said we would fight this war together. We may be on different sides, but we're partners. You've given me the Mackinnon name, and you can't take it back."

His kiss deepened. The whistle of the approaching train parted them. "Before I met you, the war was my friend, and I swore to do my duty. Now it's our enemy. I fear it will tear us apart."

"We won't let it," Jess said. "Do you love me?"

"*Wi' aw mah heart mah loove.*"

"Then we'll fight for our love," Jess said. "Swear you'll fight to stay alive. You'll survive to come to me at Mermaid's Mirth."

"I swear."

Chapter Twenty-Nine

Morgan kissed Jess until the train was ready to leave the station. He jumped on board at the last minute, paused in the doorway, and his gaze locked on hers. Would it be the last time? After her figure faded from sight, he took a seat in the back near a window. He drew his hat low over his face and kept his eyes downcast. The Union army occupied this part of Virginia, and a few times, Union soldiers paused to study him. He ignored them, praying they wouldn't confront him. He was going to stay alive until the end of the war. He was going to return to Jess.

When more Union soldiers boarded the train, Morgan couldn't avoid contact. One of them sat next to him and struck up a conversation. "Where are you headin' mister?"

Morgan knocked his hat back to reveal the ugly scar still visible on the side of his head. He drooled and mumbled some gibberish.

"Sorry. I didn't know you were a veteran."

Morgan exited at the next stop. He didn't want to chance another encounter. His haversack was packed with food, and items for cooking, shaving, and washing. His bed roll contained a blanket, shirt, and two pairs of socks. He had a knife in his boot and extra cylinders for his gun in his pocket.

When he found a quiet spot, he removed the

photograph of Jess from his coat and ran his fingertips along the worn edges before he returned it to the inside pocket. Not even a day, and he missed her.

The landscape became familiar as he neared Richmond. He entered from the northwest where supplies arrived by railroad. He told the sentry his commanding officer was Colonel Chauncy LaDonte and discovered he was at one of the hospitals. He'd been wounded at Spotsylvania. But his commanding officer could wait. He had another matter to take care of.

He reached the business district where familiar sites greeted him. The hotel Blake's father had owned had been renamed the Southern Cross. A couple blocks away, he stopped in front of his father's store. The Mackinnon name had been replaced by Neely.

His stepmother was at the counter. "May I help you?" Faye gasped when she recognized him. "Morgan. You're alive? We heard you had been killed at the Wilderness."

It was an obvious mistake. Jess had placed his uniform on Eric Prior's body, a man with no face. He retrieved the letter Tootie had written. "This is from your daughter."

Faye's hand tore open the missive. She sat on the stool behind the counter. "Lies. Lyle told me Theresa seduced him. She stole from the store when she left."

"You met Lyle less than a year ago and have known Tootie all her life," Morgan reminded her. "You're lying to yourself, Faye."

Faye's hands shook. "Where is she?"

"She's married. He's a damn Yankee but a good man. He makes her happy."

313

"She married a Union soldier?"

Had she missed the part about Tootie being happy? "Sid is a civilian."

"Doesn't matter. She's dead to me."

There would be no reconciliation between mother and daughter. "Where's Lyle?"

Faye stiffened. "He's out."

"When is he due back?"

"I'm not sure."

He slammed his hands on the counter. "Don't lie to me, Faye."

"He went to the Gallego Mill to pick up our ration of flour. He has to wait in line for hours."

Morgan looked around the store. "How is my store doing?"

Faye gasped. "Your store?"

"My father left it to me, and since I'm not dead, it still belongs to me." Morgan searched through the clothing until he found gray trousers and a gray coat for a uniform. He added undergarments, two shirts and boots. He tried on a wide-brimmed hat.

"You were wounded."

Morgan stroked his hair over the scar she had seen. "Minor scratch." He piled his clothing on the counter.

Faye shuffled through the merchandise. "That'll be two hundred…" She reddened. "Habit."

Morgan held out his hand. "Let me see the books."

Faye hesitated but produced the bound ledger.

Morgan carried his possessions upstairs. He changed into the clothes and removed his father's watch and photograph of Jess from the plain coat. He studied Jess' face. "What mother doesn't believe her daughter? I was going to show Faye some mercy, but she can rot

314

with Lyle." He smiled at her picture. "I knew you'd agree."

He flipped through the ledgers and frowned. "You're hiding something, Lyle." He removed a picture of George Washington from the wall and opened the safe behind it.

Morgan packed his belongings and the contents of the safe in a canvas travel bag. He went to his former bedroom and removed two boards from the floor. A wooden box was hidden in the hole. Inside was a square of velvet, and in its folds was nestled his mother's wedding ring. It had been handed down from mother to son for generations. The intricate silver and gold pattern was decorated with precious stones added by past Mackinnon brides. He had promised it to Jess. He shoved the ring into his pocket and added the box to his haversack.

His stepmother was unpacking China from a crate when he joined her. He returned the ledger and found a loaded revolver behind the counter. "Trouble with customers?"

Faye dropped a plate, which shattered. "Some people don't like to pay our prices."

"You should wear a mask for what you're charging." He put the gun in his bag.

"Times are hard, food scarce, but you wouldn't know about that."

"I wouldn't know about starving? I'm in the Confederate army, Faye." Morgan handed her a broom.

Lyle walked in, his hands full. "You clumsy old woman. How am I going to sell a set of dishes with a missing plate?" He put the bags of flour on the counter and turned to Morgan. "How may I help you?"

He removed his hat.

"Morgan." Lyle froze. "I thought you were dead."

"A lot of people are under that misconception."

He reached beneath the counter.

Morgan removed the gun from his bag. "Looking for this?"

Sweat dripped from Lyle's high forehead. It could have been the July heat. Morgan was betting on nerves. Civilian or soldier, the threat of death could be more terrifying than the assurance. "I've looked at the books. I'm going to sell you the store."

"I already own it."

Morgan waved the gun in his direction.

Lyle screamed and raised his hands into the air. "Don't kill me!"

"For what you did to Tootie, I ought to drop you dead on the floor." He looked at Faye. "You're making me nervous. Go stand by your worthless excuse for a mate."

She scurried to his side.

"Hands where I can see them."

"You don't trust me?" Faye asked.

"I don't believe you any more than you believed Tootie."

"I never touched the girl," Lyle defended.

"She has a husband who will kill you if you ever meet," Morgan said. "I have another way to seek vengeance. I'm going to sell you the store. It's what you wanted all along. Isn't that the reason you married Faye? You thought I'd be killed, and you could take it over. Too bad I didn't stay dead."

"There's always the chance…"

"True, which is why I'm going to sign over the

316

papers giving you title to the store."

"Why?"

"I never wanted the store. I only kept it to support Tootie. She doesn't need it now. So Lyle, the store is all yours for as long as it lasts."

"What do you mean?"

"Haven't you noticed we're under siege?"

"Lee will defeat Grant."

"That's a good attitude." Morgan signed the deed he'd removed from the safe. "You sign here."

"This says I'm paying you five-thousand dollars for the store."

"It's worth more, but it was all the gold and silver in the safe."

Lyle looked at the ceiling.

"Did you think I'd forget the combination?"

He opened the register. "I'll pay you in Confederate notes instead."

"You believe in the Confederacy, so I'll let you keep their paper currency," Morgan said. "I studied the ledger. You've let inventory run low."

"It's difficult to receive shipments."

"It's harder to pay for merchandise when you've been investing profits into gold and silver. Planning to go for a trip, Lyle?"

"What?" Faye appeared surprised by his news.

"I have no intention of fleeing."

"Good. You'll stay here in Richmond and suffer with the rest of us."

"You can't let us starve," Faye said.

"Starvation is a long way off, and with the store you'll do better than most." He grabbed the crate with the porcelain dishes.

"What do you want those for?"

"I like to dine in style, and like Lyle said, you can't sell an incomplete set."

Morgan passed the Capitol square and headed toward the train depot. He ducked into a shed and removed the loose lid to the crate. The dishes were packed with cotton to protect them in shipping. He removed the outer plates and bowls and placed the pouch of coins he had taken from the safe in a center bowel, stuffing the loose space with cotton. He withdrew a carved boat from his wooden box and placed the velvet square with the ring in the cargo hold. He arranged the remaining dishes around his treasure and enclosed a note.

"Your mother read your letter but is standing by Lyle. I sold him the store. This is payment. Half is yours. The other half belongs to Jess.

Jess, darling, I won't be there to place the ring on your finger, but it is a token of my love. We'll build a life together after this war is over. The boat is for Jake. Tell him it's from Uncle Morgan. I wonder how Blake will react to the news I'm his brother-in-law.

Your devoted husband,
Morgan"

He used a rock to nail the crate closed and mailed it to the Mermaid's Mirth. A box of china with a bit of rattling would hopefully be overlooked. He almost boarded the train. What was he doing in Richmond fighting a lost cause when he could be with the woman he loved?

Morgan crossed the center of town. Across the James River was Belle Island. The desolate pile of dirt had no buildings for the prisoners, and they lived under tents or makeshift shelters. Most of the Union soldiers had been transferred to Andersonville prison. Anything was better than Belle Island.

Morgan recognized Roe Greystone in one of the medical facilities near the canal. The battles against Grant had been costly, and the hospital was full. Roe had been promoted to captain. "I heard you had been killed at the Wilderness."

"I nearly was," Morgan said. "My wife nursed me back to health."

He stared at the side of his head. "You survived a head wound. You're lucky she's a good nurse."

"Headaches and double vision for more than a month," Morgan said. "Is Colonel LaDonte here?"

"Was," Roe said. "I'll take you to the house we're sharing. It's down the street. You're welcomed to join us. Most of the men in the regiment are with Early."

"I heard about Ewell. What did he do to be demoted?"

"He browbeat his men during the battle of Spotsylvania," Roe said. "Lee said if he couldn't control himself, how did he expect to control his men?"

Theo stood in the hallway when they entered. He looked haggard. He needed a haircut and his eyes had bags under them as if he hadn't slept. "It's the doctor," he called to the parlor. "And Major Mackinnon."

"Theo hasn't left the colonel's side since he carried him off the battlefield."

"No wonder the colonel thinks he's indispensable," Morgan said. He noticed another stripe on Theo's arm. He'd been promoted to sergeant.

Chauncy was seated in a winged-back chair with his bandaged leg propped on a footstool. "Major, I thought you were dead."

"Someone misinformed us," Roe answered. "Mrs. Mackinnon nursed him back to health."

"Miss Jessie?" Theo asked.

Morgan nodded. "And Chauncy Theodora is the prettiest little girl you'll ever see."

Theo smiled and lost ten years from his face.

"You were in Washington City?" Chauncy asked.

Morgan nodded. "I wasn't acting as a spy, but this is a fight we can't win."

"Lee believes in miracles," Chauncy said. "We'll fight until the general orders us to surrender."

"So will I," Morgan said. "How are you feeling, sir?"

"I was shot in the leg," Chauncy said. "Missed the bone but shredded the muscle."

Chauncy updated him on the situation. "Grant is commanding the Army of the Potomac and the Army of the James with eight corps and cavalry."

"And we have three corps?"

"Yes, and an additional ten-thousand men under General Beauregard, but his army consists of boys, old men, and wounded veterans," Chauncy said. "They're guarding the trenches. Lieutenant General Richard Anderson is in charge of the First Corps while Longstreet recovers from his neck wound."

"So he'll survive?"

"He's too ornery to die, but we miss him," Chauncy said. "Lee misses him. Hill has the Third Corps, but the Second Corps lost too many men at Spotsylvania. Lee blamed Ewell and assigned him to garrison duty in Richmond. He ordered several of the Second Corps regiments to help Early. Captain Baker and your men are with him."

"I thought about finding Early, but common sense prevailed," Morgan said. "Jackson always kept us on the run in the valley. It would have been impossible to find them."

"Early's orders are to keep the Union distracted and keep the railroads and supplies open to Richmond," Chauncy said.

"What are my orders?"

"Weren't you raised in Richmond?"

"Yes, sir."

"Then you'll keep supplies flowing from Richmond to Petersburg so the Union can't starve us out."

Morgan acquired supplies in Richmond, which were distributed to Petersburg. Trenches and barricades were built on the eastern side of Richmond. Two arcs created double fortifications and extended from the James River across the main roads the Union would take north. A trench ran south from the James River to Petersburg where a trench extended from the east side, south of the city, and south of the railroad. Any shipments from the east were blocked by Union forces.

Lee had his miracle early in the morning of July 30 when a huge explosion rocked the earth. Union forces had dug a mine shaft beneath Confederate lines and filled it with explosives. The resulting crater was huge, measuring a hundred-seventy feet by eighty feet and thirty feet deep. Although Confederate soldiers were killed or wounded in the initial blast, Union troops moved into the deep crater with no way out. Major General William Mahone gathered Confederate soldiers around the rim and began firing at the helpless men.

Union losses were more than double the Confederate casualties. Grant called it a catastrophe.

On the same day, Early reached Chambersburg, Pennsylvania, and burned the town in response to the Union cavalry burning the Virginia Military Institute in June.

But the destruction escalated with Grant ordering Phil Sheridan to take over the Army of the Shenandoah with the objective to tear up the rails, burn crops, and confiscate animals and supplies that might aid the enemy. But Sheridan also burned homes, leaving women and children with nothing but the clothes on their backs.

In October Early returned to Richmond, and Sheridan reported to Grant in Petersburg. Morgan greeted his men. A hardness was in their eyes that had been absent a year ago. Destruction in the past had been limited to military supplies. Sheridan had burned personal property that took a lifetime to acquire and hard work to maintain. Families would be homeless and starve this winter. If the siege lasted all winter, the Confederate soldiers could face starvation.

When Lincoln was reelected November 8, the future of the South was sealed. Lincoln would not compromise on his goal of unity. There would be no independent Southern Confederacy.

Chapter Thirty

Jess and Tootie had received the package of dishes with the money hidden in a tea pot along with a short note. Jake found her ring when he banged his boat on the table. She unwrapped the velvet square and showed it to Tootie.

"It's been passed down from mother to son for the new Mrs. Mackinnon."

Jess slipped it on her finger. "It's beautiful."

Jess and Tootie split the coins between them and stored them in the hotel's safe. Tootie told Sid about Morgan being her brother when he saw the money. He had ranted and raved, but in the end had forgiven her for the deception. He hadn't forgiven Jess. "How could you fall in love with a Reb?"

"What do you think Tootie was?"

"She converted. Why didn't Morgan take the oath?"

"It's not easy for an officer to leave his men. You've never forgotten the men in the Seventh Ohio."

Sid shook his head. "He could have had it nice and easy at the Mermaid's Mirth."

"Instead he's living in trenches, starving, and waiting for the Union to attack."

Sid grunted. "My brother-in-law is a fool."

Jess gasped. She hadn't realized that Sid was related through marriage. "You can't complain, Sid.

We're family."

Lincoln had declared Thanksgiving a national holiday, and everyone had gathered to celebrate. They enjoyed a luscious dinner of turkey, dressing, and vegetables with several fruit pastries and pumpkin pies for dessert. When the dishes were cleared, everyone settled in the parlor. Cole read her latest letter from Blake.

"Atlanta lies in ruins. What the Rebels didn't burn when they left, we torched. Sherman wanted to make sure nothing was left for the Confederacy. We have orders to obtain clothing for a fifty-day campaign and an extra pair of shoes. We're heading east, and it looks like they expect us to do some marching. Don't expect to hear any news from us for some time."

Jess sat next to Cole. They had always been close but having absent husbands had made them draw on each other's strengths.

Jess and Tootie wrote Morgan regularly, alternating between the military address and the store in the hopes he would receive them. They had received a few letters from Morgan, but the messages were not in response to anything they wrote, and it was evident few of their missives were getting through the lines.

****

Logan took Jem, Cole, Jess, and the children to Ohio to celebrate Christmas with the Beecher family. It was bittersweet because Blake and the boys would not be joining them. They were somewhere in Georgia. No one had heard from them since their departure from Atlanta.

Jess shared the news of her marriage to Morgan with her parents and younger sisters. Sterling examined the ring on her finger. "Real husband?"

"Yes, Papa."

He lowered his gaze. "Real baby?"

Jess had believed the full skirts would hide her pregnancy, but her father was a doctor, after all. "Real baby, Papa."

"When is the baby due?" Maureen asked.

"April."

"Morgan must be excited to be a father," Maureen said.

"I'm not sure if he knows, Mama."

Her mother and father exchanged glances.

Maureen stated the obvious. "Have you written him?"

"Yes, but he doesn't mention the baby in his letters. He may not have received mine."

Cole put her arm around Jess. "I haven't heard from Blake, either. Maybe the letters are only delayed."

News of Blake was in the paper before any letter arrived. General Sherman had reached Savannah and had given the city to President Lincoln as a Christmas present.

A map had been pinned in Sterling's office to track the war's battles. Jess ran her finger from Atlanta to Savannah. "That's a long way to walk."

"No wonder they needed two pairs of shoes," Cole agreed.

Blake's letter arrived after the New Year.

Cole scanned the pages and began reading.

"You're bound to hear stories. When we were given the orders to march, we didn't know the supply wagons wouldn't be able to follow. We were ordered to live off the land. Some of the generals encouraged the

men to leave a swatch of destruction to cripple the South. I want you to know we took food from the farms and homes along our path, and we burned warehouses and factories that aided the Confederacy, but we didn't harm any women or burn any homes. I'm sorry I can't say the same about the other armies. Some of Billie's boys have no discipline, and they will regret their actions in their later years. A group of deserters from North and South we call bummers followed the armies and left their own brand of destruction in our wake. They robbed and pillaged anything we had left behind."

"Phil Sheridan and Jubal Early did the same thing in the Shenandoah Valley," Jess said. "We saw some of the destruction when we traveled home."

Cole looked at the other side of Blake's letter.

"I'm tired, Cole. I ache to hold you in my arms. I look forward to holding our son. The next few months will be the worst. We are exhausted, more of war than of body. But the South is driven by hatred. They seek revenge. I don't know how President Lincoln is going to unite the two sides in peace after this.

All my love,
Blake"

"He must think Jake is a baby." Jess scooped the toddler from a chair where he had climbed to reach a pretty glass bowl. "You don't sit still long enough for anyone to hold you."

****

When Logan and Jem returned to Washington City, Cass joined them. Cole and Jess took a longer route through Cleveland and Albany to visit Blake's hotels. With everything running smoothly, they returned to Washington City in late February. War was on hiatus during the winter months, but spring was approaching.

Cole and Jess were in the front parlor playing with Jake and Chauncy when Logan and Jem arrived with Cass and Deidre. They had gone to hear President Lincoln sworn in.

"I don't understand why he chose a different vice president," Cass said. "And a Southerner."

"The President is looking at healing the wounds of the war," Logan explained. "Uniting the North and South."

"The war has to end first," Jess said.

"The war is bankrupting the nation," Logan said. "It costs more than four million dollars a day to pay for it."

"Four million?" Cass repeated. "I can't imagine how much that is."

Someone knocked at the door. "I'll get it," Jess said.

"We have two rooms available," Cole reminded her.

Jess returned with Sergeant Zach Ravenswood leaning on crutches. He had a letter from Blake to deliver.

Jem and Cass helped him to the sofa, and Cass placed a footstool beneath his injured foot.

"What happened?"

"We were making a bridge through the swamps in North Carolina, and a sharpshooter took out the man next to me. I grabbed for him, and we tumbled to the rocks below. Broke my leg," Zach said.

Jess pointed at his sleeve where three chevrons decorated the dark blue wool. "When did you become a sergeant?"

"In Savannah," Cass said. "Didn't he write you?"

"No," Jess said. "He's been too busy writing letters to you, little sister."

Zach reached into his coat. "Blake sent this letter for Mrs. Ellsworth."

Cole snatched it, tore the envelope, and scanned the contents.

"Cole darling,

We're fighting Joe Johnston but each step takes us north and closer to you. I've sent Zach to the Mermaid's Mirth for some healing. I considered injuring myself so I could join you. But the end is close now. The Rebs are wearing rags, shivering from the winter, and hungry. They have to know they're beat. Grant is tired of waiting for Lee to surrender. He'll be knocking again at Petersburg to reach Richmond. It'll end the war, and I'll return home to you and Jake.

All my love,

Blake"

The words haunted Jess. Grant would attack soon, and he was known for showing no mercy. "Morgan," she cried. "He'll never see his child."

****

It had been a difficult winter for the men in Petersburg and Richmond. Every attack on Union lines had failed, and the Confederate lines were crumbling. Sheridan's cavalry had joined Grant's army and were poised to strike.

Morgan's men were skeletons, surviving on minimal rations that barely kept them alive. The cold winter had taken its toll on the entire Confederate army, and many had deserted or surrendered in exchange for a meal. Some soldiers had taken wool Union overcoats from dead soldiers to keep warm even though it made them targets to their own side.

Colonel Chauncy LaDonte called Morgan, Otis, and Roe to his tent for a meeting. He spread a map on the table. He ran his finger along the Confederate defenses south and west of Petersburg. "The men are stretched thin along twelve miles of trenches. Grant attacked the Petersburg lines this morning. A. P. Hill was shot and killed. Our boys are holding the frontal assault temporarily, but Lee has given the order to evacuate. Any ships docked in Richmond are to be burned. Some officials, veterans, and sailors will march with Ewell. We've been assigned to help him."

The news was reeling. Grant was delivering a death blow, and Lee was struggling to survive. "What about the citizens of Richmond?" Morgan asked.

"President Davis has been notified." He pointed to the map. "We're to take the southwest road and meet up with Lee's forces at Amelia Court House."

"How many men do we have?" Otis asked.

"About thirty-thousand total. Grant has four times that." Chauncy took a deep breath. "Lee hopes to join General Joe Johnston in North Carolina and take a stand."

A final stand. The war would be over, but it could mean every man in gray would be dead first. Morgan made a stop at the Neely Store. Faye was seated behind the counter. She was gaunt with a vacant stare he had seen in too many eyes to count. "Where's Lyle?"

"He ran off with a whore," Faye said. "He abandoned me after all I did for him. Don't matter. They told me he was shot crossing the lines. I told them they could leave him there to rot."

His sympathy surfaced. "Is there anything I can do?"

"Put a bullet in my brain."

"I can't do that, but you'll be out of your misery soon. The Union troops will deliver supplies."

"Handouts from the Yankees?" Faye snarled. "I'd rather starve."

"We've lost," Morgan said. "The sooner you accept that, the better off you'll be."

"Never," she vowed. "I'll hate the Yankees 'til I die. If you hadn't been cowards, we would have won this war."

Morgan wanted to slap her. No man left in the Confederate army was a coward. No need for her to write Tootie and ask for forgiveness or a place to live. She'd never accept Sid as her benefactor. The proud folks of Richmond would fend for themselves. He paused by the door. "Did you write Tootie?"

A crooked smile creased her face. "At the Mermaid's Mirth?"

He stepped toward her. "Yes."

"I received some letters from her addressed to you. Maybe she thought they'd reach you."

Morgan crossed to the counter and grabbed her wrist. "Where are they?"

"Lyle opened them thinking she was sending you money, but all that was inside was a letter from a Jessica Mackinnon." She laughed. "Your wife."

"Those letters belong to me. I want them."

She pointed to the stove. "I burned them to stay warm. Your wife and sister think you're dead." She cackled. Faye had gone mad.

He dismissed his stepmother's evil deed.

330

Hopefully, his letters had reached Mermaid's Mirth. He didn't want Jess to give up hope. He had to return to her.

Morgan headed for the troops. The men were cold and hungry, but glad to be out of the trenches. Those who didn't have shoes, wrapped their feet in newspaper and rags for the march. It was near dawn when they took a break.

"I don't remember the fires being that big," Otis remarked, pointing behind them.

"They weren't when we left," Morgan said. "Richmond is burning." He would never go back. It was better to remember the city as it had been when he was a boy.

Morgan kept the men moving, but they were traveling on empty stomachs and sore feet, damaged from living in water logged or frozen trenches. His boots had holes in the soles, but he had lined them with newspaper.

Some soldiers showed signs of gangrene, and Roe did what he could. When they marched, their feet left a bloody trail behind. Rumors spread that rations of smoked meat, bacon, biscuits, and coffee waited for them at Amelia Court House, but their destination was forty miles away. They marched in silence. Frustration was added to depression when they reached Genito Bridge only to find the pontoon bridge had not arrived. They marched south and crossed the Appomattox River on the Richmond and Danville Railroad Bridge after placing planks over the gaps.

They made camp about a mile west of the bridge isolated from the rest of Lee's army. Morgan posted sentries in case Union cavalry searched the area.

The next day they marched through a cold rain and arrived at Amelia Court House a day after the main army. The train was waiting for them, but crates, harness, and carts were scattered in the railroad yard.

"Where's the food?" Otis asked.

Morgan read the lettering on the crate. *Ammo*.

"There's only one result when you eat a bullet," Theo remarked as he sat on the ground. He covered his face with his hands and sobbed.

"Don't get comfortable," Chauncy said. "We have orders to head for Danville."

Morgan peered over his shoulder at the map he had unfolded. "Where is Danville?"

Chauncy lowered his voice, "It's a four-day march." He turned to the men. "Lee has ordered rations to be sent to Danville."

Morgan didn't voice his fears. Many of the men wouldn't survive. General James Longstreet took the lead with the best wagons and artillery pulled by the healthiest horses. The remaining heavy equipment was placed on railroad cars or burned. The sickly animals were destroyed.

They hadn't gone far when Chauncy received orders Union forces had set up barricades at Jetersville. Danville was no longer the destination. Chauncy pointed at a route on the map. "We'll follow the South Side railroad to the town of Farmville where rations will be waiting."

"Are we sure about the food?" Morgan asked.

Chauncy folded the map and tucked it in his coat. "If we don't keep moving, we can be sure of death."

Chapter Thirty-One

Rain pelted tired bodies as they made their way through the woods and swamps only to wait while a bridge was repaired at Amelia Springs. Morgan was wet, hungry, and exhausted in equal measures. When he counted the men as they prepared to march, almost a third were missing. They had gone home. He couldn't blame them. The war was lost. The most important thing of value was a loved one at home. He removed the photograph of Jess from his pocket. It was worn, and the picture was marred in a few spots, but her face was clear, smiling, and comforting. He returned it to its haven and ordered the men to keep moving.

During the night of April 6, they set out for Rice's Station on the South Side Railroad. Longstreet led with the combined First and Third Corps followed by two divisions led by Lieutenant General Richard Anderson and the wagon train followed by Ewell and his mix of civilians, sailors, and war-weary soldiers.

Colonel LaDonte's regiment was placed at the rear of Major General William Mahone's division and in front of Anderson's troops.

"Longstreet has cavalry with him and cavalry with Major General John Gordon's Corps in the rear guard, but we have neither cavalry nor artillery," Morgan said. "Does Lee understand how vulnerable we are in the middle?"

"Our best bet is to keep moving." Chauncy pointed to a bluff as they crossed a small bridge across Little Sailor's Creek. "When we reach that high point, survey the road for Anderson's men. They've fallen behind."

"Should we wait for them?"

"We stay close to Mahone's men," Chauncy said. "Gaps invite trouble."

Morgan and Otis shouted to the men, urging them to pick up the pace. When they heard shooting behind them, they didn't need encouragement. Fear drove them.

Morgan stood on an overlook. He peered through his field glasses and searched for any sign of the remaining third of the Confederate army.

Otis joined him. "Any sign of them, Major?"

"I see smoke." Morgan focused. "Union cavalry attacked Anderson's wagons."

"Should we return?" Otis asked.

"Looks like they've driven the Blue Coats off," Morgan said. "They're passing Marshall's Crossroads."

"Any sign of Ewell?"

"He's closed ranks with Anderson and has crossed the creek." Morgan scanned the surrounding area. "The Union cavalry is heading north to Marshall's Crossroads. Ewell's infantry is heading for the same destination." They were on a collision course.

Anderson recognized the cavalry threat and organized his lines along the road but without artillery, the mounted Federals charged over their makeshift breastworks, slashing at the men with their sabers. Ewell was at a right angle to Anderson's line, dug in as Union artillery from the farm on the far hill bombarded them.

Ewell commanded veteran soldiers who prepared their guns under taunts by Union soldiers waving white flags.

"We should help them," Otis said.

"Tell the colonel what is happening and inform Mahone we're under attack."

Morgan turned as Ewell gave the order to fire. The men mowed down Union soldiers as they crossed the creek. Initial success was temporary as Union artillery allowed their forces to regroup and attack. The men engaged in hand-to-hand combat, but they were surrounded and had no choice but to surrender.

Anderson's lines had collapsed under the constant attacks by Union cavalry. A group of Anderson's men retreated toward him. "Come on, boys!" Morgan shouted as he fired toward the Blue Coats. Shots rang out behind him. Mahone's division had returned. General Lee was with him.

They gave the men cover and waited for more that never came. Chauncy shared the numbers with Morgan and Otis. "We estimate a loss of three-hundred wagons, seventy ambulances, and eight-thousand men, half of Lee's army."

"Half? How can that be?" Morgan asked. "We had thirty-thousand when we left Petersburg and Richmond."

"They've been walking away every time we stopped to rest. Those who remained are too weak to fight anymore."

But Lee wasn't ready to surrender, and his men followed, trusting him with their lives.

The next morning they headed toward Farmville with Union cavalry tracking their trail. By the afternoon they set up entrenchments on high ground at Cumberland Church and held off the Union cavalry. During the night they headed for Appomattox Court House where rations waited.

On April 9 news arrived that remnants of the Southern cavalry had beat back the Union cavalry and opened a road to Lynchburg where supplies waited for the Southern troops. Lee ordered his army through the village and across the Appomattox River. Morgan's men pushed toward the promise of food, heedless of their sore and bloody feet.

But with the prize in sight, they were surrounded by Union troops on three sides and could no longer advance.

Morgan stood next to Colonel LaDonte near the front of the lines facing Lynchburg. "It looks like they're going to attack."

"We need to form lines," Chauncy said. "It's too late to dig any trenches, but have the men find cover."

Morgan turned to his men. They were scarecrows, eyes vacant, and arms too tired to lift their rifles. He ordered the regiment to form lines, facing Lynchburg and supplies. A few skirmishes broke out between the other lines, but Morgan ordered his men to wait until Union forces rushed them. They were low on ammunition, and every bullet would have to count.

The Union forces multiplied into a sea of blue. A bugle sounded, and riders formed a line. Their raised sabers glistened in the sunlight, ready to butcher the last of the Southern Rebels.

A lone rider headed toward them from the rear. He carried a white flag of truce fluttering on the end of a staff. "Step aside," Morgan ordered.

The men were silent. Even the Union troops, poised to attack, fell quiet as the rider approached their lines. Everyone understood what the flag meant, yet four years of fighting had taught them that war was unpredictable.

"Keep your fingers off the trigger," Morgan warned.

The soldiers protested. "He can't give up. We'll fight to the death!"

"Enough blood has been spilled," Morgan said.

"It's not our decision now, boys." Chauncy joined them. "Lee has surrendered the Army of Northern Virginia."

Morgan looked at the colonel. He had tears streaming down his cheeks. Theo stood a short distance behind him, his hat in his hands, his head bowed. Lee had surrendered. What did it mean to him and his men? Would they be made prisoners of war?

Chauncy conferred with the other officers and relayed the news. Lee and members of his staff had ridden to the Wilmer McLean house where they would meet with Grant and his officers.

"He was wearing a clean uniform and his boots shined so bright, you could see your face in them," Chauncy said. "He rode Traveler like a man claiming victory not defeat."

Morgan walked among his men, who were reclining along the road. "Get up, you slackers. Do you want General Lee to see you like this? Straighten your coats and stand smart. Make him proud."

The men stood, brushed the dirt from their torn and ragged uniforms, some more civilian than military. They polished any metal and shared a rag to buff shoes and boots if they wore any. Morgan ran his fingers through his hair. It had grown in a tangled mess along with his scraggly beard. Jess wouldn't recognize him. Jess. He'd have to wait out the rest of the war in a prison camp.

Theo was running toward them from the Yankee lines. "He's coming! General Lee is coming!"

"Attention, men!" Morgan shouted as Lee approached. They were an ugly bunch of fighters, but none of these scrappers had deserted. None had run the other way. And many had families who had written, pleading for them to return home or there would be nothing to return to. Crops needed planted and barns needed rebuilt.

Lee's approach was like his arrival at Hagerstown and Williamsport. They had been defeated at Gettysburg, but Lee made them proud. They reached out to touch Traveler, stroking his gray coat. No one dared to touch Lee. Tears streamed down their dirty, scarred faces. Each took personal blame for the defeat.

Suddenly the next group of men lining the street burst into wild cheers. Lee stopped and waited for the men to quiet. Morgan pressed forward to hear what he had to say. He caught a few lines.

"Go quickly and quietly to your homes," he said in his resonant, calm voice. "And be good citizens as you have been soldiers."

Go home? Had Morgan heard correctly? Wasn't the Union going to punish them?

Lee issued General Order Number Nine that declared the end of the Army of Northern Virginia. The surrender terms were widely circulated. The Confederate soldiers would be paroled instead of being sent to prison-of-war camps. The officers could keep their side arms and personal property would be respected. Grant also provided rations to the starving Confederate soldiers. In addition Grant ordered his men not to celebrate. Grant, the butcher, had showed mercy.

Morgan was anxious to return to Washington City. He could take the Southern railroad from Appomattox Courthouse to the Orange and Alexandria Railroad at Lynchburg. But he was forced to wait until April 12 when his men formed lines for the last time to formally surrender and receive their pardons.

Three days seemed like an eternity. He filled his belly with Union rations and made sure his men had their fill. He borrowed a razor to shave, and Theo trimmed his hair.

"Do you think Miss Jessie will recognize you?" Theo asked.

Morgan examined his reflection in a small mirror. Not hardly. His cheek bones were prominent against the shallows in his cheeks. He examined his worn-out uniform. "Do you think you can wash my clothes?"

"Yes, sir," Theo said. "I don't guarantee they won't fall apart."

Morgan took a bath, using a hard bristle brush to remove months of dirt. He dressed in his clean uniform and put his few remaining personal items in his pockets for the trip home.

The men lined up by regiments, some with so few men, they wouldn't qualify for a unit in a company.

"Should I play my drum?" a boy asked.

"Give us a steady beat," Chauncy said. The familiar cadence had led them across cornfields, over fences, and into the face of the enemy. Now it led them on their last journey together.

The men marched into the Union camp with rows of Federal soldiers gathered to witness the surrender. No one cheered, jeered, or spoke except the officer in charge of the surrender procedures.

"This is our final march," Chauncy said. "You'll remember it for the rest of your lives."

Morgan looked at the men he had spent four years with in camps and on the battlefield. Most were from the Richmond area and would go home to whatever was left of their homes. The men formed their lines, shoulder to shoulder. They were asked to stack their guns in groups with bayonets interlocked or piled on the ground. They dropped their military equipment, including cartridge belts, haversacks, blankets, and tents on the ground. Officers did the same but retained their swords and side arms.

The flag bearers placed rolled flags on top of the stacked muskets. The Union soldiers would discover later that many of the flags had been reduced to a narrow panel wrapped around the staff. The men in the regiment had cut pieces of their colors and hid the remnants in their coats. Morgan had a square folded and hidden beneath his shirt. Each man waited in line for an officer to sign his parole. Some men tucked the paper in their caps, others in a coat pocket. The pardon would keep them out of prison. It would allow them to return home.

Morgan shook hands with each of the fifty men remaining in his regiment, once a thousand men strong. "Like Lee said, go home, men. Go home."

Morgan said goodbye to Colonel Chauncy LaDonte, Captain Otis Baker, Captain Roe Greystone, and Sergeant Theo Jameson. "You'll have to come visit Washington City," Morgan told them. "See that pretty girl named for you."

"You think they'd let me in Washington City?" Theo asked.

Morgan pointed at the paper tucked in Theo's hat. "That pardon lets you go anywhere you want."

"Do you have money for the train?" Chauncy asked.

"I traded items to Union officers for enough coin to see me there."

He saluted. "Then don't keep Miss Jessie waiting."

Morgan saluted, and Chauncy grabbed him in a bear hug. "Kiss Chauncy Theodora for us."

****

Morgan had shown his pardon to every Union sentry from Appomattox Court House to Alexandria. He should have changed from his uniform, but he had no other clothes, and he was in a hurry to reach Jess. The Long Bridge led to Maryland Avenue and Mermaid's Mirth. The guard examined the pass and asked a passing officer to look at it before he allowed him to cross into the city.

All of Washington City was decorated to celebrate Lee's surrender. Bunting and flags hung from railings and windows. A group of men and women were gathered on the corner singing songs. The leader of the band looked in his direction and directed the men to play *Dixie*. Morgan tipped his hat and quickened his pace when he saw the sign with a mermaid. The porch wasn't decorated. Not even a flag was displayed. Morgan entered the front parlor. It was empty. Where was everyone?

The thud of a wooden peg echoed in the hallway. It was Sid. "Hey, Reb."

Morgan stared. "Yank."

"I can't believe Grant pardoned you." Sid extended his hand. "Welcome home, brother."

Morgan shook his hand.

Sid gave a poor imitation of a Rebel yell.

"Keep the noise down." Tootie walked down the hallway from the kitchen. "You don't want to wake Miss Jessica. She needs her rest." Her hand covered her heart. "Morgan, you're home."

Home. His home was with Jess. "What's wrong with Jess?"

Tootie looked upstairs. "Jessica is in bed…"

Morgan didn't wait for an explanation. Jess was ill. There was no other reason for her to be in bed in the afternoon. He took the steps two at a time, pausing before he opened the door. The draperies were closed, shielding the room from any sunlight. "Jess." Her name caught in his throat. She was in bed, covers pulled to her chest, her flaxen hair braided to one side. He knelt by the bed. She was asleep. He took her hand, which rested on top of the covers. His fingers traced the ring he had sent. She had to know he loved her. "Jess."

She groaned and shifted in the bed. "I'm tired. What is it?"

Morgan kissed her hand. Her eyes fluttered open. "Who is it?"

"Morgan." He choked on the words. "I've come home."

"Morgan?" Jess reached for him and brushed his hair back from his face. "Why are you crying?"

"You're dying."

"Me?" She struggled to sit. "I'm not dying."

He placed a pillow behind her. "What are you doing in bed if you're not ill?"

Jess frowned, then her eyebrows rose in surprise, followed by a gay laugh. "Oh, Morgan. How long have you been gone?"

"Nine long months."

"A lot can happen in nine months. Didn't you receive any of my letters?"

"A few." Terror gripped his heart. "You're in love with someone else."

"I think you'll love him, too."

What did she mean? "Are you trying to torture me? Tell me now in person if your heart belongs to another. I don't blame you. Nine months is a long time to wait for a man."

"Look over there." She pointed toward the wall where a crib was placed between the windows.

He stood and turned to peer into the small bed. "It's a baby." Nine months. He turned. "Is this my baby?"

Jess folded her arms across her chest. "And whose baby would it be but yours?"

She sounded like his Jess.

"Born yesterday. Sid heard Ewell and his men had been captured. I was afraid you were in a prison camp, but our son must have known you were coming home and wanted to meet you."

He sat on the edge of the bed and took her in his arms. "And you, Jess, are you glad to see me?"

Jess examined him. "No missing arms or legs. Did you bring me your heart?"

"Yes." He paused, his mouth close to hers. "And

my lips."

"I'd almost forgotten about them."

"Let me remind you." He kissed her, and the months apart disappeared. "I've worn your picture to a thin layer, but you inspired me to keep living. All I wanted to do was come home to you."

"We beat the war, Morgan. We both won."

A word about the author…

Laura Freeman has been a reporter for the past twelve years and covers the historic town of Hudson, Ohio. She has won the Press Club of Cleveland's Ohio Excellence in Journalism award twice and the Ohio Newspaper Association award several times.

Her novel, *Impending Love and Capture* is the sequel to *Impending Love and War*, *Impending Love and Death*, and *Impending Love and Lies*. *Capture* takes Jessica Beecher from Gettysburg to the end of the war, first as Major Morgan Mackinnon's prisoner and then as his nurse.

Laura lives in Ohio where she is working on her next book, *Impending Love and Madness*.

Visit her on:

Facebook.com/laurafreeman.5648

Twitter @LauraFreeman_RP

or at her blog: Authorfreeman.wordpress.com

www.ingramcontent.com/pod-product-compliance
Lightning Source LLC
Chambersburg PA
CBHW071517260626
47170CB00002B/410